NEW LAND, NEW RULES

The manager of the Yellow Jacket leaned his elbows on the desk. "Mister Hartland, these mountains are not tame. Compared to your Eastern hills, they are as bucking broncos to thoroughbreds, an' don't you forget it. Now I happen to be the manager of this mine…unless you want to put in another." He eyed Hartland askance, but Hartland made no sign. "If there's anything in Butch Allen's life he wouldn't forget on a bet, it's what happened tonight. It means war between the Huntley an' the Yellow Jacket. Butch will see to that. An' whatever else it might mean, it means that I won't be bulldozed or allow my men to be molested without fighting Allen at his own game an' with his own weapons. That means brute force and singing bullets in this country, Mister Hartland."

Other *Leisure* books by Robert J. Horton:

RIDERS OF PARADISE
GUNS OF JEOPARDY
THE HANGING X

FORGOTTEN RANGE

Robert J. Horton

LEISURE BOOKS NEW YORK CITY

A LEISURE BOOK®

May 2009

Published by special arrangement with Golden West Literary Agency.

Dorchester Publishing Co., Inc.
200 Madison Avenue
New York, NY 10016

ISBN 10: 0-8439-6174-0
ISBN 13: 978-0-8439-6174-4
E-ISBN: 978-1-4285-0675-6

The name "Leisure Books" and the stylized "L" with design are trademarks of Dorchester Publishing Co., Inc.

Printed in the United States of America.

10 9 8 7 6 5 4 3 2 1

Visit us on the web at www.dorchesterpub.com.

FORGOTTEN
RANGE

Chapter One

At the Rameses night club 2:30 A.M. meant that the morning had just begun. Colored lights played upon white shirt fronts, bare shoulders, white tablecloths littered with glasses in which gleamed liquid rubies, beryl, topaz, the emerald of creme-dementhe, and the soft, saffron sapphire of champagne. The booming of drums, clash of cymbals, squawking of saxophones— jazz. Smoke pencils from 300 cigarettes. A dancing team, scantily attired, winning yawns. A tumult of voices, laughter, hand clapping, calls for waiters— bedlam. Dancing in a space the size of a rug.

Roger Hartland looked out upon all this with a stupid, bored expression. He was drinking martini cocktails this night, and now, as he raised his glass, he dropped it on the table. He didn't bother to pick it up. Merely held up a finger to a waiter. The signal was instantly answered. Hartland had a way of winning respect and service from waiters. And he was a good tipper.

He looked across at the woman who sat on the other side of his table. A brunette, tall, dark-eyed with a certain mysterious beauty and an expression usually unfathomable. Her white shoulders were shapely. None could have told her age. Even Hartland didn't know.

As the waiter left, Hartland waved an arm taking in the scene about them. "Sucker stuff," he said disgustedly, "and I'm the biggest sucker of them all."

"Why, you don't spend as much as any of the

butter-and-egg men who come here," said the woman languidly.

"I don't mean that," said Hartland with a frown. "I mean I'm a sucker to come here at all. I'm a fool, Rose."

"You mean you're drunk," she returned, fitting a scented cigarette into a long, ivory holder. "What kind of a mood are you in tonight, Roger? You know I'm the victim of them all."

He looked at her with new interest. "Yes, Rose, I guess that's so. Well, you're a pretty good sport, and I'm willing to pay for it."

Rose Raymond arched her brows. "You consider me an employee, then?"

"Oh, don't talk drivel," he retorted irritably. "Don't you see that I'm sick of all this sort of thing? What do we get out of it?"

"Well," she answered with a wry smile, "you get a good souse out of it every night."

"That's just it!" exclaimed Hartland, slapping the table with the palm of his hand. "That's just what I get. My life at present is one round of night clubs. I end up at home with the sunrise, soused to the gills, as you say. Along about two o'clock, Fredricks comes in with whiskey and absinthe. I have a bath and another bracer. A bit of breakfast and I'm off for cards at some fool club. The theater, maybe, supper, and . . . you know the rest. Every day the same. Now isn't that a fine life?"

"It might be worse," Rose observed with a shrug.

"Yes . . . it would be worse working on the docks, I suppose," said Hartland moodily.

"Why don't you go into business?" Rose suggested, knowing full well the mockery of the idea.

"Business!" he snorted. "What business could *I* go

into? Father left everything in stocks and bonds. I know of no business I control. And I wouldn't know where to start if I had one. Rose, I'm bored to death. I'm all fed up with life. It seems as though I've been everywhere, seen everything, done about everything I want to do. Damn!"

"Well, why don't you. . . ." She bit off her words. She had been about to ask him why he didn't get married. But that would be fatal for her. Hartland was her meal ticket.

But he anticipated what she had meant to say. "Get married?" he said with a cynical ring to his voice. "And where would I find the woman? I believe most of them can be bought. The ones that can't are undesirable, married, or not in my set. I'm fed up on the woman question, too."

"Well, you're in bad shape, Roger," Rose commented. "Why don't you get yourself a fine big boat and jump off in the middle of the ocean?"

"Why the middle?" He smiled grimly. "Sandy Hook would do and it wouldn't be so expensive. No, none of that, Rose. *You* may do it someday, though." He looked at her and was startled to see that her face had gone deathly white. "Oh, I didn't mean it, Rose. Come, don't look at me that way. Let's order champagne."

"What you say might come true, Roger," she said in a low voice. Then with more spirit: "Roger, it's spring. Paris is wonderful in spring, as you know. Let's take a trip over to Paris." She gazed at him out of shrewd eyes.

"Not me." He laughed. "But I'll stand the gaff if *you* want to go."

"I may take you up," she said. Roger was a good sport.

He was looking about and frowning again. A waiter passed and accidentally tipped a silver tray. Several bills fluttered down on Roger's table. The waiter gathered them up with profuse apologies.

"There it is again," said Hartland. "Money. Get the money anyway you can. That's the code here."

"Well, you shouldn't worry," said Rose sarcastically. "You've got plenty of it."

The waiter served champagne.

"If there was only something new," Hartland complained.

"There's a new revue up at the Cortez they say is very good," said Rose.

"Oh, the devil. New revue. If I could only get into a fight, or something. If I had the slightest fancy for it, I'd go big-game hunting in Africa."

Rose laughed softly. "Your moods change with the drinks," she said, and asked him to dance.

At dawn they left the club. As Hartland's car pulled up, a laborer on the way to his work passed so closely in front of them that he jostled Rose.

"What're you doing?" Hartland snapped. He took the man by the arm and jerked him around with such force that his lunch pail was knocked from his hand.

The man pulled free and struck Hartland in the face. Next instant Hartland's right flashed and the blow caught the man flushly on the jaw. He went down in a heap.

A policeman came on the run.

"Don' get 'cited, officer," said Hartland unsteadily. "Man jostled the . . . lady, here." He was groping for a card, found it, and handed it over.

The policeman looked at the name and address.

"Well, you better get along home," he said, and went on down the street.

Hartland took a bill from a pocket and gave it to the man who was recovering his lunch pail, thoroughly beaten. Then he handed Rose into the car.

It was Fredricks, Hartland's man, who let them into the apartment, looking with surprise and haughtiness at Rose.

Hartland led the way into his sitting room. "Whiskey an' soda, Fredricks!" he called back.

Rose Raymond stared in wonder at the luxury surrounding her. Rare paintings and etchings, tapestries, bronzes, knickknacks picked up in many lands, soft divans, deep rugs, antique furniture, weapons, a gold-figured Japanese screen.

Hartland was lighting a cigarette. "Sit down, Rose," he said. And when the drinks had been served: "Rose, I brought you up here tonight for a certain reason." He paused. He was drunk, yet his mind seemed clear—if such a thing could be possible—and his articulation was slow but perfect.

She eyed him askance.

"Rose," he said, "without meaning to offend you in any way, you are a woman of the world. You have been somewhat of a comfort to me because I have been able to take my . . . my spite, you might say, out on you. But you've got brains. Now I want you to try and think up something I can do to break this fearful monotony that is eating me alive. But remember . . ."—he held up a wavering, warning finger—"it must be original."

Behind the curtains the man Fredricks was listening intently.

"Is that all?" asked Rose, rather astonished.

"That's the order," Hartland replied.

"And it's a big order," said Rose with spirit. "But I'll try it. And there might be some expense attached to my investigations and researches."

Hartland tossed her a roll of bills. "Good night, Rose," he said drowsily.

Fredricks showed her out, and she looked at him twice because of the curious expression he wore. Then Fredricks proceeded to put his master to bed.

Chapter Two

At the breakfast table in the morning, or what Hartland called the morning and what was really early afternoon, Hartland sat frowning at his soft-boiled egg, bit of toast, and coffee, and looked at Fredricks suspiciously.

"Fredricks," he said sharply, "those drinks you served me this morning seem to be taking unusual effect."

"In what way, sir?" Fredricks inquired solicitously.

"Why, they seem powerful strong in one way, and in another they appear to give me a somnolent feeling," Hartland complained. "I feel more like sleeping than like eating."

Fredricks, being an English butler, coughed discreetly behind his hand. "If you will permit me, sir," he said solemnly, "perhaps it is . . . ah . . . if you'll excuse me, you were quite touched last night."

"I see," said Hartland with a glare. "You mean I'm nursing a hangover and that those two drinks floored me."

"I wouldn't quite say that, sir," said Fredricks. "They were of the usual strength."

Hartland drank the coffee, ignored the egg and toast, and went into his living room to lie down. He was soon asleep. Fredricks told several who telephoned that Hartland was out. Later he went out himself. He went first to a doctor and next to a drug store. When he returned, Hartland still was asleep.

Fredricks liked Hartland. He had worked for his father for twenty-two years; in fact, it was the elder Hartland who had brought him over from England. He had worried about the young man's present mode of living for some time, had endeavored to formulate a plan by which he could help him, but had failed. Subtle hints had merely brought scowls from Roger.

It was the visit of Rose Raymond the night before that had given him a sudden and great inspiration. He now had his plan. Roger wanted something new. Very well, he would give it to him. He had seen the young man toss Rose the roll of bills and had muttered gold digger to himself. This explained the look Rose had thought was curious, but that really was one of contempt.

When Hartland awakened, he called: "Fredricks, I feel groggy! Bring me a drink."

"Quite right, sir." Fredricks did as he had been ordered.

"I'm late for the club," Hartland grumbled, looking at his watch. It was a quarter to five. He dressed hurriedly and took himself off.

As soon as he had left, Fredricks became active. He packed a trunk, putting in all his master's sporting togs, a rifle and shotgun and other outdoor paraphernalia. He had this taken to the express office to await instructions for it to be forwarded as addressed. He then packed another trunk with clothing and this he sent to a railway terminal. After this, he packed a bag containing Hartland's shaving kit, toilet articles, and such things as he would require on a train journey. Fredricks proposed to take his master away whether he wanted to go or not. He knew very well that to suggest to Hartland that he go to the place Fredricks had in mind would be futile. Hartland would only laugh scornfully. Therefore, Fredricks was taking drastic measures, although his action might mean his dismissal.

Hartland came in at dawn fearfully drunk. Fredricks helped him to a chair.

"Going . . . to . . . the dogs," Hartland stammered. "Ought go to . . . lodge."

The lodge? Fredricks smiled. This was playing right into his hands. Hartland had a lodge on Lake George and he would think he was going there.

"Just the thing, sir," said Fredricks loudly. "Just the thing. I'll have everything ready."

"Want drink," muttered Hartland.

"Very good, sir."

Fredricks hurried for a mild drink of whiskey and water into which he put a few drops of a mixture from a bottle. He roused Hartland and actually compelled him to take the drink. Then he undressed him and put him to bed.

At 2:00 P.M., he awakened his master who got up sluggishly. He accepted the drink Fredricks offered him as a matter of course. Fredricks helped him with his bath and helped him to dress. Another drink followed. Hartland had not said a word. He took his coffee and ate his egg as a man in a dream. "Something's THE matter," he muttered.

"You'll be all right at the lodge, sir," Fredricks said. "You ordered preparations made to go to the lodge and everything's ready. We'll go right over to the train. Splendid idea, sir. Splendid!"

Hartland could not seem to collect his faculties.

"Suppose ... might as well," he muttered, his head nodding. "Sleep on train."

"Quite right, sir," Fredricks assured him. "Everything is arranged."

Meanwhile Fredricks had attended to the matter of closing the apartment for a considerable period of time. He was staking everything on Hartland's common sense when he would be himself again, upon the change of environment, and upon a business proposition that he hoped would interest his master.

Shortly after 3:00 P.M. they were in Hartland's car. They drove to Grand Central where arrangements had been made for the immediate occupancy of a drawing room on the *Twentieth Century*. Fredricks had the lower berth made up at once and Hartland lay down upon the blanket and was off to sleep. Shortly afterward they were on their way to Chicago.

Hartland woke late that night. Fredricks had put a blanket over him and made him comfortable.

"Not there yet?" Hartland mumbled.

"Not yet, sir," Fredricks answered. "Do you want anything?"

"Sure. Want ... drink."

Fredricks had anticipated this. It was something of a mechanical answer. He gave his master a drink of whiskey and water, and again the few drops went in. Hartland sank back upon the pillows and went to sleep immediately.

In Chicago next morning, Hartland still was dazed. He took the drink offered him automatically, asked no questions about the taxi ride to another station, entered another train without protest. All he wanted was sleep and he didn't care where he got it. He was in a torpor. He was mumbling and muttering as Fredricks undressed him, put on his pajamas, and put him to bed in the drawing room.

He was sleeping practically all the time for a day and a night and a day, rousing only when Fredricks made him do so to give him nourishment.

"Still on the train?" he would say sleepily. "It's a long night, Fredricks."

"It is, indeed, sir," said Fredricks. "We have that little change to make, you know, at the junction, and then we'll be there, sir."

Hartland nodded stupidly.

Fredricks got him dressed late in the afternoon and they made the change to the little train that ran up into the mountains without trouble. At 9:00 P.M. they left the train at its terminal in Silver City. They went to the Central Hotel where rooms were ready for them, Fredricks having made the arrangement by wire. Hartland was taking things as a matter of course and here he again went to bed.

Fredricks sighed a long, deep sigh of relief.

"Well, I did it," he said aloud. "Now I wonder what he . . . what he . . . I wonder?"

He unpacked the bag and arranged Hartland's toilet articles, laid out the one suit of clothes the bag contained, fresh linen, under things, and socks. Then for the first time in three days he got a good night's sleep.

He was up early. He looked out the windows at

the pine-clad mountains, the sparkling stream—green everywhere save for the mine dumps on the slopes above the town. The air was clean, cool, stimulating. The breeze that came in through the open window made Fredricks's nerves tingle. He recalled the time when he had first come to this place in the Montana mountains years before with Roger's father. The elder Hartland had sought a rest in Silver City more than once.

Well, if this doesn't fix him up, nothing will, he mused.

He heard Hartland stirring in the other room and went in to him. Hartland was sitting on the edge of the bed, rubbing his eyes. But Fredricks saw they looked better this morning. He had discontinued the drops. His master looked at him stupidly.

"Just a moment, sir," said Fredricks, "and I'll bring you some black coffee. You're much better, sir."

He hurried away and soon returned with two large cups of black coffee. They made strong coffee in that country as he well knew.

Hartland willingly drank one of the cups and the strong potion picked him up as if by magic. When he had drained the other cup, the cobwebs were nearly cleared from his brain.

He looked about the room with a puzzled expression. "Fredricks, where are we?" he demanded weakly.

"We're in Silver City, Montana, sir," Fredricks replied.

The clouded look of perplexity in Hartland's eyes increased. He rose unsteadily and, with Fredricks aiding him, went to the window. There he looked out upon the squat buildings of the mining town, the dusty street, the mine dumps on the slopes, the stands of pine marching up to the shoulders of Old Baldy, snow-crowned, gleaming in the sun.

"Good Lord," he groaned, "it's the end of the world."

Chapter Three

Hartland turned from the window. The dullness was almost gone from his eyes. He was gaining in vigor every minute. His mind was clearing fast. "Fredricks," he said sternly, "bring me some more of that coffee and order some eggs and toast. Bring the coffee first."

"Quite right, sir," said Fredricks in his old form.

While his man was gone, Hartland continued to gaze out the window. The cool, mountain breeze fanned his face. It was bracing, this air. He had to concede that. Well, he had seen better scenery in Switzerland. How had Fredricks managed it? He intended to find out.

When Fredricks returned with the coffee—two cups again—Hartland drank one cup before he began interrogating.

"Fredricks, how did I get here?" he asked.

"You . . . ah . . . slept most of the way, sir," Fredricks evaded.

"Yes, I know that, or I would never have got here," Hartland snapped. "And I didn't sleep on whiskey, either, I can tell by the groggy feeling in my head."

"You've had practically no whiskey in more than

three days, sir," said Fredricks. Might as well have the thing over with, and he didn't intend to lie.

"You drugged me, then?" Hartland inquired mildly.

"In a moderate way, sir," replied Fredricks.

Hartland dropped down on the edge of the bed and stared at Fredricks in utter astonishment. "You mean to stand there before me and deliberately confess that you drugged me to drag me out here to this ungodly place?"

"I do not think you would wish me to lie to you, sir," Fredricks returned with dignity.

Hartland stared again. "You seem to be proud of it!" he exclaimed.

"If it accomplishes the purpose I had in mind, sir, I will indeed be proud," said Fredricks.

"What purpose did you have in mind?"

"To satisfy your wish for something new, to show you that you have at least *one* business that is your very own, and . . . you'll pardon me, sir . . . to take you away from the liquor."

"*Humph,*" grunted Hartland sarcastically. "You do indeed seem to have my interests at heart. How'd you know I wanted something new, as you say?"

"If you'll pardon me again, sir, I heard you make a statement to that effect to the . . . ah . . . lady who visited you in the apartment."

"Eavesdropping!" Hartland snorted. "You think *this* will be new? Mountains? I suppose you've forgotten we've been in Switzerland. And what's this talk about a business?"

"You have a mine here, sir . . . a silver mine. Your father bought it years ago. I was here with him when he acquired it. Your father used to like to come out here for a rest. He built a bungalow at the upper end of town. Yours is the largest mine in the camp and is known as the Yellow Jacket."

A thin smile appeared on Hartland's lips and he gazed at Fredricks with elevated brows. "So you thought that because I own a hole in the ground here, it would be best to drug me and haul me out here to see it?"

"It was the only way I could get you here, sir," said Fredricks, his dignity returning. "And I thought you might be interested in the development of the mine, since it is a business you can direct yourself. I have heard you hint, sir, that you would like to be in business."

"Well, you've taken a lot on yourself," said Hartland angrily.

"Roger," said Fredricks slowly in an earnest voice, "I have your best interests at heart. You cannot imagine how it has worried me to see the rut you got into in New York. I have lain awake nights trying to figure out some way in which I could help you. I am not a fool, Roger. I am calling you by your first name because I was in your father's service for twenty-two years and have known you from the time you were a little boy." He paused, wet his lips, looked out the window. "When I saw that woman that night," he resumed, "I did eavesdrop. Not only that, but I peeped through the curtains and I saw you toss her a roll of bills. I know her kind, Roger. Anything new she could show you would bring you evil. Right then and there I decided to get you away from her and her kind. I know we have been to Switzerland. Your father and I were often in Switzerland. But he always referred to this mountain range as the hills. You were here once when you were a little boy. Perhaps you do not remember. I thought you had forgotten the hills and that, if I brought you here, and told you why, it might make an impression. I'm your servant, Roger, but I love you just the same."

Hartland sat staring at the floor. He had been on the point of dismissing this man! Still, Fredricks's act rankled. Love or no love, his father's man for twenty-two years or not—he had taken a great liberty. In many ways Hartland was an aristocrat. He was what is known as a gentleman. He could not throw off the cloak of arrogance in a moment's time. Although he realized that he had to submit to what he considered effrontery on the part of Fredricks, he had no intention of appearing to condone it.

"About the apartment, Fredricks," he said in his usual voice. "You saw to things?"

"Everything is taken care of, sir," replied Fredricks, reverting to his rôle.

"You brought some things along?"

"There is just one suit here, sir, and linen . . . at present. There is a trunk coming that contains sufficient changes and another trunk in which I put your sporting togs, guns, and fishing rods. There is very good fishing here, sir."

"No doubt," said Hartland grimly. "Well, there should be something here."

There was a knock at the door. Fredricks responded and brought in Hartland's breakfast.

To his surprise Hartland ate heartily and enjoyed the food, which was hardly as well prepared as it would have been at Fredricks's hands. After breakfast, he had a bath, shaved, and dressed. He did not know that he had one of the two baths on the upper floor of the hotel to himself. In fact—had he known it—anything and everything in Silver City was at the disposal of Roger Hartland.

The news of his arrival had spread through the camp like wildfire. The effect of his arrival was electrical. Excitement was at fever heat. "Hartland is here!" was the word that passed from mouth to mouth and men's eyes widened and then kindled with hope. Was he going to increase the development operations at the Yellow Jacket. The main shaft of the Yellow Jacket was the deepest in the camp, although it was only 600 feet down. Did he intend to sink? That seemed to be the moot question—would Hartland sink? On the short, dusty street and narrow sidewalks of the camp groups of men gathered and conversation buzzed. Had anyone seen him? None had, and none knew what he looked like. Many who had known the father were anxious to see the son. Silver City was experiencing a genuine thrill—one of those thrills so dear to a mining camp, which are its heart and soul.

The excitement was greatest at the Silver King, the camp's largest resort—a combination refreshment and gambling establishment. Here bets were being made as to the reason for Hartland's visit. All knew his father had come to the camp on occasion for relaxation. The purchase of the Yellow Jacket had been a whim, an excuse enabling him to claim business there. He had never taken much interest in it. But the son was a young man, not over twenty-six it was understood. *He* would not need to come there for relaxation. Besides he was of a generation that seeks relaxation in fashionable resorts in Europe and the like. No, he probably meant business. Bets to this effect increased.

Hartland was standing at the window when there was a knock at the door. Fredricks answered.

"I'd like to see Mister Hartland," said a deep bass voice.

"Who shall I say is calling?" said Fredricks in his best Park Avenue manner.

"Come in!" called Hartland from the window.

He turned to see a tall, powerful man, sandy-haired, blue-eyed, smooth-shaven, with strong features. He wore corduroy, boots splashed with what appeared to be gray clay, and held a stiff-peaked cap with a brass holder for a miner's lamp in his hand.

"You are Mister Hartland?" he said in his deep voice.

"Yes," answered Hartland shortly.

The man advanced and held out his hand. "I'm Jim Miller."

Hartland took the hand and winced with the other's grasp. "Yes?" he said in a puzzled tone.

"Manager of the Yellow Jacket," said Miller, seeing Hartland's look of perplexity.

"Oh, yes," said Hartland. "How do you do, Mister Miller?"

"I heard you were in town," said Miller, somewhat taken aback by the other's manner and rather awed by Hartland's aristocratic appearance, "and I thought it best to report."

"No occasion for it whatsoever," said Hartland.

"Didn't mean to butt in, Mister Hartland," said Miller, irritated. "I suppose you'll be up to the mine and I'm at your disposal any time, of course. Well, I'll be going."

"Good morning," said Hartland, and again he turned to the window. "Wonder what that bird expects me to do," he said with a frown. "Say, Fredricks, what am I supposed to be in this town?"

"As owner of the Yellow Jacket, you are the principal operator, sir," Fredricks replied. "In addition to that, you are the camp's hope."

"The camp's hope?" Hartland exclaimed.

"They hope you will increase your development here, sir," Fredricks explained.

Hartland laughed. "Well, being a hope is something new anyway, Fredricks. I'll give you credit for that. Did you bring a stick?"

"One of your favorites, sir," replied Fredricks who knew Hartland would be lost without a stick.

He brought the cane, and, putting on his hat, Hartland went out the door without another word.

Chapter Four

Roger Hartland's appearance on the street caused an immediate and profound sensation. Everyone recognized him at once. His immaculate attire and the stick stamped him at first glance as the distinguished visitor. But more impressive than anything else was the air about him, the hauteur of a cultured, traveled man, the aristocratic way in which he held his head. This manner was, of course, natural with him, and none who saw him thought he was putting on airs.

As he strolled up the street, men stepped off the sidewalk to give him free passage. This amused him. In fact, he got a thrill out of it. He was being paid the homage of a mining camp of which he was the hope. This amused him even more. He saw all eyes turned on him. The hum of conversation among the groups of miners ceased. *Absurd,* he thought to himself. It was like a scene from a comic play. But if it were carried on, it would no longer amuse him; it would annoy him.

In due time he came to the wide-open entrance of the Silver King resort. He looked within and the scene attracted him. He had never seen anything like it before. A long bar lined with men, many tables at which cards were being played, a roulette wheel and other mechanical devices. He decided out of pure curiosity to go in.

As he entered, a high-pitched voice sounded from the lower end of the bar.

"Gorblimey, 'ere's a blooming toff!"

It was Monocle Joe. Joe had come into the camp from nowhere seven years before wearing a monocle. The camp had gasped, and then ridiculed and chided him. But he continued to wear his monocle, and, when it was ascertained that he was no mean hand at cards, he was accepted, given the sobriquet of Monocle Joe, and the monocle itself accepted as part of the camp furniture. In fact, the camp was ever fascinated by the way in which he handled his eyeglass. It helped him at cards, too. He was short, bowlegged, and red-faced.

"What's a toff?" someone asked.

"A gentleman," was the scornful retort. "Whatja tink?"

Meanwhile, Hartland was strolling leisurely down the bar, the cynosure of all eyes.

"Has to carry a cane for fear he'll catch cold."

The sneering remark came from a man on Hartland's left. Hartland stopped and regarded him coldly. Only three years before Hartland had been a champion boxer at Princeton. Since then, his only exercise had been golf, but he remained more or less fit despite his period of dissipation.

Still holding his stick in his right hand, he walked over to the man who had made the sneering remark and brought a lightning uppercut to his jaw. There was power behind that blow. The man dropped to the floor as if he had been shot, knocked out.

The proprietor came running around the bar in a rage, grasped the man by the ankles, and dragged him out into the street. He hurried back to Hartland, who had stepped in where a place had been made for him at the bar.

"Sorry, sir, very sorry," he said. "Just a no-good loafer. Didn't know who you were, I expect. He won't come in here again, I'll tell the world that."

The look in the eyes of the men who were openly or furtively regarding Hartland changed from amazement to respect. Here was not only a gentleman, but one who would defend his right to carry a cane with his fists.

"D'ja see the bloody hook he passed him?" whispered Monocle Joe.

The proprietor, Big Mose, had hastened around behind the bar to serve Hartland personally.

"Have you any good whiskey?" Hartland asked.

"My own," said Big Mose. He hurried to his little office in front and returned with a bottle. "Would you have one with me?" Big Mose asked, when his customer had taken his potion and placed a bill on the bar.

"No, thanks," Hartland returned. "And I only took that one out of curiosity."

This was lost on Big Mose who walked back to his

office with the bottle, his face wearing a blank look. Queer bird, this. Well, whatever he said went.

Hartland turned to look over the gaming section. As he stepped from the bar, he was approached by a portly, florid individual who wore a black-and-white checked vest with a large chain across it from which was suspended a huge charm.

"I guess you're Mister Hartland," he said pompously. "My name is Mann." He held out a pudgy hand.

Hartland feigned not to see the hand. "Yes?" he said, lifting his brows slightly.

"I'm president of the Consolidated," Mann explained, his face showing chagrin.

"And what has that to do with me?" Hartland inquired.

"Why . . . being mining men I thought we . . . ought to meet and discuss conditions," Mann stammered.

"Well, I'm not a mining man, so get that out of your head," said Hartland curtly, and went on toward the wheel to watch the play a few minutes.

Mann's face went red, then darkened with anger as he strode to the bar for a drink. Monocle Joe's laugh greeted him. The interest in Hartland was more intense than ever.

At last, Hartland turned away from the wheel and beckoned to Big Mose who came in a hurry. "If there are any Yellow Jacket men here," he said, "pick one out who will take a message to the mine for me." Several men who had overheard this came forward at once. "Go up and tell Miller I want to see him at the hotel," Hartland told one of them. The man hurried away at once.

Hartland went out of the place and strolled back down the street. He was quite well satisfied with himself and the events of the morning. More had happened in less time than would happen to him in New York in weeks. Again the sidewalk was cleared for him and he nearly laughed outright. *I guess I'm getting a kick out of this, he thought to himself. Or maybe I'm still working under that dope Fredricks fed me.* When he reached his rooms, he surprised Fredricks by sitting down on the edge of the bed and laughing heartily.

Miller arrived in less than half an hour.

Hartland motioned him to a chair. "Miller, what is this Consolidated?" he asked.

"So far's I can see it's a condition of the mind," was Miller's reply. "Still they've got the Huntley, next to us, under option with an agreement that they can work it for a year to determine if it is worth further developing. I don't know what they paid for the option . . . if they paid anything. And they've taken options on two smaller mines and a lot of claims. That's all I know about them."

"But who are they?" Hartland asked.

"Well, a fellow by name of Mann is the president, old Gordon, the banker, is in the deal, and who the others are I don't know."

"Mann came up and introduced himself to me this morning," said Hartland. "Said us mining men should discuss conditions. I turned him down flat and told him I wasn't a mining man, which I'm not."

"He's considerable of a braggart, I reckon," said Miller. "But there's something behind his operations. I'm thinking they've been getting the options on these mines and claims mostly on wind in the hope of selling the lot to a big company and taking a big profit."

"This Mann popular here?" Hartland asked.

"He is, an' he isn't. He's mighty popular with those who have given him options and hope he'll take 'em up. But outside of them an' the bums who hang around waiting for him to buy a drink for the house, he isn't liked very well. He's too loudmouthed."

Hartland nodded. "I didn't fancy the way he approached me. I understand I have a bungalow up here, Miller."

"That's right. It's up at the upper end of town. Nice place, too. Your father built it. The furniture he put in is there yet."

"Is it in good shape?"

Miller nodded. "I've seen to that," he replied.

"Well, suppose you have it opened up," Hartland suggested. "I may stay here for a time . . . for the fishing." He saw a shade as of disappointment cloud Miller's eyes. He rather liked this manager. "How's the Yellow Jacket coming along?"

"Good as could be expected considering the fact that no money has been put into it for years."

"Is it paying?"

"Paying expenses, that's all," Miller answered with a wry smile. "I've had to cut down my force. Mister Hartland"—he leaned forward with an eager light in his eyes—"we should sink."

"What do you mean by that?" Hartland asked.

Miller now talked in dead earnest for it was his chance to tell the owner of the property what he wanted most to tell him. "We have a shaft six hundred feet deep. That isn't going down very far, but it's the deepest shaft in camp. Now there's every indication of copper beneath these silver deposits. We have copper stain galore. Butte, you know, started as a silver camp, and, when they went down, they got the copper. If we should sink our shaft a few hundred feet lower, I'd bet anything we'd get the copper. I've been a mining man all my life, Mister Hartland, and I know the signs. If you would only put in enough capital so we could sink, I believe it would pay you thousands of times over. It's worth the chance."

Hartland rose and waved an arm indicating that the interview was ended. "As I said before, I'm not a mining man."

Chapter Five

Both Hartland's trunks arrived on the night train and Fredricks busied himself looking after their contents. Hartland went to bed early. He would not tell Fredricks, but he confessed to himself that the air of the mountains was doing him a world of good. Moreover, he was beginning to feel rather grateful to Fredricks for what he had done. He was resolved that there would be no more drink for him. That day he had had not more than one. The experience was indeed something new.

In the morning he donned a gray soft shirt, leaving it open at the throat, riding breeches and boots, a soft gray hat, and took up a riding crop. In this attire, Hartland was a striking figure. Six feet tall, of superb build, wavy blond hair, gray eyes, a firm chin and clear-cut features, he was indubitably handsome. But the way he carried himself was most striking of all. Hartland possessed that indefinable knack of looking like somebody and commanding attention without effort. There was nothing superficial about him. There was not an iota of conceit in him. At all times, under all conditions, Hartland was merely his natural self.

Hartland walked up the street, tapping his right boot with his riding crop, and, if he had been a sensation the day before, he was a double sensation on this bright spring morning. Again the sidewalks were cleared for him; again men looked after him; again surmises and speculations ran riot. For it was the general opinion that Hartland took after his father in the matter of being astute, reticent, and self-willed. He would tell no one his plans until he got good and ready. And the whole camp had discussed, with more or less satisfaction, his deliberate snubbing of Mann the day before.

When Hartland reached the upper end of the street, he saw the bungalow on the slope across the creek. It was screened by pines and the creek was bridged at that point. He crossed the bridge, and, when he passed through the pines, he saw that his father had indeed selected a delightful site for his home in the mountains.

The bungalow was in a little park. A brook ambled through this park and along its banks golden willows grew. His father must have imported these. There were little clumps of alder, quaking asp, and fir. Around the broad verandah were lilac bushes. They were in bloom and the air was fragrant with their scent.

Many men were working about the place. The windows had been boarded up, but these boards now were removed and piled on the lawn. Miller was there superintending operations in person. He came down the steps as Hartland approached.

"Good morning, Mister Hartland," he greeted. "The place is about ready for you. We've been working since five o'clock. You'll find everything just as your father left it. I inspected it every week myself."

"That was kind of you," said Hartland. "It looks pretty good from the outside."

"An' it looks better inside," Miller assured him as they mounted the steps.

His words proved to be true. Hartland looked about him with amazement. It might almost have been a room transferred from a Park Avenue apartment. The walls had been covered with beaverboard and then papered. Reproductions of old masters hung upon them. On the mantelpiece of the wide fireplace was a splendid model of a sailing ship, and at either end a tall antique candlestick. In the center was a large library table with a big, shaded lamp. The table runner, which covered half its surface, was a delicate piece of tapestry. A long bookcase was on the wall opposite the fireplace. A Japanese cabinet in one corner was adorned with bronzes. There were deep, easy chairs, and a large divan. A thick rug in a dark green pattern covered almost the entire floor.

"The *pater* did it up right," Hartland observed.

Miller nodded, and they went on to inspect the two bedrooms, servant's room, bath, and kitchen. There was a hot water heater and Miller explained that the water was piped down from the mountains giving an excellent pressure.

"Well, this will do," Hartland decided. "We'll move in this afternoon if everything is ready."

"Everything will be ready," Miller assured him. Of all things Miller wanted to do, it was to keep Hartland there.

"All right, I'll take a look over the grounds by myself, and then I'll be going," said Hartland.

He found the little park to be a veritable beauty spot. As it was spring in the mountains, flowers grew everywhere, and on the slope behind were wild roses, larkspur, columbine, and berry bushes in full bloom. *Switzerland hasn't anything on this for flowers,* he mused.

On the north side of the park he found a wide, smooth trail leading into the pines. He wondered where it led to and decided one day to explore it. At this moment the soft pound of hoofs came to his ears. Someone was coming on the trail. When Hartland glimpsed the rider, he gave a low whistle of surprise.

"Enter the girl!" he exclaimed aloud. "And on a good horse, too."

She slowed her pace and rode toward him. He saw she was beautiful—dark brown eyes and hair, rose-petal cheeks, a pretty mouth, well-formed, too, as her riding habit attested.

She pulled up beside him, looking down at him from under long, dark lashes. "You must be . . . are you Mister Hartland?" she asked sweetly.

"He and I are the same." Hartland smiled, removing his hat. *By Jove,* he thought to himself, *she's not hard to look at or listen to.*

The girl dismounted. "I'm Margaret Cram," she said as Hartland bowed. "My father, John Cram, heard you were here and sent me over to see you."

"That was kind of him," said Hartland with another flashing smile. "I'm glad he did."

The girl flushed slightly. "My father supplied the horses your father used when he visited here and he thought perhaps you would want some mounts."

"Well, now, so I do," said Hartland. "I forgot to mention horses to Miller. But I don't need more than one horse, a good one. I haven't inquired about saddles."

"Your father had saddles," she said, "and they're probably in your store room. We have a fine black gelding Father thought you might like to try out."

"Is your father in the stock business?" Hartland asked.

"No, Mister Hartland, my father has a mine . . . the Oriole. It isn't much, but now that you've come to stir things up, he will probably be able to get capital to develop it. We have a small place two miles above here and Father always raised a few horses. I believe you would like the black, Mister Hartland."

Hartland was frowning slightly. "What do you mean by saying I've come to stir things up?" he asked mildly.

"Why . . . why . . . if you do what they say you're going to do up at the Yellow Jacket, it will make the camp," she stammered, "and, of course, all the mine owners will profit as well as yourself."

"And what do they say I'm going to do up at the Yellow Jacket?" he asked. *Jove, she was just like a mountain flower.*

"They say you're going to sink," she answered, her eyes widening as if she were surprised at the question.

"Great Jupiter!" he exclaimed. "That's all I hear. Sink, sink, sink! Like being in a rowboat at sea. And why should I sink?" Anything to keep her talking in that delightful voice of hers.

"To get the copper, of course."

Hartland laughed softly. "Girlie, we might have to

go right on through to China, and then only get a brass idol."

"But aren't you going to sink?" she asked, her face clouding prettily.

"Well, Miss Cram, I'm not going to disappoint you or imbue you with any false hopes, so I'm not going to answer your question," he replied. "What I'm most interested in right now is that black. Will you have him brought over this afternoon?"

"I'll bring him over myself. Father has to keep pretty much to the mine. He's working it alone."

"Good," said Hartland. "And, Miss Cram, will you go riding with me in the morning?"

She flushed at this and was undecided.

"To show me the trails and roads," Hartland explained. "You know I'm a stranger here."

Something in his voice attracted her. And what a fine pair of eyes. "Very well," she said. "Nine o'clock, from here. Providing you like the black, of course."

"I believe I'm pretty sure to like him, since you recommend him," said Hartland gallantly. No man had more of a way with women.

He started forward to hand her up into the saddle, but she mounted gracefully and turned her horse.

"Good morning, Mister Hartland!" she called back.

He waved his hat in reply. *If they come like that up here, I guess I'm in for a stay*, he said to himself. He went back to the hotel.

"Fredricks, go up and look over the bungalow and order what you need," he told his man. "We're moving in this afternoon."

On the way up, Fredricks suddenly stopped dead in his tracks. Approaching him was Monocle Joe. He drew up as he saw Fredricks staring at him.

"Where'd you get the monocle?" Fredricks blurted, overcome with astonishment.

"An' 'ow is that any of your blooming business?" Joe inquired, fixing Fredricks with his eyeglass.

"Really!" said Fredricks with the proper accent.

"Strike me pink if 'ere ain't another limey!" Joe exclaimed.

"Ridiculous!" Fredricks exploded.

"An' 'ow's what ridiculous?" Joe inquired.

"Wearing that monocle up here," said Fredricks.

"You're that toff's man, ain't you?" asked Joe.

"That hardly concerns you," said Fredricks, cloaking himself with dignity.

Strange to say, this had the effect of silencing Joe. The monocle popped out of his eye. Class distinction had instinctively been revived by these two, and a gambler could hardly be classed on the same plane as a gentleman's gentleman. Fredricks carried his dignity up the street.

That afternoon, Hartland started for the Yellow Jacket afoot.

Chapter Six

Hartland was trudging up the road to the Yellow Jacket, clipping leaves from shrubs along one side with his riding crop, when he saw two men coming down. As he neared them, he recognized the man who had insulted him in the Silver King the night before. With him was a burly individual with a red stubble of beard and small eyes, set close together.

He wore a gun. They veered in and confronted Hartland as they met.

"Say, you tailor's dummy, what was the idear of that stunt you pulled yesterday?" demanded the man Hartland had hit.

"Get out of my way," said Hartland, his eyes narrowing.

The man looked at his companion, then back at Hartland with a sneer. "You won't get through until I tell you a few things, you damned upstart," he said threateningly.

"I'm not here to listen to anything you have to say," Hartland returned sharply.

"Well, you'll listen whether you want to, or not," snarled the other. "An' if you want to keep that lily-white skin of yours whole, you'll clear out of here *pronto.*"

"Do you think I'd take any notice of a threat from you?" said Hartland angrily.

"Then maybe you'll take notice of this!" cried the man hoarsely.

He swung viciously, but Harland easily ducked the blow. Then Hartland's anger rose and red burned before his eyes. As the man made another swing, he ducked under and gave him the same left uppercut that had floored him the night before. It staggered him but did not knock him down. Then Hartland himself staggered from a blow behind the left ear. The two of them were attacking him!

With two against him, he swung his riding crop. It struck the man ahead squarely in the face bringing the blood spurting from his nose and sending him to his knees. Hartland turned just in time to avoid another blow from the man behind. He swung his crop, but missed. There was a lightning move of the man's right hand and Hartland just caught a glimpse of the gleam of metal before the gun roared. It was as if a red-hot iron seared his left side.

Guns. He had never been up against them before. They wanted to kill him! He leaped aside as the gun spoke again. Then his riding crop came down like a flash of lightning on the gunman's wrist, bringing a howl of pain as the gun *thudded* into the dust.

Hartland dived for the gun. But he had forgotten the other man. A flying weight flattened him in the dust. He twisted, choking, and managed to get hold of the gun. The second assailant pounced upon him, and, as he squirmed to free himself, a hand came under and gripped him by the throat. He felt his right wrist gripped, and, with every iota of strength he possessed, he heaved upward and jerked the wrist free. Sinking down in a twinkling, he whipped the gun around over his left shoulder and fired.

The fingers clutching at his throat relaxed. There was a shout and the weight upon him lightened. He flung off the load on his back and leaped to his feet. The gunman lay on his side where he had been flung. The other was standing to one side, a white pallor spreading over his face.

Hartland looked down at the gunman and his face, too, went white. A little pool of red was forming under the man's right temple. Hartland stopped and turned him over. He had a sickening feeling in the pit of his stomach as he saw the bullet hole in the temple oozing blood.

Then he turned on the other man in a fury. "This is your fault!" he shouted. "You rat, I've a mind to drop you, too!"

"Don't," the man quavered. "I didn't know he was going to pull a gun in the first place."

"You lie and you know it!" Hartland accused. "You knew from the moment you saw me you'd use the gun if you had to. Who is this man? Talk straight or I'll let you have it. You attacked me and I've got every excuse in the world."

"He was Ed Mercer," said the other quickly.

"What'd he do? Where was he from?"

"The Huntley," came the speedy reply.

Hartland considered this. He recalled that Miller had said the Huntley was the mine next to the Yellow Jacket and was under option to the Consolidated. But there could be no connection between that fact and this attack. Such a thought was absurd.

"Walk along ahead there," he told the man before him. "You're going to the Yellow Jacket with me."

Hartland took his man into Miller's private office and there they waited while Miller was sent for. It was some twenty minutes before he appeared.

"I was on the six-hundred foot level," he explained.

"There's a dead man down the road," said Hartland crisply, putting the gun on Miller's desk, "and this fellow wants to tell you about it. Tell him!" he commanded, scowling at his captive.

The man cleared his throat and related exactly what had happened, trying at the same time to make his part in the affair appear insignificant.

"This fellow started it, and I finished it," said Hartland when the man was through.

"What's your name?" Miller demanded.

"Finch," was the reply.

"Well, you can go," said Miller, "but don't leave the camp!" When Finch had left, Miller smiled at Hartland. "That means he'll light out as fast as he can, an' that's just what I want him to do so he won't be wandering around shooting off his mouth."

Hartland nodded, and Miller drew up a chair.

"This is rather serious business, Mister Hartland," he said. "It'll more'n likely mean trouble with the Huntley crew. They've got a tough bunch over there an' a gunfighter by the name of Butch Allen. He's a killer. What Mann's got him around for, I don't know." He paused in thought while he rolled and lighted a cigarette. "You see, they wanted to cut across our claim and join our road, an' I turned 'em down. We can do enough damage to that road in winter and spring with our own ore wagons without them coming in, too. But that isn't it. Mann's got something up his sleeve. Maybe this killing . . . accident, will bring it out. Anyway, it wasn't your fault an' you were lucky you didn't get plugged yourself."

"Hadn't we ought to do something about the . . . the body?" Hartland inquired in uncertain tones. "I've never killed a man before, Miller, and I don't like the sensation."

"I'll send down the spring wagon," said Miller. "I reckon you better go on down. I'll send a man with you to show you the short cut."

Hartland went to the bungalow and found Fredricks installed there.

"Fredricks, did you bring anything strong with you?" he asked.

"Why . . . yes," Fredricks replied, noting that his master looked rather pale.

"Then I'll take one stiff drink," said Hartland, sinking into a chair.

During the late afternoon, all through the excellent dinner Fredricks had prepared, and that evening, Hartland strove to thrust from his mind the picture of the dead gunman, the pool of blood, the bullet hole in the man's temple. Frequently he would shudder.

He tried to read, but it was no use. Then late in the evening, there came a knock at the door. When Fredricks opened it, Hartland saw Mann's bulky figure in the doorway.

"Come in," he invited, glad of anything to divert his thoughts.

Mann entered. "Mister Hartland, you killed one of my men this afternoon, so now I guess we can talk."

"Sit down," said Hartland.

As Miller had predicted, the affair of the afternoon had brought results.

Chapter Seven

As they sat by the table in the glow of the shaded lamp, Hartland saw there was a difference between Mann on this night and his look and demeanor of the day before. There was more force to the man than he had suspected.

"Will you have a drink?" Hartland inquired hospitably.

"No, thanks," replied Mann with a gesture of his pudgy hand. "Drink and business do not mix, Mister Hartland."

"Very well," said Hartland quietly, "state your business."

This direct assault caused Mann to frown. "It's a serious business to murder a man, Mister Hartland," he said impressively.

"Oh, has someone been murdered?" asked Hartland, elevating his brows.

"Now, don't start that with me," said Mann pompously. "Finch has told me all about it. You hit him with your riding crop, grabbed Mercer's gun, and shot him down like a dog. He was one of my best men. This is serious business, Hartland."

"Hasn't Finch left town yet?" Hartland inquired mildly.

"Of course not," Mann replied sharply. "Why should he leave town?"

"I don't know," Hartland answered. "I merely asked out of curiosity."

"Don't you people come down on Finch," said Mann, shaking a forefinger at Hartland. "He's under my protection."

"I expect that gives him license to lie," Hartland remarked dryly.

"I'll take Finch's word any day!" thundered Mann, bringing a palm down on the table.

"Well, you have it." Hartland smiled. "What do you propose to do . . . have me arrested?"

"Ah . . . not at present," replied Mann. "Perhaps not at all. It'll depend, of course. Yes . . . it'll depend."

"Depend, I suppose, on what I think of this business you say you have to talk over with me," said Hartland, amused.

Mann bristled. "This isn't a joke," he snapped. "I suppose you know we are working the Huntley Mine, next to the Yellow Jacket, on option for a year. Now we want to cut through a corner of your property to build a road to join the road from the Yellow Jacket. This will enable us to transport more ore and we are willing to pay you reasonably for the right of way. We are doubling our force of men next week. The road will not injure your property and someday it might be of use to you. Miller has refused to consider this proposal but you, as owner, can consider it." He looked closely at Hartland.

"Who do you mean by *we?*" Hartland asked.

"The Consolidated, of course," answered Mann sharply.

"And just what is this Consolidated?" Hartland persisted.

"We'll come to that later," said Mann irritably. "What we are discussing now is the matter of the road. We need that road, and, as I say, we're willing to pay a reasonable sum for the right of way across your property."

"You want a road through there so you can transport more ore and you're putting on more men," said Hartland as Mann nodded in confirmation. "You must intend to gut the Huntley in a year."

"We're paying a royalty on every ton," Mann declared angrily. "But that has nothing to do with the matter we're discussing. Do we get the road? That's what I want to know."

"I'll answer your questions when I've heard all you've got to say," Hartland retorted calmly.

Mann frowned. "Well . . . Hartland, would you consider giving an option on your mine?" he asked.

"I told you," said Hartland in a rising voice, "that I'd answer your questions when you were through."

"Very well," Mann acquiesced. "Now I've got two propositions to put up to you, Hartland, and there's money for us both in either of them. I've got a year's working option on the Huntley. I've options on the Silver Queen and Susan Mines. They're small, but then they haven't been developed, although both have good ore showings. In addition, I have options on nineteen undeveloped claims. These are all grouped together, understand?" Mann was talking very seriously now.

Hartland nodded. "But you speak of us making money, and of you having these options," he pointed out. "Where does the Consolidated come in?"

Mann shook his head impatiently. "I mean the Consolidated, of course. But I'm the head of it, which is why I speak the way I do. Now, listen. There is a large body of low-grade silver ore here that could be handled profitably by a big company that could put in a mill and develop on a large scale. With the Yellow Jacket added, many of the others would come in. We would have a big property to offer. I don't take any stock in this copper talk, but a big company would just as soon have a big body of low-grade ore as a single mine of high-grade ore. Understand?"

"Sounds reasonable," Hartland admitted.

"Good." Mann rubbed his hands. "So there's another question to be answered when I'm through. Will you put the Yellow Jacket into the pool and come in with us? Now next, Hartland, is a proposition where you'd make more than any of the rest of us. I believe this will interest you. In fact, I was going to write you in detail about both these propositions if you hadn't shown up when you did. It was a fortunate thing you came at this time. Very fortunate."

Hartland made no comment on this.

"Hartland," said Mann, leaning on his elbows on the table, "capital is a great thing. You have it. You're a millionaire, I understand. But I've never heard of a man yet who had so much money that he didn't want to make more. Now here's a chance for you. Handle this thing by yourself. Either buy our options outright, or we'll go in with you. You, or we, can form a company, secure outside capital while retaining control, erect a mill, and develop this low-grade proposition. With a mill, and developing on a large scale, anything from four dollars a ton up will pay. And we're bound to run into streaks of high-grade ore. They've run into patches in your own mine that have run as high as eleven hundred dollars to the ton. And I've got all this stuff of ours tied up tighter than a drum."

He waited for some comment from Hartland but none was forthcoming.

"You would only have to invest some five hundred thousand, or even less," said Mann. "And you could hold control. Or we might take stock in the company and put in our options. What do you say?"

"Is this all?" Hartland asked, without looking at him.

"That's all, but the last proposition is the best," Mann replied.

Hartland rose. "Now I'll answer your questions," he said grimly. "You cannot put a road across my property. I will not give you an option on the Yellow Jacket. I will not put the Yellow Jacket into what you call your pool. I will not buy your options, or undertake the development you suggest under any of the conditions you have stated. Now that you have your answers, you can go. Fredricks!"

Fredricks came in at once.

"Show this man out," Hartland ordered.

Fredricks went to the door and opened it.

"I'll fix you!" Mann shouted. "I'll. . . ."

He got no further. Hartland leaped from his chair, grasped him by the collar, and hurled him through the door. He fell on his face on the porch.

"Good night!" Hartland called. "Fredericks, close the door."

Fredricks obeyed, and stepped softly around the table. His face was white. Strange happenings, these.

"What's the matter, Fredricks?" said Hartland, seating himself. "You look a little white about the gills."

Hardly had he got the words out of his mouth when the door burst open. Hartland looked around quickly to see a tall, rough-looking man framed in the doorway. He was of swarthy complexion with small, glittering black eyes. In his right hand he held a gun with which he covered Hartland.

Butch Allen! thought Hartland as he remembered Miller's mentioning that Mann had employed a gunfighter by this name.

The man strode into the room, his cruel eyes holding Hartland's gaze. Behind him came Mann. Doubtless Mann had brought him along to intimidate him.

"Now, I reckon you'll hear what this man has to say," said the gunman. "An' don't try any funny capers . . . I'm telling you."

"I suppose you're Butch Allen," said Hartland coolly.

"I'm glad you've heard of me," said Allen, "for you'll be knowing what you're up against. Go ahead, Mister Mann."

"Just a minute!" Hartland's words broke sharply. "Do you think you can come here and scare me with that gun? You know what my position is and what it would mean if you were to shoot me. I have no intention of listening to anything more this man has to say. Maybe he can talk in the dark, but it won't be very impressive. Fredricks, turn down the wick and blow out the light."

"Stay where you are!"

Fredricks was unable to move under the spell of the gunman's eyes and his tone of voice.

"Oh, very well," said Hartland, "I'll do it myself." He rose and leaned over the lamp.

"Don't try it!"

Hartland straightened. "Do you mean to tell me I'm not the master of my own house?" he said sternly. Then, before Allen could interfere, he turned down the wick and blew out the light. The room was plunged into darkness.

"Why don't you shoot?" he asked derisively.

"I'll give you twenty-four hours to reconsider!" Mann shouted. "Remember that. Come on, Butch."

"I wouldn't give him twenty-four minutes," said Allen as they went out.

Fredricks struck a match. His hand was shaking so that he couldn't light the lamp. Hartland took the next match, lit the lamp, then closed the door. His face was set and stern. But he looked at Fredricks curiously.

"Although I don't suspect you knew you were do-ing it," he said slowly, "you certainly have given me a taste of something new. Make some tea."

He went to the mine telephone and rang. A short wait, then: "Oh, I took a chance on your being up, Miller. Mann and his gunman were up here tonight. I'll tell you about it tomorrow. Put on a full crew, Miller . . . all the men you can use and pick them carefully, if that's possible. And you better keep an eye on the Huntley outfit. Mann's putting on more men over there. That's all. Good night."

He sat down and thought steadily until Fredricks brought in the tea.

Chapter Eight

Next morning Hartland was up, almost with the dawn.

"Did that girl bring the horse?" he asked.

"He's in the barn, sir," replied Fredricks. "I looked after him. A splendid beast, sir."

Hartland smiled. "Well, I've no intention of making a hostler out of you, Fredricks," he said. "You've enough to do as it is. We'll have to look around for a man to tend to things on the outside. I don't know but that we may be here for some time."

"Very good, sir," said Fredricks in a tone of relief. Horses were not in his line.

Hartland went out to the barn and found that the black gelding was indeed a splendid animal.

"You'll do," said Hartland aloud, and, as he spoke, the horse threw up its head with ears alert.

In the little room at the front of the barn, Hartland found several English saddles and a stock saddle that had been left by his father. They were all in good condition. There was a riding crop, too. He wondered if Miller's men had found his own crop when they went for the body up there in the road. His face clouded again with the mental picture of the dead man, but he shook off the unpleasant feeling by sheer willpower.

Hartland went in and saddled the black. He mounted and crossed the little park to the bridge. Across the bridge he came into the road leading up the valley. He galloped for a mile and came back at a canter. He put up the animal, well satisfied, and went in to breakfast, refreshed and hungry. He no longer was the Roger Hartland of Park Avenue.

Miller came after breakfast. He brought Hartland's riding crop, explained that the body of Ed Mercer had been turned over to the Huntley outfit, and then listened intently as Hartland explained what had taken place the night before.

When Hartland had finished, Miller chuckled. "So that's the lay," he said. "Mann has bitten off more than he can chew an' he figures to bulldoze you into taking the load. He hasn't got the capital to put his scheme through." Miller paused thoughtfully. But," he added, "his scheme is feasible. If you were going to sink, Hartland, I'd say get hold of the option on the Huntley anyway."

"I'm not a mining man," Hartland said again, crossly. "I can't start a lot of work here, Miller, for I'd want to be on hand to see how it went and I can't tie myself up here. But this Mann has, in a way, roused my old football fighting blood. He's not going to put anything over on me. How about the men?"

"I'm going to pick some up around town an' the rest will come from down the line," Miller replied. "I won't take just any man into the mine because he's a miner. I'll have a full crew an' be working all levels, save the hundred an' two-hundred, within the next forty-eight hours."

"Good." Hartland nodded. "Do you know Margaret Cram?"

Miller looked at him quickly, and, Hartland thought, a bit suspiciously. "So you've met her," he said. "She's old John Cram's daughter an' a mighty nice kid."

"I could make that out myself," said Hartland

dryly. "She came over yesterday. Said her father supplied Dad with horses. Brought me over a fine black. Tried him out this morning. I'm going riding with her at nine o'clock, so I guess you better toddle along."

A queer expression had come over Miller's face. It betrayed commingled suspicion, resentment, and speculation. He rose. "John Cram thinks a lot of that girl," he said slowly in a tone that conveyed a subtle warning. "She was born in the mountains an' . . . hasn't been around much." He looked Hartland straight in the eye and the owner of the Yellow Jacket frowned. "I'll be going," he concluded, and went out the door.

Hartland stared through the open doorway, his frown deepening. Then it suddenly gave way to a laugh, and he went out to the barn for his horse.

Margaret Cram was on time to the minute, and, when Hartland saw her this morning, he gave a low whistle. He might still have been a little befuddled the morning before, but the girl looked better at second sight than at first. *Mountain flower is right*, he thought to himself. Then, aloud: "You match the scenery this morning, Miss Cram, and I've just been deciding that the scenery is beautiful."

The roses bloomed in her cheeks, but she ignored the compliment. "You like the black, Mister Hartland?" she asked.

"Very much," he answered, patting the horse's neck. "What's his name?"

"Father named him Pete," she replied as though apologizing. "I know it's a horrid name. But Father says a good horse should have a good, honest name and he seems to think Pete is such a name."

"It's an easy name to remember and an easy name

to say," he said, smiling. "And I have no doubt but that it is honest. Where are we going, Miss Cram?"

"I thought we'd go over the ridge into Moon Valley," she replied. "It's about the best trail I can show you, Mister Hartland, and I can point out others on the way."

"Fair enough," said Hartland. "And it's very kind of you to go to this trouble, Miss Cram."

"Oh, I ride every morning," she said. "Besides, it's the duty of everyone in Silver City to see that you enjoy yourself here and get a good impression of the country."

Hartland looked at her admiringly. "Miss Cram," he said, smiling again, "you are more than clever. You are adroit."

"We had better start," she said hastily, and whirled her horse to lead the way into the trail that ran north into the pines.

Scarcely were they out of sight when Monocle Joe came walking jauntily up to the house from the bridge. He went around to the rear door and by chance found Fredricks on the little latticed porch back there.

Fredricks had a sudden inspiration. "Do you know anything about horses?" he asked.

Joe looked up in such surprise that his monocle dropped. "Do I know anything about 'orses?" he exclaimed. "Do I know anything about 'orses? An' me once working in Lord Longdale's stables! Wot don't I know about 'orses?"

"Very well," said Fredricks, much pleased. "Mister Hartland wishes to engage a man to look after his horse, and things about the yard. Would you like the situation?"

Monocle Joe screwed in his glass with a thrill.

Into service again. And with another Englishman in the same service. It wouldn't interfere with his card playing of nights.

"Gorblimey, I'm asking for the place right now," he said.

Thus Monocle Joe entered Roger Hartland's employ.

Hartland and Margaret Cram trotted along the firm trail through the pines until they came into a trail leading east and west. They turned west, Margaret explaining to Hartland that the east trail led down to the road to town. They climbed a high ridge and rode down into a long, narrow valley through which ran a small, clear stream.

"This is Moon Valley," the girl explained. "There is a fine trail leading up the valley and over to the left clear up to the north Divide. You'll enjoy riding up here."

She had checked her horse and Hartland remembered that they were not supposed to be out merely for a ride. He was being informed as to trails.

"There is another trail across the stream halfway up the valley that goes off westward and over the main range, although I doubt if you'd ever want to ride that far."

"Let's get a drink," Hartland suggested. He dismounted and drew a collapsible drinking cup from a pocket. She got off her horse, also. He had noticed her stealing furtive glances at him on their ride, and she looked at him curiously now as he handed her a cup of water. When they had both taken a drink, she spoke suddenly, impulsively.

"It must be wonderful to have so much money, Mister Hartland," she said.

"Eh, what?" The spontaneity of her remark startled him. "What makes you think I've got so much money . . . if you meant me?"

"Father says you've got all the money in the world and it'll never do anybody any good," she replied. "He said your kind. . . ." She caught herself and placed a hand over her mouth in dismay.

"I might as well hear all of it," he said wryly. "What about my kind?"

"I shouldn't have said that," she answered in confusion. "I can't tell you. Anyway, Father blurts out things without stopping to think."

"Everybody seems to think I ought to be here to play Santa Claus to this camp, Miss Cram," Hartland complained. "Well, I'm not here for that purpose. I'm here for pleasure. And please don't let us talk about money. There are plenty of other topics. Yourself, for instance. Have you always lived here in the mountains?"

"Except for the winters when I went to the lowlands to school," she replied. "I keep house for father."

So she had no mother. Hartland could sympathize with her for he had lost his own mother when a boy. "I gather that you like it up here," he said.

"It's my home," she said simply.

"You've had a longing to see more of the world?" he ventured. She must have some vulnerable spot. All the women he'd ever known had.

She shook her head. "No. I've merely wondered about it."

"What would you and your father do if he were to make a big strike at his mine and sell out at a handsome figure?" he asked curiously.

"I've never thought about that," she said soberly.

"If it should ever happen . . . which I doubt . . . it would then be time enough to make our plans. This isn't a big strike country, Mister Hartland. It's mostly low-grade silver or galena. The big strike will be made only by sinking for the copper."

Hartland shrugged. Back to business again. Then a thought struck him. Had her father told her to attempt to influence him? He looked at her searchingly. "Would you be glad if I were to take a chance on the copper?" he asked pointedly.

Her eyes widened. "Of course," she said frankly. "The whole camp would be glad."

He shook his head impatiently and took up his reins. He knew better than to attempt to help her into the saddle, for she already had proved that she scorned such assistance. They had hardly found the stirrups when a wild, hatless figure of a man, with hair disheveled and features strangely distorted, burst through the willows along the stream and peered at them from under thick, bushy brows. The man was stooped, his great shoulders hunched; his huge hands hung at his sides and were covered with matted hair. Hartland thought instantly of a gorilla.

The man turned to Margaret Cram, saying something in a hoarse, croaking voice that Hartland could not understand.

"Go away, Creeps," said the girl sharply.

She started to turn her horse, but the man grasped a rein near the bit. Hartland instantly swung his horse in and struck the man's wrist a smart blow with his riding crop. The rein was released and the girl spurred her mount with Hartland following.

"Who, or what, was that?" Hartland asked her as they started back up the trail.

"That was Creeps Hallow," she replied. "Called that, I guess, because he gives folks the creeps."

"Did you understand what he was trying to say?"

"Yes. He wanted to know who you were," she replied.

"Well, I don't like his looks a little bit," said Hartland. "Got a claim, I suppose."

"On the east slope, halfway up the valley," answered the girl. "I've always thought he was crazy."

"And I believe you're right," said Hartland.

When they reached the intersection of the trail to Hartland's place on the other side of the ridge, Margaret drew rein.

"I'll be going on home," she said, smiling. "Father'll be wanting his dinner. Someday I'll show you some trails down the creek. But the ride up Moon Valley or up the main road north is always good."

"Miss Cram, won't you come over to my place and have tea some afternoon?" he asked.

She hesitated and appeared uneasy. "I . . . don't know," she stammered. "It wouldn't be . . . no, I don't think I could."

"But my man will serve tea on the porch," he pleaded. "And you know I'm not acquainted here. You've been very kind. Suppose we go riding down the creek one day this week, and then have tea. You said it was the duty of everyone here to see that I enjoyed myself, you know."

She looked at him quickly and saw he was smiling. He had a good smile. Millions at his command, and the future of Silver City in the palm of his hand. She looked off to where the Divide traced its jagged outline against the sky.

"Well, perhaps," she said, and, with a wave of the hand, she was off.

Hartland sat down at noon to his luncheon in a queer state of mind. He was puzzled and satisfied by turn. "Well, anyway, she's a little mountain queen," he muttered.

"Beg pardon, sir?" said Fredricks.

"It's nothing," said Hartland irritably.

On a crude bench before a log cabin, high on the east slope of Moon Valley, Creeps Hallow sat in the burning sun, staring stolidly at a red welt on his right wrist.

Chapter Nine

The afternoon was warm and Hartland lay down upon the divan to catch forty winks. When he awoke, it was nearing sunset. Fredricks was preparing dinner. He went out for a stroll about the park, as mountain meadows are known, and, when passing the barn, he saw Monocle Joe leading the black in from water. Fredricks had told him about Joe, saying that he had taken him on, and Hartland looked curiously at the diminutive figure with the single glass screwed in his right eye. Joe saw him and saluted. Hartland nodded and passed on. It occurred to him that Joe might prove useful someday as he must possess a vast fund of information about the inhabitants of Silver City.

After dinner, Hartland sat in a wicker chair on his porch. He wondered about Rose Raymond back in New York. Well, she had nothing to complain about, so far as he was concerned. There had been plenty in that roll he had tossed her before leaving. Then his thoughts reverted to Margaret Cram. He lit a cigarette and frowned. He couldn't expect class and cleverness, adeptness and brains in a simple mountain girl. She wasn't his kind, of course. He was interested in her merely because she was the first girl he had met here and would probably prove the best-looking of the lot. Nevertheless, he had to have diversion.

His thoughts were interrupted by the appearance of a visitor who came walking briskly up from the bridge. This man was of slight build, and, as he neared the porch steps, Hartland saw he had a grayish complexion that was in direct contrast to the tan and sunburn of most of the men about. He wore a bristly, iron-gray mustache and his eyes were dark with a quality to their gaze that could not be described as otherwise than sharp.

He halted at the bottom of the steps. Good evening," he said. "Mister Hartland, I believe?"

"I'm Hartland," said Hartland, rising. "Will you come up?" He motioned to a chair.

"I'm Alex Gordon," the newcomer announced as he came up the steps. "I have the bank in Silver City."

Hartland nodded. He was not particularly interested, except that he remembered Miller's mentioning this banker as being connected with the Consolidated.

Gordon took a chair. "I understand, Mister Hartland," he said slowly, putting the tips of his fingers together before him, "that you are about to start extensive development at the Yellow Jacket, and I wanted to tell you that I will be able to provide all the banking facilities you will require." He looked at Hartland keenly. "It won't be necessary for you to go to an outside bank," he added with a smile meant to be pleasant.

"Where did you obtain your information about this extensive development you mention?" Hartland inquired.

"Oh . . . ah. . . ." The banker waved a hand in a comprehensive gesture. "Everyone knows that a young man like yourself, with the world's playgrounds to choose from, wouldn't come to Silver City just for an outing. We are not such fools as you might think, Mister Hartland." Again his smile strove to convey good feeling. "Besides, Miller has been taking on men . . . a lot of them."

"I told him to put on a full crew, which means both day and night shifts," said Hartland. "The Yellow Jacket has been breaking even, nothing more. It must pay interest on the investment. It must pay some kind of a profit. But I contemplate no extensive developments, so get that out of your head."

Gordon's face clouded. "There's an excellent opportunity here, Mister Hartland." He was genuinely in earnest in this.

"Maybe so," said Hartland calmly, "but my father knew far more about business than I, and he didn't see fit to go ahead with any extensive developments."

"That was because your father was not a mining man."

"I'm not a mining man, either," Hartland interposed. He looked at the banker speculatively. He had often heard of the power of money, but as yet he had only found that it meant luxurious living quarters, travel, limousines, amusements, orgies, and the obsequious attention of menials. Then he remembered.

"Mister Gordon, what is your connection with what Mann calls the Consolidated and what is it?" he asked suddenly.

"I have invested some money in the Consolidated," replied Gordon readily, "which is a company being promoted to bring one of the big mining or smelting companies in here to develop the camp. But such money as I have invested is my own, and has no connection with the bank. I am very conservative when it is a matter of the bank's funds, Mister Hartland."

"I suppose so," said Hartland dryly. "I presume you know that Mann is trying unsuccessfully to bulldoze me into taking up this development proposition?"

"I believe he said he intended speaking to you," Gordon evaded, "and I think you would realize heavily on your investment, Mister Hartland. In fact, as a banker who knows this country, I recommend it."

Hartland smiled. Then he bethought himself of something else. Perhaps it would be well to make an impression on this shrimp of a banker at the start. He excused himself and went into the living room to his desk. When he returned, he handed a slip of paper to Gordon.

"I think I'd best augment the Yellow Jacket's bank account," he remarked simply. "Our payroll will jump."

The banker looked at the slip of paper and started. It was a check on a New York bank for $150,000. He looked with bright eyes at Hartland, and this time his smile was genuine.

"I'll have to bring in more cash," he said with some excitement. "The men are paid in cash, you know. Oh, I get it all back in my vault eventually. This must mean that you are going ahead, Mister Hartland, but I won't ask any more questions." He rose, actually beaming.

"It might be well for you to remember that's subject to my orders," Hartland said casually, "and don't spread any false reports."

Gordon walked back down to the bridge with a sprightly step, leaving Hartland frowning on the porch in the gathering dusk. He had intended starting back to New York in two weeks, but here he was becoming embroiled in a network of activities about which he knew nothing. Mann's threats and aggressiveness had aroused his fighting instincts, and there was Margaret Cram.

"Confound it!" he ejaculated aloud. "Has it taken me thirty years to find out that I'm crazy?"

The purple veils of dusk were darkening. Fredricks lit the lamp in the living room, but Hartland remained on the porch. Night flung its Cimmerian robes over the mountains and lighted the heavens with stars. A cooling breeze idled in the meadow and the air was sweet with the scent of lilacs.

Finally Hartland went inside. He had letters to write informing his bankers and brokers of his whereabouts. He must write to his sister, too. She was living in Paris. And Rose Raymond had wanted him to take her there. For a moment he thought whimsically of writing to Rose, but he decided against it. What would be the sense of it?

He wrote his letters slowly. Fredricks was busying himself about the kitchen. Joe had gone off to town where he was to stay. He would have a night at cards, be back at dawn, to have Hartland's horse ready for an early ride, and catch catnaps during the day.

He had just finished the last of his letters—the one to his sister—and was sealing the envelope, when his faculties were suddenly alert with an intangible sense of another presence in the room. The feeling that came over him was so uncanny that it sent a chill up his spine. He overpowered the impulse to leap to his feet, finished sealing the letter, and put it with the others. Then he turned about in his chair. What he saw gave him another chill. He could not resist getting to his feet.

Leaning on his great, hairy hands on the farther side of the table was the gorilla man—Creeps Hallow. The twisted features were more contorted than they had been that morning. The mouth drooped on the right side and lifted on the left, and two long, yellow teeth showed against the thick lower lip like fangs. But it was the look in the eyes that gave Hartland the chill. The flashing pinpoints of red made of the man a monster. Now the lips moved.

"You're Hartland!" he said in a hoarse, guttural voice, pointing a fearful forefinger. "I found out. You're Hartland!" A horrible cackle of sound issued from the monster's mouth and Hartland took it that the man was laughing. The lips writhed. "I know you!"

"What of it?" Hartland demanded sharply. To save his life he could not have helped being awed, almost frightened by this awful creature.

Again that horrible, croaking laugh. Then the lips screwed themselves into a hideous grimace; the skin at the corners of the eyes bunched, and the thick, scraggy brows came down. It was as if the man were wearing a trick mask.

"I want my money." The words came in a deep

tone as from a well. "You hear?" The question burst from the distorted lips as if shot from a gun.

There was a short space in which Hartland stared at this formidable visitor with a puzzled expression. Then he suddenly became angry. Everybody here seemed to want something from him. Even the one girl he had met had harped on the matter of doing this and that for the camp. What was Silver City to him? He worked himself into a rage—a wild, burning rage that this uncouth creature should enter his house by stealth and demand money.

"You get out of here!" he commanded harshly.

Creeps Hallow stepped around the end of the table with his queer, ape-like gait; his massive shoulders were hunched and his left hand hung like a talon.

"Your father promised to buy my claim," said Creeps Hallow, baring his yellow teeth. "He died. Good! Now you buy it. I want the money." He chuckled in his throat.

A great beast of a man, Hartland was thinking, with the mind of a child and the strength of a giant. He was all the more dangerous because of his low order of mentality. And where was Fredricks? In the next room, listening and shivering and rubbing his hands in a fright, doubtless. His appearance might at least distract this monster's attention and disconcert him. But Hartland knew it would be useless to call. At this moment, Hallow started around the table.

Hartland backed away from him, then leaped for the Japanese cabinet. He grasped one of the bronzes and held it aloft, ready to hurl it at Hallow's head. The man's snarl was like that of a wild beast. Then came footfalls on the steps and porch. The screen

door was jerked open and Miller came in, just as
Hallow leaped. The missile Hartland flung struck
him fully in the face, but didn't stop him. Hartland
leaped madly out of reach of those clutching fingers
and powerful arms.

Next moment Miller had flung himself on Hallow's
back. It seemed as though Hallow merely shrugged
or shook his shoulders, but Miller was thrown against
the wall. His hand went inside his coat, and, when he
whipped it out, the yellow rays of lamplight gleamed
on the blue barrel of a six-shooter.

The change in Hallow was magical. He backed
away and cringed before the black bore of the gun.
Another of those lightning changes of expression
left his face bearing the frightened look of a child.
He paid no attention now to Hartland. He could not
take his eyes from the weapon Miller held.

Miller rose. "You get out of here!" he thundered.
"Never come again! He'll have one next time . . . understand?" He shook the gun and pointed to Hartland. "Now go . . . an' never come back!"

Creeps Hallow slipped noiselessly out to the
porch and disappeared into the night.

Hartland took a long breath. "Crazy," he muttered
through dry lips.

"You said it, I reckon," said Miller. "He pestered
your father some. Your father used to ride up into
Moon Valley where this Hallow lives, an' I guess he
was going to buy his claim to get him out of there. I
told him not to, for goodness knows what Hallow
would do next. If he ever starts anything again,
shoot. Don't let him get his hands on you. Here are
some things I had up at the office. I had the silverware and other valuables up there, too, for safekeep-
ing." He had secured the package from the table

where he had thrown it when he entered and was unwrapping it. "I'd keep this article handy," he said. He put an ivory-handled .45 on the table before Hartland. "There's a belt an' holster around here somewhere," he added.

Hartland hardly heard what Miller went on to say about securing additional men for the mine. When the Yellow Jacket manager had gone, Fredricks crept into the room, rubbing his hands nervously. He found Hartland, a bit white, staring down at the gun.

Chapter Ten

The fresh element of danger and uncertainty that Creeps Hallow had precipitated into the involved situation in which Hartland found himself caused the Yellow Jacket owner to consider leaving the camp and returning East. He could not see why he should stay and have his life threatened. On the other hand, if he did go, he would be hooted and jeered at and branded as a quitter, and perhaps a coward. No—he couldn't go. Not at once, anyway. But he resolved that henceforth he would go armed.

Next morning after his ride and breakfast, he sent Monocle Joe to town for ammunition and began pistol practice. It was a new diversion. He rather expected to hear from Mann during the day, as the Consolidated head had given him forty-eight hours in which to change his mind with regard to his proposals. But Mann had no intention of communicating with him. He expected, foolishly, that Hartland would send word to him.

Silver City was pretty well informed as to the nature of Mann's activities. Although he was not generally liked personally, the men of the camp had faith in his plans. It was known that he had approached Hartland in the matter and the camp was eagerly awaiting his report. Mann had permitted it to be noised about that Hartland would give his answer by evening.

Soon after sunset the Silver King was thronged. Many miners from the Huntley were there; twenty of the twenty-three owners of the nineteen undeveloped claims Mann had optioned were present, as were others who were interested in the Silver Queen and Susan Mines. Gordon dropped in, an interested spectator since he represented Wright & Harris of Butte, who owned the Huntley. There were Yellow Jacket men on hand, too, and Monocle Joe was at his usual station at the lower end of the bar. "Hit's a Fourth of July mob," he said to another gambler. And so it was.

Mann was the center of attention. He looked at his watch from time to time, and, as the dusk deepened into night, the excitement became intense. Butch Allen was at Mann's side, his face glowering, and, although Mann repeatedly cautioned him, he drank steadily. Of course, Mann knew by this time that he would receive no word from Hartland. He didn't much care. His next move was to turn the sentiment of the camp against the Yellow Jacket owner. He had hated Hartland from the moment when the latter had snubbed him in this same resort. He could have killed him when he was literally thrown out of the bungalow. He felt that his dignity had been offended and believed Hartland was a snob. The treatment he had received at the hands of that rich son-of-a-bitch rankled and bit deeply into his pride. It was now a personal affair that he endowed with as much importance in his mind as his scheme for making a fortune for himself out of the Consolidated.

It was going on 10:00 P.M. when Mann took out his watch and looked at its face intently for some little time. A hush came over the place, and, when Mann pocketed his timepiece and held up a hand, there was absolute silence.

"Well, boys," said Mann in a loud voice, looking about at the scores of anxious faces, "Hartland's turned us down."

The silence held for a space of several seconds, then there was an outburst of exclamations in which oaths were sprinkled liberally. Only the Yellow Jacket men remained silent. They were gathered at the upper end of the bar around a tall, fair-haired giant named Sandy Anderson. They merely looked on curiously.

The turmoil subsided as Mann again held up his hand. "Boys," he said, shaking his head," I did my best. I went up to his place and explained what we wanted to do to make this one of the liveliest camps in the West. I asked him to trail along with us by putting in the Yellow Jacket and he refused. I offered to turn our options over to him, take stock in a company he could form in return. In fact, I offered to let him be the whole works and make the biggest profit. He turned that down, too. I gave him forty-eight hours to reconsider. The time is up and I haven't heard from him." He paused and nodded his head impressively. "Boys," he continued, "this

Hartland ... this damned dude ... doesn't care a snap of the finger for Silver City. He doesn't care whether you mine and claim owners ever get a cent out of your properties. He doesn't care whether you miners have work or not. He can make this camp by speaking a few words, but he won't speak 'em because he thinks we're a bunch of rough necks and fools. He told our banker he was putting on more men because his mine had to pay a profit. It would be nothing out of his pocket if he put in with us, and, if he took the Consolidated over, it would put money in his pocket, but all he wants is a profit for himself, and the rest of us and the camp can go hang."

Unreasonable as was Mann's short argument, it caught the temper of most of the men in the place. The swelling murmur of disapproval grew in volume until the place was in a tumult. None stopped to consider. Hopes, which had been running high, were dashed—scattered to the winds. In the minds of those who were interested in Mann's project, Hartland became a tyrant, a double-crosser, and the camp's chief enemy almost instantly. In contrast, Mann, as he had hoped, was looked upon now as a benefactor. And Mann had a deeper motive than just personal revenge. After making himself solid with the camp, he proposed to form a company himself, and wring every dollar he could out of Silver City. As yet, although none knew it, only he and Gordon were behind the consolidation project. Most of the options had been obtained on promises. Gordon had arranged the Huntley option and they stood to make considerable out of that mine whose owners were too much interested in larger propositions to pay much attention to it. Then there was a chance of Hartland giving way and coming in, or taking over the project. There was a chance, too, he figured, on interesting one of the big smelting and refining companies. His glowing forecasts made to Gordon had convinced himself. He was living the first part of a glorious dream.

The men milled about, talking excitedly, and surged to the bar in relays. Although he was absolutely in the right and within his premises, Hartland was put in the wrong by these impressionable miners and prospectors who had looked forward for years to the time when Silver City would come into its own. Now that Hartland was on the ground, there was a tangible target against which to hurl their full force of ambition, hope, or animosity. Their feelings were unleashed.

Gordon touched Mann on the arm and drew him aside. "This is liable to result in serious trouble," he said in a worried tone.

"I can't help it," said Mann with the air of a martyr. "I had to tell them, didn't I?"

"But don't you see that it's liable to drive Hartland out of camp?" Gordon protested. "And after he's just made a deposit of a hundred and fifty thousand. You can't tell what he's got up his sleeve. And he's not the kind that will stand for a lot of rough stuff, for he doesn't have to. There . . . you see." He pointed down the room.

An argument evidently had arisen between some of the Yellow Jacket men and some others. Now a fight was in progress. The huge Scandinavian, Sandy Anderson, was pushing his way to the front. He dived into the thick of it, picked up a man, and threw him bodily into the mass before him, knocking several down.

The Yellow Jacket men formed solidly about him

and backed, fighting, to the door. In the foremost ranks of their opponents were the Huntley men. They were led by Butch Allen, who, like Mann, had a personal grudge to settle. Ed Mercer had been a friend of his, and his death had made the Huntley gunman wild with an insatiable rage.

Bottles and glasses, hurled from behind, shattered the front windows. Anderson and Allen tried to get at each other, but the press was too great. Then the Yellow Jacket men began backing out the door. The mob within the place pushed and shoved. The din was terrific.

"Stop!" shouted Mann. "Stop! Stop!"

He clawed futilely at the backs of the rear rank in a vain effort to get through. Again and again he shouted, but he couldn't make himself heard above the uproar. Nor was there any likelihood that his command would have been heeded even if it had been heard. His control over Butch Allen in such a crisis would be negligible. The sweat broke out on his face and forehead as he renewed his efforts; he shouted himself hoarse, and then leaned weakly against the deserted lower bar.

Alex Gordon stood white-faced—powerless for once. As the Yellow Jacket men crowded through the door to the street, the mob followed *en masse*. There was a jam and men were wedged in the doorway. Some went down as they burst through. Others piled on them. Next there was a struggling, cursing mass in the doorway, and just outside it, in the street, Sandy Anderson could be heard roaring orders. Then a portion of the flimsy front wall of the building gave way. There was a shower of splintered glass and blood spurted. The mob plunged into the street, picked itself up, and looked about for opponents. But the Yellow Jacket men, greatly outnumbered, had taken advantage of the opportunity to quit the scene of combat. Not a man was in sight.

Butch Allen was like a maddened bull. "We'll go up to the mine!" he roared amid the cheers of the Huntley crew.

Mann struggled through to his side, hatless, his coat torn, his tie askew—a fat, round, puffing, ridiculous figure. "Don't," he pleaded in a voice that now was nothing but a squeak. "Do as I say, Butch. . . ."

Allen paid no attention to him. "We'll go to the Yellow Jacket!" he shouted in a tremendous voice. "We'll meet their midnight shift coming an' going!"

"To the mine!" The cry went up from the Huntley outfit as one mighty shout. Then the men started for the road, leaving Mann and Gordon, trembling and frightened, in the street.

Out the shattered entrance of the Silver King came a slight figure. A single glass glistened in the right eye. It was Monocle Joe, making for a telephone.

Chapter Eleven

At the foot of the road leading up to the Yellow Jacket, Butch Allen admonished his followers to make as little noise as possible. He punctuated his warning with a flow of crisp profanity. Then the crowd, with the Huntley men in the lead, started up the road. It was a threatening procession. The Huntley men were out, first of all, to avenge the death of Ed Mercer. The beating up of the Yellow Jacket crew in a free-for-all fight seemed to them a more impressive way of getting even than merely to move on Hartland alone. He would come later. Butch Allen had said so.

Behind the Huntley outfit marched a horde of miners and prospectors whose grievance concerned what they considered Hartland's unfairness in refusing to associate his interests with those of the Consolidated. There were also many shady characters and the riff-raff of the camp.

Meanwhile, during the interval after the clash in the Silver King, Sandy Anderson had rallied the Yellow Jacket men, and had started for the mine in advance of the mob. Monocle Joe had no success in getting the mine from the first telephone he tried. He started up the street, walking briskly at first, and then running until he came to the bridge leading to Hartland's park. He crossed and hurried up to the bungalow. There was no time to give his message to Fredricks. He knocked boldly on the screen door—knocked so loudly and vigorously that he brought Hartland himself to the door.

"I tried to get the mine on the phone from town but was out of luck," he told Hartland breathlessly. "Call Miller on your private wire an' tell him Butch Allen is leading a mob of dirty swine up there to make things hot for the night shift. They're on the way now."

"Come in," said Hartland, pushing open the flimsy door. "Tell me quickly about the trouble. There must have been some."

"We 'aven't much time, sir," said Joe very seriously. "That Mann did some talking down in the Silver King an' the Huntley an' Yellow Jacket crowds got into a fight. The Yellow Jackets got away an' now Butch Allen is leading 'alf the town up the road to your mine. You better get word to Miller right away, sir."

Hartland waited for no more information. He got Miller on the mine phone and told him crisply what Monocle Joe had said.

"We'll be ready for 'em," Miller flashed back. "Now, don't you try to come up here."

"On the contrary, that's just what I'm going to do," said Hartland grimly as he hung up the receiver. He turned back to Joe. "You know the short cut up the hill?" he asked.

"Lor' an' I do," replied Joe. "But after wot was said tonight, I wouldn't go up if I was you, sir." The little man screwed in his glass and looked genuinely concerned. His well-meant advice was not heeded by Hartland who speedily buckled on his gun belt and weapon, put on a coat and hat, and motioned to Joe to go out.

"Lead the way," he ordered sharply.

Joe had no alternative but to do as he was told, and they started for the steep trail as Fredricks came rushing out upon the porch, his face gray with apprehension. They ran across the bridge and on the farther slope began their climb, and behind them crept the bulky, swaying figure of the gorilla man— Creeps Hallow.

Miller was out of the mine office in a twinkling after he received Hartland's message. He was not disposed to argue with Hartland about his appearance on the scene and the effect it might have. If Hartland wanted to take the risk, it was his own business.

The Yellow Jacket shaft was reached through a

tunnel of nearly half a mile, the bore piercing the mountain. Miller ran through the tunnel and sent down word to the shift boss. Soon the cage was dropping regularly to the levels on which men were working, bringing up as many miners as could crowd in each trip. They were a hard lot, these men. Moreover, they were appreciative of the fact that they had had work the year around when other mines had closed. They armed themselves with drills and pick handles—anything they could lay hands on that would serve as a weapon. They came flooding out the mouth of the tunnel and gathered in the open space in front of the office.

Miller gave six-shooters to the shift boss and a few other men who he knew he could trust not to lose their heads. At this juncture, Sandy Anderson appeared with his small following. He told Miller in crisp sentences what had taken place down in town and explained that they had seen the procession from the upper turns of the switchbacks. Although it was not time for the midnight shift to come on, many of the miners who were on that shift were with Anderson. Miller gave the order for the Yellow Jacket men to wear their miner's lamps lit on their caps.

The procession led by Butch Allen had reached the first of the switchbacks. One of the men who had hurriedly procured an axe for the occasion had cut pine knots from dead trees and distributed them among the Huntley men. When the highest switchback was reached, and the road ran straight to the level space before the mine, these pitch torches were lighted and the mob came on holding them aloft, illuminating the scene with a weird, yellowish flare under which the dark forms of the marchers seemed to multiply until the advance took on the aspect of an army.

They came to a halt almost in front of the mouth of the tunnel, out of which stragglers from the mine still were running. It was Miller, with a six-gun on his side, who stepped forth to meet the attackers.

"Allen," he said in a sharp, clear voice, "you've come here looking for trouble. I don't know what your excuse is, an' I don't want to hear it. You're on Yellow Jacket property an' I order you off." He took another step toward the Huntley leader. "You understand?" he said loudly. "I order you off!"

Allen swore in his face, but Miller held himself in check. If possible he wanted to avoid a clash. But Allen's reply showed that the fight was inevitable.

"That hound pup, tenderfoot boss of yours shot one of our best men an' turned the camp down flat when it had a chance to go ahead!" he shouted so all his followers could hear. "He's goin' to come in with us or get out . . . clear out of these mountains. An' we want to know the idear in some of your bunch startin' a row down town tonight. Talk, you goddamned bastard. . . ."

The profane expletive had hardly left Allen's lips when Miller leaped and struck, the blow landing flushly on the Huntley man's jaw.

Allen staggered back against some of the men behind him. Then his voice roared and he made for Miller. The crowd behind him closed in about them as the Yellow Jacket crew leaped forward. The fight was on. Torches were flung aside. The Yellow Jacket miners' lamps were put out, one by one, but not before many of the men on both sides had been burned. The battle raged in the dim illumination of a few calcium lights. A ring of spectators formed about the struggling factions.

Miller and Allen, exchanging blow for blow, were finally forced apart by the forces about them. It became a free-for-all mêlée with combatants often hitting men of their own side by mistake. Sandy Anderson was cutting a swath with his swinging fists and arms serving as flails. Men went down with their heads split by steel drills, or knocked senseless by the pick handles. But the fighting was too close for effective use of these weapons and a struggle ensued for their possession. In a minute or two the conflict resolved itself into a writhing mass of cursing, sweating, maddened humanity in which it was impossible to tell friend from foe. Then the mass went down. There were muffled groans, curses, cries of rage and pain and terror. And this was the sight that greeted Hartland's eyes as he came up from the short-cut trail.

He ran toward the writhing pile, and, as he did so, a form passed him, leaping with great shoulders hunched and long arms hanging so low that the fingers of each hand nearly touched the ground. Despite himself, Hartland paused in amazement at what he saw. It was Creeps Hallow, converted into a demon of the dark places—ruthless, cruel, barbarous—a real gorilla man. He reached the mass of struggling miners in three bounds and began tearing them off each other. He picked up men with his great hands and flung them right and left, leaving many of them stunned on the ground. Some got up and hurled themselves upon him, but he shook them off, hitting out in lightning punches, every one a knockout. Thus the struggling combatants were separated and brought to their feet, or sent crawling away.

In the center, disheveled and bloody, Butch Allen unbuttoned the flap of his holster and drew his gun, looking about him in enraged bewilderment. Creeps Hallow flashed past Hartland in great, surging bounds and disappeared in the shadows.

Then Allen saw Miller. The Yellow Jacket manager was standing a few paces away. He was covering Allen with his gun. He made a grotesque figure, the white of his face accentuating the bloodstains, his eyes burning, his clothes in tatters. But the hand that held the gun was steady as a rock.

"Put up your gun, Allen!" he commanded in a ringing, keen-edged voice. "An' before I shoot, for the last time, I'm ordering you off!"

Allen's brutal features were contorted in futile rage and malice. He heard men behind him walking away, stumbling, dragging their feet, spent with the force of the struggle. He whirled about with an inarticulate curse. Then he started after them.

Chapter Twelve

Roger Hartland's thoughts raced in turmoil, caught in the net of confusion, always coming back to the start of their trend, which was the overwhelming realization that he was responsible for what he had seen. "They have the minds of children," he murmured, but without contempt.

Looking about him, Hartland saw men being carried toward the offices. He hurried to the building and found the injured miners being taken into a room that was fitted as an emergency infirmary with neat, white cots and a large case with first-aid necessities. Miller met him inside.

"I've sent for the doctor," he said. "Some of the men are badly cut."

"I'll help," said Hartland shortly. He had had experience in this sort of work during his university activities and on big-game hunting expeditions.

He set about his self-appointed task with deft fingers, cleansing and bandaging wounds. As he worked, it was evident by the looks the men he attended gave him that they appreciated his efforts. It was brought home to him with compelling force that these men had been fighting to protect his property— fighting for him.

When the doctor arrived, Hartland went into Miller's private office. He was nursing the germ of a plan—perhaps the most startling and important idea he ever had had in his pampered life. And he was absent-mindedly tracing dollar signs with a stub of pencil on the blotter on Miller's desk.

Moreover, he was wrestling with a problem. Why had Creeps Hallow plunged into the battle, throwing his great strength on the side of the Yellow Jacket? It was easy to understand that he might have been to town and thus have learned of Butch Allen's intended attack, and had seen Hartland and Joe starting for the mine, and had followed them. But why he should take part in the affair was a mystery. Hartland arrived at a double conclusion—either Hallow had believed Allen's men were getting the worst of it and wished to enable them to get away, or he was seeking to gain favor with Miller and himself. He was inclined to the latter belief. Hartland did not know that Monocle Joe had stood behind him, with his hand on a gun hidden in a shoulder holster, ready to fire the instant a hostile move was made against his employer.

When Miller finally came in, Hartland saw his manager's face was set and grim. He tossed his hat on the desk and sat down, frowning at Hartland.

"It was luck," he said slowly, "that nobody was killed tonight. If one shot had been fired, it would have been different. An' you can paste it in your hat that the next fight will be to the tune of gunfire."

"You think there's going to be another?" Hartland asked blandly.

"Another!" Miller snorted. "I see you don't know Allen's breed. Well, that isn't your fault. Listen here"—Miller's tone was sharp—"Allen's kicked over the traces, an' Mann's control of him is gone. It's a personal matter with Butch now. He hasn't been used to being beat at any game. He's red-hot inside this minute. Mann wouldn't dare let him go, even if he wanted to, for Butch would take every man on the Huntley with him. There's only one way to fight guns, an' that's with guns."

"Meaning we should stock an arsenal, I suppose," Hartland commented with a hint of sarcasm.

But Miller was not offended. "You're wrong," he said, deadly serious. "I'm going to stock one gun."

"A machine gun!" Hartland ejaculated.

Miller shook his head. "One gun," he said earnestly, "an' the man who owns it." He nodded as he saw Hartland's eyes kindle with interest.

"I gather that you're beginning to get my drift," he went on, leaning his elbows on the desk. "Mister Hartland, these mountains are not tame. Compared to your Eastern hills, they are as bucking broncos to thoroughbreds, an' don't you forget it. Now I happen to be the manager of this mine . . . unless you want to put in another." He eyed Hartland askance, but Hartland made no sign. "If there's anything in Butch Allen's life he wouldn't forget on a bet, it's what happened tonight. It means war between the Huntley an' the Yellow Jacket. Butch will see to that. An' whatever else it might mean, it means that I won't be bulldozed or allow my men to be molested without fighting Allen at his own game an' with his own weapons. That means brute force and singing bullets in this country, Mister Hartland."

"I suppose you mean that there are going to be more fights and gun play, as you people call it, until one side or the other is exterminated," Hartland scoffed.

Miller tapped with the fingers of both hands on the desk and looked his superior squarely in the eyes. "It means," he retorted lowly and earnestly, "until certain parties are exterminated."

"Well, I'm not hiring men to engage in pistol duels and barroom brawls and free-for-all affairs as this tonight," said Hartland sharply. "I'm hiring men to mine, to get out enough ore to make the Yellow Jacket pay!"

"You're not hiring any men, Mister Hartland," said Miller slowly. "I'm hiring the men."

"You mean to tell me I can't manage my own mine?" cried Hartland hotly.

"You can take over the management of the mine this very minute!" Miller exclaimed, rising and taking up his hat. "But I'll bet a lot of money you won't have a man on any level within two weeks!"

"That's a threat!" Hartland shouted. "You'd take

'em away just as you say this ruffian of an Allen would take 'em away from the Huntley."

"I won't speak a word to a single one of them," Miller declared, shaking his head. "But I won't leave town an' let Allen say I'm a quitter."

"Oh, sit down," Hartland ordered impatiently. "This is all a bunch of damn' foolishness, but I'll hear you out. Now what is it you want to do?"

Miller resumed his chair. "I once did a favor for a man right in these same mountains. He was in a tight hole with two posses on his trail. I showed him the way out. I won't tell my reasons. They do not concern you, or the Yellow Jacket. I know where this man is at present an' I propose to bring him here an' hire him at his own price for an outside job . . . understand?"

"Who is he, and what is he, and what is the outside job?" Hartland demanded.

"He's Squint Evans," Miller replied. "He's *the* Squint Evans. He's short, squint-eyed, bowlegged, docile-looking. Might be some wistful prospector, drifting in from nowhere. And he's faster than light with his gun an' never missed a mark in his life."

"A killer, I suppose," said Hartland sarcastically. But he showed interest despite his tone.

Miller nodded his head. "Exactly . . . if he has to be. He has a few notches on his gun, I believe, but I've yet to hear of a man he drew down on first, or without sufficient provocation."

Hartland suddenly burst into laughter. He thumped the desk and then stared at Miller incredulously. "Why, this is rich!" he ejaculated. "Say, Miller"—his tone suddenly became confidential— "you know how I happened to come out to this godforsaken place? Of course you don't. Well, I was smuggled out here by my man, Fredricks . . . yes, kidnapped. I won't tell you how or why, but it's not exactly a funny story. Anyway, I'd said I was bored to death, and, when he got me out here . . . the devil . . . he said I'd forgotten this range and he wanted me to see, or rather he wanted to show me something new. And I'll hand it to him, for he certainly has. I wish I'd brought some friends along to enjoy the entertainment."

"You think it's an entertainment?" Miller asked dryly.

"Is it!" exclaimed Hartland. "Why it's worth the price just to see that little cockney wandering around with a monocle on! And here I'm wandering around wearing a pistol! And now you want to bring in Dead-Eye Dick the Squint and have him do his stuff against Butch Allen. Well, if it should happen, be sure I'm there. Why . . . why, it's a three-ring circus, side show and all."

"If it wasn't because you're a tenderfoot Easterner, I'd think you were a damn' fool," said Miller slowly. "As it is, there are many excuses for you."

"You needn't mention any of your excuses," said Hartland irritably. "And now I'm going to put on a little show of my own and demonstrate how a tenderfoot Easterner does things. Instead of gunmen fighting with bullets, I'm going to fight with these."

He pointed with his pencil to the dollar signs he had drawn upon the blotter.

Miller's lips drew into a wry smile. "I had expected some such thing," he said, his tone tinged with sarcasm. "It's natural for you to think that money will do anything."

"On the contrary," said Hartland cheerfully, "I've never had such a thought until this minute. Money to me, Miller, has never meant anything except being able to get about comfortably and have what I wanted to have. But I believe there's more to it. I now am inclined to the belief that there is something in what you say. I propose to try it out. I have a tidy sum of it, and, if I lose a bit, it won't exactly inconvenience me. What's more, my dear manager, I've heard that you Westerners were more or less sports. Well, I'm a bit of a sport myself. I'll make you a bet in the nature of a proposition. It'll be a bet you can win, in a way, but, unlike most bets, you won't make any money out of it. Now, what do you say?" He leaned back and took out a cigar.

"What's the proposition?" Miller asked curiously.

"It's this. I'll start the fight with dollars, and, if I don't win . . . you send for Squint Evans."

"Yes, start by buying up everything in sight," said Miller in derision.

"I'm a sport," said Hartland dryly, "but I'm not so foolish as to put out that much money."

Miller studied this man of millions across from him. "All right, I'll take you up," he decided.

"Shake on it!" cried Hartland enthusiastically, rising.

"When do you start?" Miller inquired as they clasped hands.

"I've already started." Hartland smiled.

He was thinking of the $150,000 he had deposited in Alex Gordon's bank.

Chapter Thirteen

Monocle Joe was on hand to guide Hartland down the shortcut trail and, incidentally, to guard him as well. Hartland was thinking, not of the night's happenings, or the steep trail and the danger that might lurk along it; he was already beginning to devise schemes and methods of operation to make good his boast to Miller. He felt he had to make good.

When they reached the bungalow, Hartland found Fredricks had prepared an excellent supper. As he sat down at table, it seemed to him that he approached his meal with unusual zest. He fell to with a heartiness that caused Fredricks's expressionless face to flutter slightly as if he were smiling inwardly.

"Good job, Fredricks," said Hartland when he had finished. "Had an appetite tonight, too."

"Very good, sir," said Fredricks. "Ah . . . pardon . . . did you intend to stay here long, sir?"

Hartland looked up in surprise. "Why, you had the whole summer in mind, had you not?"

Fredricks coughed behind his hand in the proper manner. "It was an . . . an experiment with me, sir. I . . . perhaps I went too far. I thought perhaps, if you intended going back soon, I could proceed with the arrangements leisurely, sir. There are not the conveniences in this kind of country, sir, for. . . ."

"You've got something else than packing or moving on your mind, Fredricks. Now, what is it?

"Ah, it's like this, sir. These mountains have

changed since I was last here with your father. We had no difficulty of any kind. It seemed to be more civilized, sir. Yes, it has changed."

"How has it changed?" Hartland demanded, puzzled.

"Well, we had no intruders, sir," replied Fredricks. "Ah . . . your father's life was never in danger."

"Do you think my life is in danger?" asked Hartland with widening eyes.

"It's that horrible brute who was here, sir," said Fredricks earnestly. "He might have . . . he might have done 'most anything, sir! He was like some jungle animal. It might not be safe for you to remain, sir, and, if anything happened to you, it would kill me."

Hartland stared at his servant a few moments, and then laughed loud and long while Fredricks stiffened and elevated his smooth, ruddy chin.

"So you want to beat it, eh?" roared Hartland in an excess of merriment. "You think Creeps Hallow might kill me. Why you're not afraid for my life, you're afraid for your own. You might have died of fright this very night." This was followed by another gale of laughter.

"I don't quite understand you, sir," said Fredricks with high dignity.

"No?" Hartland chuckled. "If you don't want me to lose my life, where were you when the fireworks started?"

"I didn't hear you call, sir," was the icy reply.

Hartland's chuckle of mirth deepened into a hoarse laugh and he clasped his hands about his stomach in an effort to stop it. He succeeded, and looked at Fredricks sternly. "Why, Fredricks, I had no idea you had cold feet," he observed with a frown.

"If you'll pardon me . . . that remark seems to be irrelevant, sir," said Fredricks stiffly.

"Oh, I don't mean that you need a foot-warmer," said Hartland with a wave of the hand. "I just mean that you would have been forgiven if you had taken part in the festivities without being called. In the future, Fredricks"—Hartland's voice became hard and stern—"at any time that I may be attacked, or that an attack may appear to be imminent, you are at once to rush to my aid, regardless of circumstances. That will be all."

"Thank you, sir," said Fredricks faintly, bowing a matter of some three inches.

Hartland lounged in an easy chair before the fireplace, in which a half log smoldered, glowing red against the chill of the mountain night. His thoughts reverted to the coincidence of Creeps Hallow's appearance on the scene in time to break up the fight. There must be something behind Hallow's action, for the man could hardly be altogether mad. Hartland puzzled his brain with the mystery. He didn't like mysteries. This one might have some tangible bearing on his own prospective operations.

"By Jove!" he exclaimed aloud as he knocked the ashes from his pipe. "I'll see this gorilla man in his den!"

Instead of taking his early ride next morning, Hartland ordered his horse ready after breakfast. When he came out, he found Monocle Joe waiting with the animal. The rising sun glinted in Joe's single glass. Hartland looked at him quizzically.

"Joe, you're a treat. How much are you getting here?"

"Sixty a month and meals, sir," Joe replied readily.

"Fredricks wanted me for forty, but I held out, sir. I knew he couldn't get anybody else as good as me. I know 'osses, sir, I do."

Hartland chuckled. "Tell Fredricks I said to make it seventy-five," he said as he swung into the saddle.

He turned up the valley, keeping on the east side of the stream that ran its length. Whatever the outcome of his venture might be, he must show Hallow he wasn't afraid of him. To do this he would have to use a great deal of tact. But he believed his task could be accomplished.

Suddenly from up the valley came a voice singing. At first Hartland could not make out the words, but the fine tenor voice arrested his attention and caused him to rein in his horse abruptly. The voice was magnificent. Then the words came drifting on the breeze:

> *You can bury me deep, where I can sleep;*
> *You can bury me wide, where I can hide;*
> *You can shovel the dirt upon my face,*
> *But please remember there's only one place*
> *Where my bones in peace can lie.*
> *I care not where,*
> *I only ask . . .*
> *Please bury me high.*

Hartland smiled because of the wording of what was undoubtedly a crude mountain song. The voice came nearer:

> *Bury me high in the hills, I pray;*
> *Bury me high in the hills, I say.*
> *Bury me high where the long winds play . . .*
> *Oh, bury me high.*

Hartland's face was lit with wonder. Then the voice seemed literally to roll in upon him. From some trees on his right a figure emerged. He rushed toward him in crouching bounds—Creeps Hallow. Hartland was struck dumb and motionless with amazement. The gorilla man! With a voice like that! Would the wonders of these mountains never cease? But he was roused to action by the leap the man made for his bridle rein. He whirled his horse. Hallow peered up at him out of his small, ape-like eyes in which glowed malice with a gleam of triumph.

"Where did you learn to sing like that?" Hartland asked sharply.

The look in the eyes changed, and then the dangerous glint was gone. It was as if this great, ungainly bulk of a man had suddenly become a child.

"You like it?" came the question in a voice of such a throaty quality that it utterly belied the notes Hartland had heard.

"Very much," said Hartland, quickly noting the change. "You can sing, Hallow."

All of the man's fierceness now had vanished. He looked around vacantly. Hartland saw his chance and took immediate advantage of it. He leaned forward in the saddle. "Listen, Hallow, we must not be enemies. You helped us out last night. Why did you do it? Was it because you thought by helping us, I would buy your mine?"

"*Ugh!*" It was a single syllable that might have been the grunt of an animal.

"Did you come up there and help us because you wanted to win favor with me?" Hartland persisted. "Do you know what I am saying, Hallow?"

A scowl came over the coarse, grotesque face.

"You go!" came the command. An arm, abnormally long, pointed down the valley.

"All right," said Hartland. "But you're welcome at my house, Hallow." He spurred his horse down the valley—baffled.

Chapter Fourteen

At the entrance to the trail leading through the trees to his bungalow, a second—and more welcome—adventure loomed. Margaret Cram came riding up the road at a fast pace, leaving a golden ribbon of dust behind her that matched her hair. Her eyes were wide as she drew up near him. She nodded at his cheerful greeting.

"Were you up in Moon Valley?" she asked in an anxious voice.

"Yes. And, as you say, Miss Cram, it's a beautiful ride."

"But . . . did you see anything of Creeps Hallow?"

There was growing concern in her tone, he imagined. "Not only saw him, but heard him sing and talked with him. Where did he ever get that voice?"

She shook her head. "It's one of those strange things that happen only in the mountains. But . . . I should have told you yesterday that it might be dangerous for you to ride up there alone. He will want you to buy his mine, and, if you refuse, he may try to do you injury. It isn't safe, Mister Hartland."

"He already has visited me and asked me to buy

his property," said Hartland calmly. "I refused and he tried to do me injury, as you say."

"And you deliberately rode up there despite that?" She stared at him incredulously.

"To beard the gorilla in his jungle." He nodded. "He did me a good turn last night. We had some trouble up at the Yellow Jacket. It was a fight with ruffians and Creeps busted in and helped us. Now why do you suppose he did that?"

"I've no idea!" she exclaimed in surprise.

"Nor have I," said Hartland. "I went up to Moon Valley to try and find out. I failed, but I believe I've made a start toward taming him so far as I'm concerned. One of the first and best moves in dealing with a fellow like that is to start him wondering, if he can wonder."

Margaret Cram surveyed him with a new interest. "You know a great deal about men?" she asked curiously.

"Perhaps I know more about women." He smiled.

She frowned. "You've had every opportunity for gaining experience."

"And have learned three things," he said somewhat bitterly. "Those three things are luxury, clothes, and jewels." He looked straight ahead and compressed his lips.

"You are not as experienced as I thought," she said. "Not nearly so experienced. You have three more things to learn."

He looked at her quickly. "And those?" he inquired.

"You will have to learn them and not be told them," was the rejoinder. "We heard about that trouble at your mine last night, Mister Hartland, and we didn't like it a little bit. Father was very angry that such an attack should be made upon your property."

"Oh, he's on my side, then? It can't be because I'm renting his horse." He saw her eyes flash. "Perhaps your father would like to sell me his mine," he suggested.

She looked him straight in the eye. "My father's mine is not for sale," she said coldly.

"No?" Hartland showed surprise. "Then it must be good. But if I went up there with a nice fat roll of bills . . . ?"

"You couldn't buy it," she interrupted.

Hartland smiled in memory of the dollar signs he had traced on Miller's desk blotter the night before. "You mean to tell me," he said pleasantly, "that if I offered your father a tidy sum for his property, he wouldn't sell?"

"That's the meaning I was trying to convey, Mister Hartland."

"Bosh!" he exclaimed irritably. "You don't know much about money, Miss Cram. We're all, as one might say, out for a profit."

"In our case, Mister Hartland," she said slowly, "we want no profit unless . . . unless it benefits the camp."

He stared. "Well, I'll be. . . ." He stifled the expletive. "In just what way do you wish the camp benefited, Miss Cram?"

"By some move that will bring a profit to all," she replied. "But I'm not going to explain, Mister Hartland, for I do not wish you to think me a nag . . . but why don't you come up and have a talk with Father someday?"

"I might do that," he promised. "And why don't you ride over and have lunch with me?" He smiled his best. "Fredricks sets out a nice lunch, Miss Cram."

"It would hardly be proper," she demurred.

Again he stared at her queerly. "Preposterous!" he ejaculated. But the idea interested him and freshened his interest in her. "Tell you what we can do, Miss Cram, if you look at it that way. We'll have Fredricks set out our lunch on the porch, where men, animals, and birds can watch us eat. I don't mind if you throw crumbs to the birds, either." He nodded seriously.

Margaret Cram laughed. "Oh, I'll try almost anything once," she said gaily, and, spurring her horse, she led him at a swinging lope along the trail.

Hartland noticed how well she rode; he noted, too, that her riding habit was smart, that it fitted, that she knew how to wear it. He remembered that her diction was perfect. She had never got those riding boots west of the Mississippi. Here was no ordinary girl of the backwoods. And he had always required a certain amount of feminine diversion!

It was cool on the wide verandah shaded by the vines and rattan screens. They sat in comfortable wicker chairs with the white cloth, china, and silver between them, and Fredricks fulfilled Hartland's promise by serving an excellent lunch.

Hartland made another interesting discovery about this mountain girl. She knew table manners. He became more and more curious about her. With the brightness of noonday glowing in her hair and a mild light of excitement in her eyes she seemed like an elf child on holiday. How had he come to think that, he wondered?

"Miss Cram, how do you amuse yourself up here?" he asked suddenly.

The elfish look in her eyes was intensified. "Why, I don't know as I ever thought much about it, Mister Hartland. It seems as if everything is interesting and amusing, my work at home, my riding, my fishing, my gossiping while shopping in town, my . . . oh, I can hardly explain it."

"But don't you go to any dances, or . . . well, things like that?"

"I go to the best ones . . . if there's any difference. They're not the kind of affairs you're accustomed to, of course. You'd think them pretty crude . . . rough, I expect. I never stay long."

"But don't you have any . . . companions?" he stammered. "That is . . . ?"

The soft ripple of her laugh broke in upon his words. "You mean men?" she asked mischievously. "Of course. I know lots of nice boys up here, although really nice boys are in the minority."

He took out his cigarette case. "Miss Cram," he said, "you do not appear like a girl of the mountains. There's something about you that . . . seems out of place here. You do not talk or act as I would expect a mountain girl to talk and act. And, what's more, you have that indescribable air or manner that signifies culture."

"Do you think culture is out of place in the mountains?" she asked, lifting her brows.

"I suppose it isn't, but where in the world did you get it?"

"My mother, to begin with," she answered, "and then I've been to school in the lowlands. I shall perhaps go to college when Father has. . . ." She paused, biting her lip.

"Have you ever been East?" he inquired hastily to cover her slight confusion.

She shook her head. "I suppose it would be a great experience," she said.

"Might be a novelty," Hartland said wryly. "Just as all this up here is a novelty for me. But I should think you'd find it monotonous, just the same. You know, Miss Cram, you're positively beautiful."

"I was expecting to hear that sooner or later," she said dryly, "but I came here for lunch and not for compliments, Mister Hartland."

"By Jove, you're clever in the bargain." He laughed, slapping the arm of his chair. "It's your own fault, for such a girl as you must expect compliments."

"Just as we must expect bad weather, Mister Hartland."

This *tête-à-tête* was suddenly interrupted in a startling manner. Around the porch came a shadow, crouching, gliding, and then at the bottom of the steps appeared Creeps Hallow. He rose to his full height when he saw them. The surprised look in his eyes burst into flame as he looked from the girl to Hartland.

Hartland rose hurriedly. "Hello, Hallow, do you want to see me?" he asked pleasantly. He did not know that behind his back, Margaret Cram was motioning to the unexpected visitor in a commanding manner.

Hallow wet his lips with his tongue, then with a bound he was gone.

Hartland ran down the steps and around the porch after him. "Wait a minute, Hallow!" he shouted. "You can see me! What is it?"

But Hallow was leaping with the long bounds of a mountain lion for his horse near a clump of trees up the meadow. He seemed literally to spring from the earth and land in the saddle. A few moments more and he had galloped furiously out of sight into the trail at the edge of the timber.

Hartland went back to the verandah, scowling. "That human gorilla is getting on my nerves," he said. "What do you suppose he wanted?"

"I don't know," Margaret Cram replied, her eyes clouding slightly. "But it seems to anger him to see you with me. I thought that yesterday."

"The man's a lunatic," Hartland grumbled. "I'll have to find some way to tame him even if I have to buy his confounded mine and ship him out of the country."

The girl smiled. "Where would he go, Mister Hartland?"

"I don't know and don't care." Hartland frowned. "Why, are you going already, Miss Cram?"

"It has been a delightful lunch," she said, putting on her hat and taking up her riding crop.

When she had gone, Hartland sat on the verandah, his brow wrinkled with thought. For the second time that day he was baffled—this time by a girl.

Chapter Fifteen

For nearly two hours Hartland sat on the shaded verandah, smoking and thinking. He arrived at two decisions that concerned his battle of dollars against bullets. The first round of the fray would be fought out with Alex Gordon, the banker, and the second round would probably have to be fought out with Butch Allen. He also decided to call his bankers and brokers in New York. He rose to do this, then looked at his watch. It was 2:30 P.M. As there was two hours' difference in time between Silver City and New York, it would be 4:30 P.M. in the latter city. Too late to get the people he wanted. He would call next day.

He took up his riding crop and donned a cap for the trip to town. He had carried a walking stick too many years to be able to go about without something in his hand. The riding crop seemed to fit in with the environment better than a stick. Among other things he wanted to sound out the sentiment in town, although, as he knew no one there on friendly terms, this would be a difficult matter personally. The information would have to come through Yellow Jacket men. Then he bethought himself of Monocle Joe and sent Fredricks for him. In barely a minute the little cockney stood at the foot of the steps, cap in hand.

Hartland got right down to business. "Joe, you went to town last night after you left here, did you not?"

"That I did, sir."

"And how did you find things?"

"I didn't find things a-tall, sir. Wot I found was a hornet's nest buzzing like blue blazes."

"All Huntley men, I suppose?" Then, as Joe nodded: "Well, let me have an idea of what was going on."

"Hit was mostly talk, sir, talk about what was going to happen to the Yellow Jacket an' as how Miller was going to get his. An' they said as how you had got Creeps Hallow for a bodyguard an' had sent him into the fight. They're scared of Creeps. There was a lot of swearing an' drinking, with Butch Allen in the center out-swearing an' out-drinking 'em all.

Then they went out, in pairs it seemed, an' it was all over before daylight. The whole crew wasn't there because a lot of 'em was hurt an' had beat it for the bunkhouses at the Huntley."

"What was the general attitude toward me?" asked Hartland.

Joe took out his monocle and polished it carefully, hesitating to reply. "Well, it wasn't none too flattering," he confessed, "but it was mostly calling you names. But the businessmen, like Big Mose of the Silver King an' others, are with you, sir. They say that it looks like a boom for the camp, you putting on a full crew day an' night. I'd say it was about fifty-fifty. But it was a good thing none of the Yellow Jackets was around."

Hartland nodded. "Keep your eyes an' ears open, Joe, and report to me when you know something . . . or even when you think something. And you might let me know in the morning what goes on tonight. By the way, when do you sleep, Joe?"

"I don't need much," Joe evaded. "I catch a catnap now an' then."

Hartland smiled. He knew Joe was sleeping on his time, but he didn't care. "You better catch a long one this afternoon," he suggested, "so you'll be fresh tonight."

"As you say, sir." And Joe withdrew.

Hartland started for town. He didn't wear the gun. In fact, he didn't intend to wear the gun at all from then on, except on some occasion that might make it advisable to be armed.

This was his first appearance on the street since he had moved up to the bungalow, and it caused another furor. But this time the excitement had two aspects. Some of the looks directed at him were hostile, while others were respectful or curious. It was plain to be seen that there were two factions in town, and he stood between them. But they readily made way for him, and, as before, he was the cynosure of all eyes and the cause of the suppression of speech. Talk had been the order of the day.

He entered the Silver King resort, curious to see what was going on there. The place was in an uproar, but a sudden silence fell over the throng at his appearance. His eye roved about the room and he spotted a tall, husky figure near him at the bar. He recognized one of the Yellow Jacket men who had been doing effective work during the fight the night before. He moved toward him and a place opened immediately for him at the bar. Big Mose hurried forward to take his order.

"A bottle of ginger ale," said Hartland curtly.

There were some snickers as the conversations were resumed, but, in the main, those present scented something significant in this attitude on the part of Hartland. Big Mose glared about, as if trying to discover who had snickered. He served Hartland with alacrity.

Hartland turned to the big man at his side. "You're a Yellow Jacket, are you not?" he asked in an undertone.

"I'm Sandy Anderson, night shift boss," came the reply in a respectful tone.

"Well, Anderson, what's been going on today?"

"Everybody's on their guard. Nobody's saying much. Looks like the Huntley crowd will keep quiet for a while now, an' then they'll try to spring something tall. But we'll be ready for 'em an' meet 'em more'n halfway. No, today's been sort of a letdown, you might say. I haven't seen Butch Allen, so I don't know what kind of a mood he's in, but then he's always ornery."

"I notice you're wearing a gun today, Anderson."

"Me an' some more of the boys are packing our guns. Those of us who know a little about using 'em. Miller's orders. Can't tell what might happen, he thinks, an' they have a soothing effect."

"I don't think it's good policy," said Hartland, frowning and shaking his head. "Anderson, do you happen to know who owns the Huntley?"

"Wright and Harris, of Butte," replied Anderson.

"Are they ever around here?"

"No. They haven't paid any attention to that property in years. They've got bigger fish to fry. That's how Mann and Gordon managed to make such a good deal on their option."

"I see," said Hartland, putting down his glass. "And now I've a little business to attend to. You put up a mighty good fight last night, Anderson. So long."

He walked briskly out the entrance that Big Mose had managed to have repaired. He saw a small crowd in the street and wondered if they had gathered because he had gone into the place. As he turned down the boardwalk, a shadow moved to the left of him and Butch Allen loomed in his path.

Hartland moved slightly to one side, but Allen again confronted him, his hands on his hips, sneering. "Look here, Hartland. . . ."

"Get out of my way!"

Hartland's clear, ringing command could be heard the length and breadth of the street and there was a rush from the Silver King.

"Oh, you'll listen to what I've got to say," Allen boasted. "I'm going to tell you that. . . ."

"If is wasn't for soiling my hands on a dirty ruffian like you, I'd knock you down," Hartland interrupted. "You're a reputed gunman and supposed to be all-around bad, but don't think for a quarter of a second that I'm afraid of you. Now step aside or I'll pet you with this riding crop."

Sandy Anderson had moved close to Hartland, his hand on the butt of his gun. There were murmurs of approval that might have come from either of the men's supporters. Butch Allen realized that, if he attacked Hartland, he might get the worst of it. He couldn't resort to his weapon. After all, Hartland was the big man of the camp—too big.

"We'll have our talk later, Hartland," he snarled as he moved out of the way.

Hartland walked on—and Silver City fairly reveled in the latest sensation.

The Gordon Bank building was a one-story frame structure with a top false front that once had been painted a brilliant green. The mountain snows and sun and wind had tempered this color to a pale blue. There were two small windows on either side of the door. There were two rooms. The larger room was in the front. This was the cage where the teller and a bookkeeper held forth. The rear, and smaller, room was Alex Gordon's private office. There was a narrow space at the left of the cage leading back to the door to Gordon's office. The place had a musty smell.

Hartland sauntered nonchalantly into the bank and spoke to the teller. "Gordon in?"

"Yes, sir," replied the teller. "Who'll I say wants to see him?"

"You know me," said Hartland curtly, and turned away from the window. He just had time to draw his case and take out a cigarette when Alex Gordon came hurrying from the rear.

"Good afternoon, Mister Hartland," he said in some excitement, holding out his hand. "You should have come right back to my office. You don't need to wait to be announced."

Hartland ignored the hand until he had lighted his cigarette. Then they shook and walked back to the private room.

"It's been a wonderful day," Gordon commented, rubbing his hands as they sat down. He plainly was nervous and ill at ease.

"And it was a wonderful night," said Hartland easily.

"It was disgraceful," Gordon declared, bringing a palm down on his desk. "Absolutely disgraceful and uncalled for. Every law-abiding citizen in Silver City is incensed over the affair. If there had been a way to stop it, if. . . ."

"I understand Mann made quite a speech in the Silver King just previous to the start of the activities," Hartland observed.

"He's a fool!" Gordon ejaculated. "I told him so to his face. He . . . he was excited. Maybe he had been drinking a little. I tried to stop him. And I had nothing whatever to do with it, Mister Hartland. I want you to know that just because . . . Mann and I have certain dealings of a purely business nature . . . I would not be involved in any way in such a thing as happened last night. I have a reputation to sustain, and a bank to protect, and I couldn't afford to be mixed up in any such outrageous proceedings."

Hartland nodded. "I shouldn't think so," he said suavely. "Where's Mann today?"

"He went to Butte," Gordon replied. His nervousness increased as he noted Hartland's cool, confident manner. "On business," he added.

"Has it anything to do with Wright and Harris of the Huntley?" Hartland asked sharply.

Gordon started in his chair. "Why . . . why no, I believe not," he stammered. "To tell the truth, I don't know just why he went. The train leaves before I get down in the morning."

"Perhaps he thought it would be best to leave town for a few days in view of what took place last night," Hartland suggested. "There's no doubt but what his talk started the ball rolling."

"But I'm sure, Mister Hartland"—Gordon was sincere in this—"that he hadn't the slightest idea that it would. He was excited. You see, his heart was set on obtaining your support for the Consolidated, and, when you . . . when he failed, it went to his head."

"I see." Hartland's voice was hard and cold. "For the last time, Gordon, what is this Consolidated?"

"Why . . . why it's a company for the promotion."

"Who's in this company?" Hartland demanded. "Is there anyone in it besides you and Mann? I want a straight answer to that."

"Well . . . well, at present," Gordon began, clearing his throat, "at present Mann and I. . . ."

"That's enough," Hartland broke in. "Gordon, when does your option on the Huntley expire?"

"Why . . . the Thirty-First of December," Gordon answered in surprise.

Hartland tossed away his cigarette end. "Gordon," he said pleasantly, "I'll have to take over your option on the Huntley . . . within forty-eight hours."

Chapter Sixteen

During a lifetime of fifty-two years, Alex Gordon had experienced some shocks. He stared in stupefaction at the man who sat across from him. Then his eyes brightened as a stirring thought was born in his brain. Hartland wanted the Huntley. Then he was prepared to pay for it. Good. They could get their own price!

"But, Mister Hartland," he said, smiling amiably, "the Huntley option isn't for sale."

"I'm not concerned with that," said Hartland.

Gordon's face glowed. Just like this multimillionaire! He'd boost the price to a figure at which it would be for sale. "But, Mister Hartland, forty-eight hours is much too short a time," he protested agreeably.

"Can't help that, either," replied Hartland laconically.

"But, you don't understand," said Gordon. "You see I can't dispose of the option alone. I have to consult with Mann."

Hartland looked at him thoughtfully. "Well, you know where Mann is and he can certainly get here within forty-eight hours. Wire him."

"That's just it," said Gordon. "I don't know where he is. I was only guessing when I told you he was in Butte, although that's where I believe he is. He can't get here in a day from Butte because of the poor train connections on this branch line. And we'd want time to talk it over."

"All right," Hartland conceded, "take three days."

"I'll try it," said Gordon doubtfully. "If I can get in touch with him, he'll be here. I assure you of that."

"Another thing, Gordon." Hartland took out another cigarette and lit it carefully. "Were you intending to convert that hundred and fifty thousand dollar check I deposited into cash?"

"Well . . ."—Gordon shifted some papers on his desk—"I have to have more cash now that you've tripled your men, and we're putting more men on at the Huntley, too. I suppose you'll keep them if you take it over," he added hastily.

"Possibly," said Hartland dryly. "I suppose your vault will resist a raid. Such a sum of money would be quite a lure for bank thieves, if they knew it was here. This building doesn't look any too strong."

"It's resisted two raids in its history," said Gordon.

"There's always a third time," Hartland drawled, rising. "I'd take a look around and make sure."

On the way out Hartland passed a man who looked at him so keenly that he was annoyed. A man of medium height, well-built, grizzled, blue-eyed—might be anywhere between fifty and seventy, Hartland thought as he went out into the street.

John Cram passed on into Gordon's office. Gordon, still nettled because of the abrupt manner of Hartland's going, looked up with a frown.

"Oh, hello, Cram," he greeted perfunctorily. "Sit down. What's on your mind?"

"My notes," Cram replied shortly. "They're due on July Fifteenth."

Gordon looked at the big calendar on the wall. "But that's some little time yet. Did you want to pay them today?"

"I wish I could," said Cram. "No, I don't want to

pay them today because I can't. But they're continually on my mind, an' I need what brains I've got for my work."

Gordon nodded. "You're right, Cram. Man needs brains as well as brawn for work . . . mining in particular. They tell me you're getting on up there and starting to make a showing. How about it?"

"It's looking a little better," Cram confessed. "Of course, I can't take out much ore yet, but when I do start, I'll try to show 'em. I'm working, that's a sure enough fact. Yes, I know it's some little time before my paper will be due, Gordon, but I'd like to arrange to renew it."

Why, Cram, I can't renew notes before they're due," said Gordon, looking surprised. "You ought to know that. It wouldn't be banking."

"I don't see why you can't," said Cram belligerently.

"Because conditions might arise in the intervening time that would make it inadvisable to renew . . . the value of the security might deteriorate, or something." Inwardly Gordon was smiling to himself. He had no intention of renewing Cram's notes, and he knew Cram couldn't pay. This was why he and Mann had not asked for an option on Cram's property. They would get it anyhow—for a little over $2,000.

John Cram leaned forward with a gleam in his eye. "Look here, Gordon, my property is worth double this minute what it was last year at this time, and you know it. You've got good security for five thousand dollars, instead of two. In fact, I'm going to ask you for another thousand."

Gordon pursed his lips and shook his head. "Not

at this time," he said with a simulated sigh. "Money's tight. Anyway, I've got to go up and look over the property. Then, when the notes are due, we'll go into the matter."

The look in John Cram's eyes was steel blue. He rose and leaned on Gordon's desk. "Gordon," he said hoarsely, "I have always worked for the good of the camp, and, if you double-cross me, I'll make you pay for it. You could renew those notes and write a new one for another thousand right now if you wanted to. I'm no fool. You don't have to wait till the notes are due and you don't have to look at the property. There's something queer about the way you're acting."

"I'm running this bank," Gordon retorted sharply. Then, in a soothing tone: "It's all I can do, Cram, whether you believe it or not. I might think there was something queer about the way you're working your prospect. . . ."

"It isn't a prospect!" Cram exclaimed.

"Well it's not a developed property as yet," Gordon said angrily. "It's no use till July Fifteenth, Cram. Then we'll talk business."

"We'll not only talk business, we'll do business," said Cram grimly as he stamped out of the office.

Gordon reached for his telephone and called a number in Butte. While waiting for the call to be put through, he rose and paced his office, rubbing his hands. John Cram was forgotten. The look on Gordon's face was one of supreme satisfaction. When the telephone bell rang, half an hour later, he responded with alacrity.

"Empire Hotel?" he asked eagerly. "I want Herbert Mann . . . no, *Mann* . . . that's right." There was a short wait, then: "That you, Herb? . . . say listen, Hartland wants our option on the Huntley ... what ... yes, and from the way he talked in here a while ago he's willing to pay any price to get it ... yes ... wanted to do business within forty-eight hours, so you get back here quick as you can ... all right, I'll be looking for you."

He prepared to leave the bank, well satisfied with the day's work.

Miller came down to see Hartland after supper that night. He looked at his employer in keen disapproval.

"Hartland, I don't know whether to congratulate you or give you thunder," he said.

"How's that?" Hartland inquired with some amusement.

"I mean that stunt this afternoon," Miller explained with a frown. "I should think you'd know by this time that Butch Allen is bad medicine. Now there are no ifs or ands about it, Hartland. He's dynamite."

"I'm beginning to think, Miller," said Hartland seriously, "that somewhere in Butch Allen's make-up there's a yellow streak. I don't mean that he wouldn't draw his gun with any man on earth. But ... well, I can't explain myself. It's a feeling I have. He's yellow somewhere about something, that's all."

"Maybe so," Miller drawled. "But I take it that the only thing that protected you today was the fact that you're Roger Hartland. He knows that to injure you would put him in bad with everybody that amounts to anything in the camp. The fact that he realizes that fact is your protection."

"I've a hankering to see what's going on downtown tonight, Miller," said Hartland. "Fact is, I'm getting a bit interested in all this. Suppose we both go down and take a look around. What say?"

There was a gleam in Miller's eyes. Hartland was becoming interested.

"Sure, we'll go down an' look around," Miller agreed.

Hartland again carried his riding crop. Miller noted that he didn't wear the gun, but said nothing. More and more he was beginning to respect this young millionaire who owned the Yellow Jacket.

They strolled down the street, and, if men had looked at Hartland before, this night their eyes fairly popped with eager interest. Miller they ignored. And, when the pair entered the Silver King, Hartland noted that for the second time that day a dead silence fell over the place. But this time it didn't last long. It was broken by the loud voice of Butch Allen.

"Here's the pretty boy from New Yawk, now," he said, raising his glass. "Here's hoping he chokes." Down went the fiery white liquor.

It wasn't so much the words Butch Allen spoke as it was the look that accompanied them. It maddened Hartland. The very world went red. He leaped forward, his riding crop whipping up high over his right shoulder. Those between him and Allen dropped to the floor. Then, almost in the same instant, another figure leaped forward. This was Sandy Anderson, who had been standing in his customary place at the head of the bar. His gun flashed from its holster. Butch Allen's right hand struck like lightning. The place rocked to the sharp report of the shot. Hartland's riding crop came down on Allen's head, dropping him to the floor. But it was too late. Sandy Anderson, who probably had saved Hartland's life by interfering, sank slowly into Miller's arms.

"Yellow Jackets, don't draw!" came Miller's sharp command.

There were tense moments, with Hartland standing over Butch Allen, from whose head blood was trickling, and Miller holding the limp form of Sandy Anderson.

Then those present awoke to the realization of what had taken place in a space of less than a minute. Four Yellow Jacket men took Anderson and carried him out, while Miller grasped Hartland by the arm, and led him, dazed, to the outer air.

In the street Hartland recovered himself, and his face went white. He turned to Miller. "Send for Squint Evans," he said grimly. "We both win."

Chapter Seventeen

Sandy Anderson was not dead. Hartland ordered him taken to his bungalow where there was a spare room and where Fredricks could look after him. Hartland went along with the doctor. Butch Allen was helped to the rear room of the Silver King, where his friends washed his scalp wound with cold water and he drank a bracer of white liquor. All the while, he stared straight ahead, unseeing, but his cronies knew the look. It meant terrible trouble for someone, and they had no difficulty surmising who that someone might be.

Miller had gone to the telephone in a store near the resort. There he put in a call to a town in the lowlands with instructions that he would talk from Hartland's bungalow. He took this precaution so that none who might happen to be in the place would overhear what he said. Then he hastened up the street and crossed the bridge to the bungalow.

The doctor decided, after examining Anderson's wound, that the big Scandinavian had a chance. The bullet had pierced the right lung but it had gone through, leaving a clean wound. It bled freely as the doctor attended to it and bandaged it. He left medicine and certain instructions with Fredricks. Anderson seemed to drift off into a deep sleep as the doctor took his departure.

The telephone bell rang but Miller answered. There were a few terse sentences spoken, but Squint Evans's name was not mentioned. Miller made no attempt to explain what had been said to Hartland. But Hartland suspected the truth. Miller had called someone he knew well, and the seemingly casual utterances had really been an order for Evans to report. Miller had been careful to impress upon whomever was at the other end of the wire, who he was and where he was, and to "tell the one to come up and bring the other." Mountain code. *Not so bad*, thought Hartland.

"I'm going to send a man down here to keep a look-out," Miller announced as he left the telephone. "But first I'm going in to town and see that Monocle Joe is on the job there. My place is at the mine. Hartland, don't go out again tonight."

"You said it," said Hartland, frowning. "It was the most dastardly thing I ever saw."

"Dastardly?" said Miller with a grim smile. "There

was nothing dastardly about it. Butch Allen had no other out. Sandy was behind you with his gun out an' you were rushing to the attack. Allen had to shoot. It was either you or Sandy, an' he knew, if he let you have it, Sandy would get him. He didn't know but that Sandy intended to shoot anyway. He let Sandy have it because Sandy could do more damage with his gun than you could do with your riding crop. Allen was drunk or he wouldn't have made that crack at you in the first place. Now he's simply got you on the books for a six-foot trench under the daisies. Think it over an' see if you can't make up your mind to be careful. Remember, Hartland, in a wild country like this, a man must keep his head."

"Meaning I didn't keep mine." Hartland scowled. "Well, I didn't. But I failed to reckon on gun play."

"Well, you've got to figure on it," Miller pointed out. "An' you've got to figure on it now more than ever. I'd keep the curtains down and the door closed. So long. I'm going."

Hartland sat for a long time, drumming upon the table with the fingers of his right hand. He was thinking it was a far cry from the Rameses night club in New York and Rose Raymond to this wild mining camp sequestered under the peaks, and Margaret Cram. How different Margaret was from the average girl he had known. She was simplicity and sweetness and frankness, he confessed to himself. He shuddered as he thought of the duplicity and unscrupulous natures of such women as Rose Raymond. How had he ever got mixed up with her? The answer was easy, of course—night clubs and high life generally and booze. Well, he was past that stage. Yes, he fully believed all that sort of thing had been left behind. He'd spend a summer in Silver City, see this trouble through, leave his property on a paying basis, and go East in fine shape physically and mentally. Such was the trend of his thoughts.

A step on the porch. Hartland drew open a drawer of the table noiselessly and took out his pistol. He slipped to one side of the door just as the knob was turned stealthily. A large, hairy hand pushed the door open and Hartland knew who his visitor was. Creeps Hallow stepped inside, and, as he did so, he looked fully into the muzzle of Hartland's gun. He shrank back, his jaw sagging, disclosing the yellow teeth.

"Sit in that chair," Hartland commanded, pointing to the chair he had vacated at the table.

Hartland closed the door, advanced a step toward Hallow.

"Now what do you want?" he demanded.

The man's eyes looked into his with a bland-like expression. There was no answer.

Hartland was annoyed. "Look here, Hallow, I won't have you sneaking around here in this way, understand? This is twice you've been here, coming like a ghost and then running away without saying anything. When you've got something to say to me, come like other people, and knock at that door before you open it. If you come in again without knocking, I'll let you have this."

Hallow shrank at the gesture Hartland made with the gun.

"How do I know who's coming?" Hartland continued. "I have enemies here who wouldn't hesitate to kill me. Now before you leave here, you've got to tell me what you want. Speak up."

"You like her?" Hallow croaked.

"Do I . . . ?" Hartland bit off his words with a

flush. "You mean Miss Cram? Well, what if I do? What business is it of yours?"

Hallow's small eyes glittered. "You be good," he grunted.

Hartland sat down across from his queer visitor and rested the hand holding the gun on the table. "Miss Cram can take care of herself, Hallow," he said sternly, "and, if you don't believe it, you ask her. She doesn't like it because you are sneaking around like this and she'll tell you that, too. She doesn't like it . . . do you hear?"

The man's eyes seemed to change color several times. His thick lips were almost in a pout. He looked away.

"Now, we'll forget that," said Hartland in a soothing tone. "We must be friends, Hallow. What is it you wish me to do? Do you want me to buy your mine?

"No."

The tone was sharper than any Hartland had heard the man use. He was surprised. Then he recalled what had been said in town to the effect that he had hired Hallow as a bodyguard. He had a brilliant idea.

"All right," he said cheerfully, "but any time you want to sell, I'll talk business with you . . . providing you leave here after the sale." He paused to let this sink in and saw that Hallow comprehended. "Meanwhile, Hallow, I'd like to hire you . . . to give you a job, at good pay."

Again Hallow's eyes became the eyes of a child, flickering with keen interest. "What kind of a job?" he asked.

"Keeping watch on this house," Hartland replied. "It would be mostly at night, I suppose. You don't mind being out at night, do you, Hallow? If you'll keep watch on this house at night and see that none of Butch Allen's . . ."—he paused and wondered as he saw a look of fury come into Hallow's eyes— "Butch Allen's crowd come up here to make trouble, I'll pay you one hundred dollars a month. There are going to be some wild times around here, Hallow. I can feel 'em coming in my bones. I need protection a great deal more than Mildred Cram needs it and you can get paid for your work."

Hallow was nodding his huge, shaggy head. "I been looking out already," he said hoarsely. "If you like her an' you be good to her, nothing shall happen to you. I go now."

He rose and stepped, cat-like, to the door, opened it, and with a final nod to Hartland went out into the night.

In the morning, Hartland put in two calls to New York. He then put in a call for Wright & Harris of Butte. He didn't know either Wright or Harris, of course, but he knew they would at least know of him. So he didn't hesitate in calling. Within an hour he had talked with Harris, learned the details of the option held by Gordon and Mann, and had ascertained that the partners were more than willing to co-operate with him. Such, then, was the power of the Hartland name. He realized it thoroughly for the first time and it gave him a thrill. He sat thinking over this until his New York calls came in. He had finished his business with the metropolis in less than ten minutes.

This morning Monocle Joe hadn't shown up to saddle Hartland's horse and Hartland had foregone his ride. Not that he objected to saddling his own horse but he had much to think about besides the telephone calls. He suspected that Miller had sent Joe on an errand and he thought he had an idea as to the nature of the little cockney's mission.

Anderson was raving and running a high fever when the doctor came. The physician stayed at the bungalow most of the day. Hartland stayed around, also. He was worried about Anderson, for one thing, and he was afraid a visit to town might result in more trouble. He didn't want any more trouble just yet.

Miller came down at dusk and announced that he would accept an invitation to dinner if it were offered him. At table he vouchsafed the information that Butch Allen had left town. "But he'll be back," he finished. "He's just staying away for a few days till things quiet down, you might say. When he comes back, he'll be worse medicine than ever."

Hartland had nothing to say to this. He listened while Miller took advantage of the opportunity to describe operations at the mine. "Now that I've got the men," said his manager, "I can do something. We won't show a profit for three months maybe. Then we'll jump above expenses in a day. It's preliminary work I'm doing now." There was a short silence. "I hear that Mann's back," said Miller suddenly. "Got in on the late train."

Hartland smiled. "I expected him," he said cheerfully. "In fact, I practically sent for him. Miller, I'm going to take over the Huntley."

Miller's eyes sparkled. "Great!" he exclaimed. "An' I'm the red-hot baby who can show you what to do to make that mine a hummer."

"It may never be worked," said Hartland dryly, and the look in Miller's eyes died.

At this moment the *clatter* of horses' hoofs came from the bridge below the park. Miller stirred in his chair and glanced surreptitiously at Hartland. But the Yellow Jacket owner remained calm, displaying little concern.

The riders dismounted at the porch steps. Spurs *jingled* on the porch floor and there was a sharp knock.

"Come in!" called Hartland.

Monocle Joe entered, looking quickly at Miller, who rose at once. Hartland took no notice of Joe but looked past him at the man he ushered in.

The newcomer was short and slight with bowed legs. The tanned face was seamed, lined, and wrinkled until it appeared as an intricate pattern traced upon cheeks, chin, brow, and at the corners of the eyes. It was absolutely hairless. The lips were thin, bloodless, the nose slender and hooked. The eyes were a watery blue with that childish, wistful light one sees in the eyes of a prospector who has searched the mountains in vain. But the man's hands, although tapered in the fingers, gave the suggestion of strength. On the right side was strapped a worn, black holster from which protruded the scarred butt of a six-gun. Quietly dressed in black, sateen shirt, black scarf hanging from the neck, blue serge trousers tucked into black riding boots—an array topped by a huge gray Stetson.

"This is . . . Mister Smith, Mister Hartland," said Miller, advancing.

"How are you, Squint," said Hartland cordially, stepping forward and holding out his hand. "We might as well call each other by our first names . . . here, at any rate." As Hartland drew nearer, he saw that he had been mistaken in the eyes. There was a light behind that misty film of blue, a light that seemed to go through Hartland and read him like a book.

A single flash, and Squint Evans held out a limp, fishy hand.

Chapter Eighteen

Hartland studied the man curiously in the brief interval after they met. He had heard of this breed of men; it was the first time he had come into contact with one.

Miller approached them. "We thought it best to call Squint by another name," he explained. "He has something of a reputation an' there would sure be some in camp who'd heard of him. So he's Ed Smith. That's good enough."

"It's simple enough," Hartland conceded. "I suppose you're right. What's he supposed to be around here . . . a miner?"

"That's the theory," said Miller with his tongue in his cheek. "You've done some mining or mucking in your time, haven't you, Squint?"

Evans looked at him for the first time. "Maybe," he said shortly. Then, looking back at Hartland: "I've had a long ride. Have you got anything to drink?" The voice was rather high-pitched and sharp. It carried a note that belied the distant mildness of the eyes and features. Hartland had made the further discovery that at close quarters the face was cold and hard. One must remain some little distance from Evans to retain the first impression of harmless stupidity.

"Fredricks!" Hartland called. "Bring some whiskey."

Evans looked about him with interest. The furnishings of the room attracted his eye. He noted with approval the easy chairs and, tossing his hat on the table, sank down in one. His hair, disclosed for the first time, was white.

Miller had seated himself and motioned Monocle Joe to a chair. Hartland took his usual place by the table. When Fredricks came with decanter and glasses, he motioned to him to serve the gunman. Squint Evans took two large drinks without so much as glancing at Fredricks.

"Would you like something to eat?" Hartland asked.

"I'll get it in town later," Squint grunted.

"All right," said Hartland. He turned to Miller. "Have arrangements been made for his quarters?" he asked.

"Joe has attended to that," Miller replied. "Ed Smith will live in town. He . . . isn't going on shift immediately."

"Very well." Hartland again turned his attention to the diminutive gunman. "I don't know what arrangements my manager has made with you," he said slowly and impressively. "I do not want to know. So far as I'll ever know, Miller has hired you to work in the Yellow Jacket. I want you to remember that point and to remember that it wasn't my idea to send for you and that I didn't send for you. You quite understand that, I suppose?"

"I'm not deaf," came the sharp reply. "Nobody but Miller could get me up here an' I'll take orders from nobody else."

"That's agreeable to me," said Hartland, rising. "Is there anything more, Miller?

"Not here," Miller replied laconically. "Come along, Squint. You, too, Joe." As they went out, he paused and spoke to Hartland: "The manager at the Huntley is Fred Crawford. He's been there a long time an' so far's I can see he's a pretty square sort."

"Don't worry," said Hartland. "I won't fire him. If that should be necessary, I'll leave it to you. And you needn't mention this Huntley business to anyone until I give the word."

When they had gone, Hartland turned his attention to the next business at hand. Mann had returned. Very well, the Huntley matter would come up the next noon. Although Alex Gordon had tried his best to conceal his elation over Hartland's proposal to take over the Huntley option, he had failed. Hartland had caught the look in the banker's eyes and the suppressed excitement in his voice. He knew the pair would try to hold him up. They would ask a large, perhaps outrageous price for the option. He smiled grimly. He was beginning to enjoy the game.

He went to his desk, took out a sheet of paper, and wrote as he had been directed by Harris:

For, and in consideration of, $1.00 and other valuable considerations, we, the undersigned, hereby agree to sell and convey the option on that mining property in Silver City, Montana known as the Huntley Mine, granted us by the said mine's owners, Wright & Harris, of Butte, Montana to Roger

Hartland of New York City, said conveyance to be made upon receipt of the legal papers of transfer.

Hartland read over what he had written. *Doesn't sound like much,* he thought to himself. *But that's what Harris said to write, and the papers are already on the way.*

He had his ride early next morning, partook of a hearty breakfast, heard with satisfaction the doctor's favorable report on Sandy Anderson's condition, and then idled about with keen anticipation as he awaited a telephone call. He expected Gordon to call him up when he and Mann were ready to talk business, and he was not disappointed. At 10:00 A.M. Alex Gordon called.

He entered the bank with a brisk step and walked rapidly back to Gordon's private office. The banker must have heard him coming for he opened the door for him. Mann was seated at one end of Gordon's desk. He rose as Hartland came in and held out his hand.

"First thing I wanted to tell you, Hartland," he said in an effort to be pompous, "is that I'm mighty sorry for what happened the other night. It's unfortunate that these wild fellows can't be controlled when they're drunk."

"Yes?" said Hartland, giving the proffered hand a single, perfunctory shake. "Funny you didn't think of that before you made your little speech in the Silver King that night. I wouldn't be surprised but what your talk had something to do with starting the trouble. You seem to be long on mouth, Mann." He took a chair that had been placed out a little from the other end of the desk. It was plain from his manner that there were to be no preliminaries and both Gordon and Mann recognized the signals.

Mann shook his head as if in sorrow, while Gordon swung about in his chair and tapped the desk nervously.

"That was a mistake, Hartland," said Mann in a tone that was really sincere. "It was a bad mistake. I was a little off that night myself, I'll admit. And I was so disappointed because you had rejected our . . . our proposition that I . . . well, I lost my head, that's all. I told Gordon, here, afterwards, that I was sorry. Now I'm telling you an' apologizing. But I think there'd have been trouble anyway, for the men were just itching for a fight."

"Of course we have no way of proving that," Hartland pointed out dryly. "I suppose Mister Gordon has acquainted you with the reason for this conference?"

"Oh, yes, yes," said Mann hastily. "Yes, we've talked it over. I understand you want to buy our option on the Huntley. Well, Mister Hartland. . . ."

"I didn't say anything about buying it," Hartland broke in sharply. "I said I was going to take it over."

"Well, well, that's the same thing, you might say," said Mann, rubbing his hands. "Of course you know, Mister Hartland, we had no idea of selling . . . disposing . . . of the option on a single mine, especially the most valuable option we hold. We had intended to dispose of all our options to a company that would develop the properties. But, as we would have a bundle of options left, we will consider letting you have the Huntley. I take it that you intend some extensive development?"

"I didn't come here to talk about my intentions," said Hartland coldly. "I came here to get a slip of paper signed that will give me your option on the

Huntley. That's all that interests me, and I don't propose to spend all day getting your signatures."

Mann and Gordon looked at each other. Hartland's talk didn't sound any too good. Still, this was probably the way in which millionaires did business. Brief and to the point. Of course. All right, they'd meet this young fellow halfway.

"Our option costs us a lot of money," Mann began. "We. . . ."

"You have an option on the Huntley Mine at seventy-five thousand dollars," Hartland interrupted in a concise voice. "It expires next December Thirty-First. You paid twenty-five thousand last January, and I suspect that you paid it out of the bank's funds." Gordon's start at this was not lost on Hartland. "You have twenty-five thousand to pay July First, which won't be paid out of the bank's funds." He paused to let that sink in, and noted that Gordon's face had gone a shade gray. "Then you have the remaining twenty-five thousand to pay next December. Meanwhile, you're working the mine on an agreement to give Wright and Harris a royalty of thirty-three and a half percent. I know enough about mining to know you haven't made much money so far, if any. You've got to clean up between now and the end of December . . . just a little over six months . . . if you're to take up the option. But first you've got to meet this second twenty-five thousand in about two weeks and you can't do it."

"What makes you think we can't do it?" Mann demanded wrathfully.

"Because you've got to borrow the money," said Hartland calmly. "No use of my telling you that, for you know it. You intended to borrow it from this bank. Oh, I know that two and two is four, gentlemen.

But I'll stop any such loan. By the terms of your option, you lose what you've paid if you miss any payment. I could hold off and let you lose the twenty-five thousand you've invested, if I so wanted. But I'm doing you the favor of taking over the option, thus practically making you a present of the amount you've sunk, and, perhaps, saving Mister Gordon from an embarrassing situation, although I suppose he has sufficient means to make the amount good. As for you, Mister Mann, I happen to know you're well stocked with nerve, but your financial rating is Z-minus."

"Where'd you get all your information?" Mann sneered.

"From Mister Harris, of Wright and Harris, Butte," Hartland replied. "Nice man, Mister Harris. Seemed much interested when he learned who he had on the phone. His tone of voice almost led me to believe that I have a certain measure of influence."

Again a look passed between Mann and Gordon. Now Gordon spoke for the first time.

"How much will you give us for this option, Mister Hartland?" he asked in a polite voice.

"I'll reimburse you for the twenty-five thousand you've paid out," said Hartland, leaning forward in his chair and tapping the floor with his stick. "And"—he sat up suddenly—"out of the goodness of my heart . . . the goodness of my heart, understand? . . . I'll make you a present, for that's all it is, of five thousand apiece to take that much edge off your feeling of disappointment at not having hooked me for a young fortune in this deal."

"Never!" cried Mann, leaping to his feet.

"Just as you say," said Hartland, simulating a yawn. "You can take that or nothing. Either way, I'm to get the option. What you do with your other options does not concern me. But the Huntley option I'll have . . . and for personal reasons! . . . if I have to break this bank and this camp. And I don't mind telling you that I've already taken steps through New York to preclude the possibility of any of the large smelting or other companies opening negotiations of any kind with you. I'll withdraw my objections, of course, when you've both affixed your signatures to this paper." He put the slip he had prepared on the desk.

"Another case of capitalism bulldozing the little man," said Mann in a voice hoarse with venom. "I suppose you call yourself a square-shooter."

Hartland's eyes narrowed. "What about yourself?" he asked in icy tones. "I came here for a vacation and not to get mixed up in this insignificant camp's activities. You try to bulldoze me into a deal for your own benefit. And when you fail, you make a talk that starts a riot and results in several of my employees being severely injured. You told your gunman, Butch Allen, to make it tough for me. Don't try to deny it! As a result, one of my best men is shot by him and lies between life and death. Is that a sample of your Western square-shooting? I don't think so. Now . . . you'll sign that paper or I'll ride you until you have to walk out of camp."

In the tense silence that followed, Alex Gordon's voice seemed to come from a great distance. "We'll sign," he said simply.

When Hartland had the slip of paper with both signatures appended, he tossed a check for $10,000 on the desk. "Split it. The other papers will be along tomorrow or next day." Without another word, or a look at either of them, he left the office and the bank.

An hour later, Mann entered the Silver King. A place was immediately made for him at the bar. When he had been served, he held his glass aloft and handed Silver City its second big sensation.

"Gentlemen," he announced in a stentorian voice, "I've put over my first big deal for the Consolidated. I've sold our option on the Huntley to Hartland!"

Chapter Nineteen

After delivering himself of the startling information, Herbert Mann found, to his great satisfaction, that the effect was exactly as he had predicted in telling Alex Gordon of his intention. He at once became the center of interest.

"How much did you get?" was the paramount question.

"Now, boys," said Mann blandly, holding up a hand, "you want to know too much. Don't ask me the price. An' it isn't the price that's so important as the fact that I've made a start. I've got this Hartland interested. You know what that means." He looked about him, nodding his head significantly. "It means," he continued, swelling out his chest and lowering his voice, "that it'll only be a matter of time before he'll throw in with the Consolidated an' we'll have the liveliest camp in the shadow of the Rockies."

The long room rang with cheers. Even the Yellow Jacket men present—loyal every one to Miller and Hartland—felt a thrill. If the big boss had taken over the Huntley, there was something in the wind. It stood to reason that he wouldn't be taking over the second largest property in the camp if he didn't intend to go ahead with some plan for extensive development. And now, with enthusiasm at high pitch, Mann played the first of what he believed were his trump cards. Again he held up his hand for silence and the crowd waited breathlessly on his words.

"Gentlemen," he began after an appropriate pause, "the Consolidated has up until now been a private company headed by Alex Gordon and myself. But it has become too big a proposition for a few individuals. Big things are in sight and capital is needed to carry out our plans. Therefore, we are about to incorporate The Silver City Consolidated Mines and Milling Company at a capitalization of two hundred and fifty thousand dollars, divided into only five thousand shares at a par value of fifty dollars a share. The stock will be non-assessable. We have, as many of you know, optioned a large number of the best mines and prospects in this district. We propose to develop and to buy, and later to merge with another company . . ."—he paused long enough to let his hearers form the impression that he had reference to Hartland—"or dispose of our holdings to one of the largest companies in the West at a handsome profit. Gentlemen, we have the ore. We have the initiative and the business ability. Consolidated stock will never sell below par. On July First we will open our offices and Silver City will have the first opportunity to get some of the rich pickings from the first block of stock to be offered. Gentlemen, Silver City was never dead. She was just sleeping. Now she's waking up. I promised you months ago that this would happen. Now it has really begun to happen right before your eyes and this very day!"

This speech met with a great reception. Although many did not quite follow parts of it, all understood the last few sentences, and the cheering broke out anew. The crowd pressed about Herbert Mann, demanding more details, but he waved them back.

"That's all, boys," he said in a benign voice, "that's all for now. If anybody thinks or says I'm talking through my hat, he'll be laughed out of town in less than a month!"

Waving his hand above his head, Mann passed through the aisle that opened for him through the crowd and left the place. But his announcement had had its effect.

"He's got something up his sleeve," was the word that was passed from mouth to mouth.

"Well, I'm goin' to ride with the Consolidated!" shouted a man, and this brought similar expressions from scores of others.

Across the street, in Alex Gordon's private office, Mann was telling the banker of his initial success. He had no need to exaggerate. The bare facts were enough. They would put over the Consolidated in spite of Hartland. First, sell stock—that was the play. Sell stock!

Monocle Joe, who now was spending most of each day and night in town, keeping his eyes and ears open, reported what had taken place to Hartland while the latter was at lunch. Joe possessed an admirable memory and he was able to quote Mann's talk almost verbatim. He finished with a description of the excited throng and the comments favorable to Mann that had been freely voiced after the promoter's departure from the Silver King.

Hartland frowned darkly, threw down his napkin, and swore under his breath. Mann's scheme was all too vividly apparent. It was true that he had taken over the Huntley. And no one, save the principals in the transaction, knew the terms. Already Mann had given Silver City the impression that a huge sum had been paid for the option. Had this been true, it would indeed have signified that Hartland had something big in view. Now, on the strength of the Huntley transfer, Mann proposed to unload a lot of stock in the Consolidated, a thing that he could easily do after incorporating. It would be a pure swindle, but it would be legal. It made Hartland furious to think that Mann, who he considered an impostor, should contrive to use his name in such a way to promote his dubious enterprise, and leave him without a come-back. But wasn't there a come-back? Hartland thought as hard as he ever had thought in his life. At last he looked at Monocle Joe with a smile.

"Joe, did you ever do any fishing?" he asked.

"Aye," Joe answered readily, "an' I caught 'em, too, sir."

"Well, there's some rods and tackle around here somewhere. Storeroom probably. Get Fredricks to show you. Pick out the rod suitable for whatever they catch around here, and the tackle and flies, and have my horse ready in an hour. I'm going fishing. Maybe I'll catch something that'll give our friend Mann indigestion."

As Joe went off to do what he was bid, he polished his monocle thoughtfully. Queer chap, this Hartland. Eccentric enough to be His Lordship!

Hartland cantered up the road, his cased rod and tackle bag tied to his saddle.

The valley narrowed until it was virtually a cañon with steep walls. The stream also narrowed, but looked deeper because of the fact.

Soon Hartland came into a large meadow on the left of the creek. Here was a tidy habitation, a small, whitewashed cabin built of logs, a small barn, corral, woodshed, and what appeared to be a miniature blacksmith shop. There was an excellent garden. A cow was resting in the shade of a cottonwood. Three horses were grazing, and one of them Hartland recognized at once. It was Margaret Cram's horse. So this, then, must be the Cram place. As if to confirm the conjecture, Margaret Cram appeared at that moment on the little front porch of the house.

"Hello!" she called. "Aren't you coming in?"

Hartland checked his horse at the gate of the fence about the house and garden. "I was just going to ask you if you wouldn't come along," he returned, touching his cap with his riding crop. "I'm going fishing."

"Oh! In that case I'll go along," said the girl with a laugh. "Will a three-pound rainbow do?"

"Just right," said Hartland, "and a few smaller ones for breakfast. I'll have Fredericks stuff and bake the rainbow for dinner. Meanwhile, if you'll open that trick gate, I'll come in and make a stab at saddling your horse."

They bantered and joked in jolly humor while Hartland saddled Margaret's horse, helped her up—a formality she permitted with a whimsical nod—and they passed through the gate to the road. They turned upstream, trotting their horses in a soft cushion of dust.

Hartland had, for the time being, forgotten Herbert Mann and his activities. This was not hard, for Margaret Cram was radiant this afternoon. Her eyes sparkled with the exuberance of youth, and health, and high spirits, and in them was a daring light of adventure. She was irresistible, Hartland acknowledged, and wondered to himself if the she knew it.

Strange to say, Margaret Cram furnished a link with the past by contrast. Hartland could not help comparing her with the average girl he had known the past three years. Margaret Cram was not a parasite, or a flatterer. She wanted nothing from him. And she possessed a natural, sweet beauty that fascinated him.

Margaret led the way off the road and through a grove of poplars to the bank of the stream. Hartland saw a long, deep riffle below a blue-green pool. Magnificent fishing water! It was as if he had said this aloud, for Margaret nodded and smiled.

"Now, girlie," he said in a boasting tone, "just you watch how this is done and learn something about fly-casting." He gave her an atrocious wink and she laughed delightedly. "I haven't any net, so I'll have to land him in the sand."

He dropped lightly off the bank to the gravel and sand at the edge of the swift-moving water. He made a few practice casts "to get his hand in" as he called to her. Then he began letting out line and casting upstream to get the distance. Not once did the fly touch the water up there. Finally the fly shot even with the rock, hung motionlessly for a moment, and dropped naturally into the white water. As it made the riffle, there was a flash of silver. The line was suddenly taut, the tip of the rod bent.

"Hooked him!" cried Hartland, stepping out into the water for the fight.

He brought it in, inch by inch, reeling in the line until the trout was close against the sand. A kick sent it flying into the gravel and he dropped like a flash, grasping it with both hands just behind the gills. He carried it, struggling mightily, up the bank and dropped it in the grass. There it lay, with its rainbow streak across its side flanked by silver.

"It's a three-pounder if it's an ounce!" Margaret Cram exclaimed, grasping his arm in her excitement.

Hartland drew a long breath and looked about proudly, then looked into her sparkling eyes, at her flushed cheeks. Suddenly he had her in his arms and was holding her tightly to him, kissing her once, twice, and once again—pressing his cheek to hers and stroking her hair.

Chapter Twenty

Hartland released the girl with a sharp intake of breath, and she drew away slowly.

"Why did you do it?" she asked quietly.

Hartland flung himself on the grass at her feet. "I don't know," he responded dully. "It was just . . . you were so alluring. I must have women in my life." He did not look at her.

"You've had many of them, Mister Hartland," she said, as if scrutinizing a fact.

"Oh, call me Roger," he said. "That's my name. Call me by it, whether you like me or not. I like to hear it now and then."

"Well, then, Roger," she said, humoring him.

"Yes, I've had lots of them," he conceded. "I've lots of money. I can buy them. That's what most of them think about . . . money, or what it will get." There was a tinge of bitterness in his tone that did not escape her.

"You'll think differently when you've learned the three things you don't know about women," she said.

"Oh, I know you are different," he said quickly, looking up at her for the first time. "You are a novelty, too. But you've a price, Margaret. Not money perhaps, but something."

"My price is, or would be, love," she said slowly. "It's a thing that cannot very well be bought with money."

He looked up at her again. Her eyes were pools of dark, deep mystery. Was she laughing at him? He was suddenly irritable. "Love is a word in the dictionary," he finished grimly.

"Until you take it out and learn its meaning," she said steadily.

"Have you been in love?" he flared. "Or are you in love?"

She shook her head. "No," she answered. "And that's just why I'll know when it comes along."

Hartland shook his head in turn. "Too wise," he said gravely. "Too wise, Margaret. But here we came to fish and we're talking of love. Is that an omen? I don't care to fish any more. It made me pretty excited. I didn't mean to be rude, Margaret. It . . . well, it just happened. I'm sorry . . . no, I'm *not* sorry. Why lie? To some women . . . yes. To you? No. Margaret, I like you."

"That's mountain talk," she said lightly with a slight flush. "Straight from the shoulder. You're not a bad fellow, Roger, but you've been petted and catered to until you're almost spoiled. You must have brains or you would be. You haven't had anything to fasten to, you've had no incentive. What you've needed is work, and I'm glad you're going to get it."

"Going to get it?" he said vacantly.

"Why, of course," said Margaret cheerfully. "You've taken the Huntley, haven't you?"

He smiled wryly. "This is a case where news travels fastest where there are fewest wires. Yes, I've taken over the Huntley, but it was for personal reasons other than for going to work. This is my summer vacation . . . if I stay long enough."

Disappointment shaded her eyes. She leaned toward him. "You wouldn't deliberately buy that mine to close it down, would you?" she asked earnestly.

Again he was conscious of that feeling of irritation with her. "Perhaps not close it down," he said gruffly. "But if it's worked, I have a manager who can look after two mines as well as one. I'm not a mining man."

"Of course, I know nothing of mining, either," said Margaret contritely.

Instantly Hartland's surliness fled. "Oh, I'm sorry if I spoke rather . . . energetically," he said. "I didn't mean to, and, for that matter, I may have to do some work after all."

The girl held his eye with the seriousness of her expression. "Roger," she said with just a hint of a timid note in her voice, "you said you liked me. Well, I like you, too. We can forget, theoretically, what happened a short time ago. It isn't the first time I've been kissed, anyway . . . although the others meant no more than yours. But what I want to say is that I don't wish to appear to be nagging you. Nor have I the right. It's just because of you that I speak of work. And I don't mean work with your hands, but work with your brains. It would be the making of the camp if you cut loose with your gray matter, Roger, and started some real development in your properties, but what is more important it would be the making of you. It would change your viewpoint, and eventually be a source of pride of accomplishment. Now, that's all. Sounds like I'd read it in a book, doesn't it? I hope I haven't offended you, and I won't speak of anything like this again. I might want another luncheon."

Her lips parted in a smile, exposing two rows of pearls.

He got to his feet. "I don't believe I care to fish any more," he said again in a bored voice. "Not today, anyway. Would you like to take the rod a spell?"

The girl declined. "When you want to come again, remember the best fishing is from here upstream, two or three miles," she said.

Her tone of voice suggested that she was dismissing him. He resented it; he liked it; it puzzled him and caused him to frown as he gathered moss, wet it, and packed the splendid fish in the creel.

They were very quiet, these two, going back.

John Cram was just returning from his work in his mine when they reached the house in the big meadow. The three of them pulled up at the gate. Hartland recognized the man he had seen in the front of the bank, subjecting him to a close scrutiny.

"This is my father, Mister Hartland," said Margaret.

John Cram leaned from his saddle and offered his hand. "I'd have known you without an introduction anywhere," he said. "You have your dad's eyes. Good eyes they were, too," he added as they shook. "The camp's gone sort of wild over your buying the

Huntley," he went on. "They've put the price at a hundred thousand, but I reckon you're not telling what it was." The blue eyes twinkled.

"I merely took over the option," Hartland explained, "and there wasn't a third of a hundred thousand involved. It's just that Mann, and Gordon, too, I suspect, are trying to boost their Consolidated project by misrepresenting the deal. Mann, anyway, is trying to make out that he did something big, leaving people to imagine that he got a big price for his option. It isn't so. I don't fancy the idea of his trafficking indirectly on my name."

"Don't blame you a bit," said Cram heartily. "But you can stop that quick enough by stating the facts."

"When the time comes." Hartland nodded. He was glad to learn that this old-timer held the same view as himself, for it was the very move he had decided upon earlier in the day.

"Won't you come in an' have supper with us?" Cram invited.

"No, I have a trout for my man to work on, thanks to your daughter who guided me to his lair," replied Hartland with a smile for the girl. "Some other time, though."

"Any time," said John Cram stoutly. "A Hartland is always welcome here."

Hartland took his leave and rode back home in the sunset. But the marvelous colors that bedecked the high skies did not distract his attention from his thoughts. "I know what's the matter," he said aloud. "I want that girl!"

Chapter Twenty-one

The doctor found Sandy Anderson much improved next morning and predicted his speedy recovery. This favorable report pleased Hartland very much. In fact, Hartland was in excellent humor. He sat down to breakfast refreshed by his early ride and shower, ravishingly hungry, and, as he ate, he wondered if he had been sincere in the decision he had arrived at the night before in concluding that he wanted Margaret Cram for his wife. Did he want her for a wife, or . . . ?

He stirred his coffee impatiently. He had taken an immediate liking to the girl's father, for he saw nothing but frankness, truth, honesty, and fearlessness in the old man's eyes. Hardy, too. A miner and a mountaineer of the old school. Hartland hoped he would have a chance to help him in some way.

He ordered Fredricks to call Monocle Joe.

When Joe entered the dining room, Hartland rose and led the way into the living room where he sat down at his desk and wrote on a slip of paper. He handed the slip to Joe.

"After the train comes in tonight, and the mail is changed, hand that in at the post office and they'll give you my personal mail out of the Yellow Jacket box," he said. "Bring it up to me."

"Right you are, sir," said Joe, putting the note in his inside coat pocket.

"Anything new in town last night?" Hartland inquired.

"Nope . . . except that Squint Evans was playing cards," Joe replied.

"Well, there's nothing remarkable in that," Hartland observed. "I expect all men of his sort play cards. Is he good?"

"If he's half as good with his gun as he is at cards, it would be sure death just to think of drawing against him," drawled Joe.

Hartland laughed. "They tell me you're not so bad yourself, Joe, and that you're not any too particular. Well, it's something to know I've got two first-class gamblers in my employ and that one of them can double in lead. Hot lead, at that. Joe, I'm curious to know the general opinion of me around town. Can you tell me?"

"Easy enough, sir," was the ready reply. "They think you're smarter than you look, that is . . . smarter than they thought you would be, sir. An' they think you've got something up your sleeve just like they think Mann's got something up his sleeve. Fact is, sir, you've got 'em guessing, an' that's what a mining camp wants. In a camp like this a rumor is as welcome as a real strike, understand? An' I believe the most of 'em, except Butch Allen's gang, like you."

"That's fair enough," said Hartland absently. "Has Mann made any more talk?"

"Nope. But he's milling aroun' with a mysterious look an' that's as good as speeches."

"I'll spike his guns," growled Hartland, rising. "Well, Joe, you look after the mail tonight. I'm expecting some important papers."

Silver City had become so accustomed to sensations that the arrival of Sheriff Robert Currie at noon, behind a pair of spanking bays after a fast drive from the county seat in the lowlands, failed to rouse any great amount of excitement. The official was a tall, spare man of military bearing.

After putting up his team, he entered the Silver King and was greeted at once by Big Mose. "Understand there's been some excitement up here," he said casually.

"Oh, nothing to speak of," said Mose with a derogating gesture. "Some of the boys got excited . . . you know how things will come up between two mining outfits. The camp's been pretty lively since Hartland, the Yellow Jacket owner, showed up."

"So I hear." The sheriff nodded. "And they're liable to get livelier. You've been pretty well behaved up here without a deputy, but I guess I'll have to name one now. How about this Anderson who was shot?"

"Coming around fine," said Mose, rubbing his hands. "All a misunderstanding, Sheriff. Anderson had his gun out an' Butch Allen thought he had drawn on him an' shot in self-defense. We all saw it. I reckon Anderson himself would tell you it was a mistake."

"Killings are seldom mistakes," the sheriff remarked dryly, "and I guess Allen meant it for a killing. He doesn't usually shoot for fun. Oh, he's got the first draw alibi, and all you folks to back him up, and so long as Anderson doesn't die, I'll let it go at that, but I won't stand for any wild camp up here, and the word's gone out that that's what it's going to be."

"It'll be a big thing for the county if Hartland goes ahead an' does things an' the camp comes back," Mose pointed out.

"I hope it does," said Currie. "I want to see that very thing happen. But it'll have to come back in law-abiding fashion."

"Well, you can always depend on me to back you, Sheriff," said Mose earnestly. "Did you have anybody in mind for deputy?"

"No, I'm just scouting around," was the answer.

"I don't want to say I'm a politician or anything like that, although I control a few votes, of course," said Mose subtly. "An' I don't suppose you're out looking for suggestions as to a suitable man?"

"I'm not asking for them," Currie retorted. "Give me three cigars . . . you know the brand."

"Certainly, certainly." Mose beamed, opening his case and taking out a box. "Help yourself, Sheriff."

Currie put down a silver dollar. "You know very well, Mose, that I pay for my cigars," he said dryly, taking three.

Mose smiled wryly as he rung up the money in the register. He would rather have made the official a present of the smokes. "You're a mighty good sheriff, Currie," he drawled, "but sometimes I think you're too damned unsociable."

Currie smiled. "I get sociable at election time, Mose," he said with a wink, "and then it's me who does the handing out. See you later."

He went out and Big Mose knew he was not in town merely to appoint a deputy. Certain hints would be passed around as to the conduct of certain places in event of a boom. And it did look like a boom. Strangers were coming into town fast. This was doubtless due to Mann's talk on the outside. For it was part of Mann's scheme to draw as many men into town as possible, to give the appearance and atmosphere of a boom before one really existed.

Sheriff Currie strolled into Alex Gordon's private office unannounced. He was greeted enthusiastically by Gordon, who was alone. "I'm afraid your man's beat it, Sheriff," the banker said sadly, after they had shaken hands.

"What man is that, Alex?" the sheriff asked as he dropped leisurely into a chair.

"Why . . . Butch Allen, I suppose," Gordon answered in surprise.

The sheriff puffed on his cigar and shook his head. "Don't want him," he said, "unless . . . Anderson dies. Then I'll get him wherever he is. No, I'm up here to appoint a deputy. With you and Herbert Mann framing a boom, things are likely to get lively and I'm passing the word around that my office won't stand for no open town stuff."

"Oh, not that bad," said Gordon. "I don't think any open town is planned, and, anyway, I'd be behind you every time. So would Mann. Whatever gave you the impression we were framing a boom?"

"Alex," said the sheriff, smiling comfortably, "I've seen the thing done too many times. I don't object. I'm not concerned with any stock-selling schemes, or such, but I am concerned with the behavior of citizens, and, when it comes to rough stuff, I'm hard-boiled."

"I know that, Sheriff," said Gordon heartily, "and, if anything starts up here, it'll take a good man to handle it. Did you . . . have anybody in mind for the job?"

"Nope, but I'll find one. Is Mann in town?"

"No. He went out this morning . . . to Butte, I guess."

The sheriff rose. "I guess that's all. If this boom comes along, you might find a night watchman handy."

"I've provided for that," said Gordon, following the sheriff out with casual remarks about the weather and conditions. He thought it queer that Currie had not spoken of Hartland, and he had thought of nothing to bring him into the conversation. But, as they stood in the entrance, he had an idea.

"It might be" he suggested, "that any boom that might come would be because of Roger Hartland. He's taken over the Huntley and there's talk that he intends big developments."

"It might be," agreed Currie, "and I've thought of that. I suppose he's up at his father's bungalow? Good. I'm going up to see him. So long."

Gordon went back to his office and put in an out-of-town telephone call.

Roger Hartland was on his verandah when Sheriff Currie strolled up the meadow.

"I'm Robert Currie, sheriff of this county," the visitor announced, "and I could tell at first sight that you're Roger Hartland." His words were precise in a deep voice.

"Well, I never would have taken you for a sheriff," said Hartland, smiling as they shook hands. "I was under the impression that Western sheriffs all wore six-gallon hats, red handkerchiefs about their necks, carried two big guns, and displayed big stars."

"Some of them do, I guess." Currie smiled in return. He had studied Hartland keenly and decided the young man gave a good first impression. It was really Hartland, more than anyone else, he had come to Silver City to see.

"Sit down, Sheriff," Hartland invited, pulling up a chair on the verandah. "You might as well break the bad news sitting down, for I suppose you've come to arrest me."

Currie sat down and again subjected Hartland to a sharp scrutiny. "Not as bad as that," he said. "I'm not arresting anybody today. How's Anderson?"

"He's pulling through fine. He's here. Want to see him?"

"A little later. Tell me what happened."

Hartland gave the details. "I guess Anderson saved my life by butting in that night," he finished.

"And that other affair . . . the attack on you and the fight at the mine?"

Hartland frowned, but recited what had taken place. "I assumed it was a case of too much white whiskey."

The sheriff nodded. "I see you're a sport and not a squealer," he commented. "I'm not going to do anything in these affairs, but there will be others . . . and then I'll act. I won't stand for the rough stuff. I'm going to appoint a deputy up here," Currie volunteered.

"Good idea," Hartland agreed. "Picked your man? No? Well, come inside."

The sheriff followed him curiously and Hartland called the mine. "Say, Miller," he began, "Sheriff Currie is here, down at my place now. He's going to appoint a deputy for the camp and is looking for a man. How many votes do we control and . . . ?"

"None of that!" The sheriff's interruption was knife-edged.

"All right, let that go," Hartland continued. "He wants a two-fisted, hard-shooting, tough bird with some common sense, honest, and who can use discretion when necessary . . . who?"

"I say that'll be Ross Milton." The voice in the phone carried to the sheriff who didn't know whether to be angry, amused, or appreciative.

"There you are," said Hartland cheerfully, hanging up the receiver. "His name's Ross Milton. Any man that Miller recommends will absolutely fill the bill."

"I've known Miller for years," said Currie in a fine drawl. "You play two kinds of politics, I see. I've a hunch you'll get on. Now I'll see Anderson, and then I'm going up to see Jim Miller myself."

Hartland led him into Anderson's room where he listened to the wounded man's corroboration of the story of the fight in the Silver King. But the sheriff's eyes were on Hartland more than on Anderson. He declined a bite and hurried away with long, swinging strides down the meadow on his way to the trail to the Yellow Jacket. Hartland watched him go and pondered over the terse interview. He realized that Currie wanted to see him to form an opinion of him, and he sensed, too, that whatever the official had wanted to get out of him, he had been successful. He hadn't inquired as to his plans. Well, it would have done him no good to probe in that direction. His big source of information would be Jim Miller. That was it! They were old friends and Currie knew what Miller told him would be reliable. And Miller could be trusted to inform him of what he should know. He was getting a line on the camp because of the increased activity. Hartland let it go at that and sat down to lunch.

When he had finished, Miller telephoned that Currie had appointed Ross Milton deputy for Silver City. Hartland laughed. The sheriff had intended asking Miller in the first place.

The fifth man Sheriff Currie talked with that day would have avoided the interview—and would have been ready to pay well for the privilege. The official came striding across the street from the mining road just as a diminutive, bowlegged man turned a corner and almost bumped into him. The little man drew back, bristled, started on. But the sheriff stopped him.

"Hello, Squint," he said genially. "Haven't seen you in some time." The official appeared extraordinarily affable—pleased, in fact.

"You ain't got anything on me, Sheriff," said Squint Evans defiantly.

"Maybe not, and maybe I could get plenty," said Currie pleasantly, "but we won't mention that. What're you doing here, Squint?"

"I'm working," came the belligerent reply.

The sheriff's brows lifted. "Well, well, well," he said as if amused. "What is it . . . dealing or behind the wheel? I thought you could make enough on the other side of the tables."

"I'm working for the Yellow Jacket," Squint explained with a frown. "Mining, mucking . . . anything."

The sheriff gave vent to a soft whistle of interest and astonishment. The look in his eyes and the tone of his voice changed. "So Hartland has hired a gunman, eh?"

"I don't know anything about that," Squint retorted. "He hasn't hired me as a gunman. If you don't believe it, ask him."

This was a challenge and Currie realized it. He leaned down a bit and his eyes were hard and cold. "Squint," he purred, "how would you like to do a ten or twenty year stretch . . . or life?"

The soft look in Evans's eyes was gone. The mask was off. His right hand was tense—chained lightning held in leash by a hair. "You want me?" The words came through his teeth in a hiss.

"Would you like it?" Currie's words were sparks of fire.

The little gunman hesitated, but he knew his man. "No."

"Then think of that before you start anything up here," said Currie slowly. "Remember, think of it. And think harder than you've ever thought before."

Two hours later, Butch Allen returned to Silver City.

Chapter Twenty-two

The arrival of the train did not interest Monocle Joe, or it never had—until this night. And this night he was interested merely because of the mail. He had to get Hartland's personal letters and he strolled down to the depot to kill time, and to see the mail sacks started on their way to the post office. Monocle Joe walked alone. He was more alone than usual of late. There was no open hostility, not even a jeer, but the manner of those with whom he had formerly associated, and with whom he still associated with at the tables, had become reserved. Joe had merely shrugged and stuck to his cards and his job.

It was about dark when the train drew in, its whistle awakening a long, lingering echo that reverberated up the valley and across the mountains. Then the scene was one of animation; passengers of many descriptions swung down the steps of the two coaches; trunks and boxes and packages, mail and poultry were speedily being unloaded from the baggage and express car; shouts, handclasps, slaps on backs—confusion. And out of all this, personally assisted by the conductor, floated an apparition that caused those on the narrow platform to catch their breaths. A tall brunette, a beauty all in red even to stockings and slippers, and she carried a flimsy lace red parasol. Whoever she might be, if she had conjured her brain for years she could not have evolved a more striking costume with which to knock Silver City off its feet.

"Anyone here from the Yellow Jacket?" It was the voice of the conductor. There was no response.

"Here's Monocle," came a voice from the rear. "He's a Hartland man. Same thing."

"This lady wants to go to Hartland's house," the conductor explained. "As there isn't any rig, I guess you'll have to take her up there. An' you better slide along before the rain comes."

"There's only one bag," said a sweet, stirring voice. "The rest of the luggage can be left here until. . . ."

"We'll look after it, ma'am," said the conductor politely, handing Joe the bag. "This gentleman will show you the way."

They set off with a path opening before them like magic, Joe in the lead, leaning far to the left under the weight of the bag on his right, the woman in red following, a smile upon her lips—which were red, too—and an amused sparkle in her eyes. As they gained the boardwalk, she moved up abreast of Joe. The wind was whipping her thin skirt about her elegant legs, tearing at the cobweb coat about her shapely shoulders.

"Is it very far?" she asked sweetly in Joe's ear.

"No, ma'am," Joe quavered. "Just at the upper end of the street, across the bridge and up the park. No, 'tain't far."

"Just so we can reach there before the rain," she murmured.

Once again men stepped right and left, clearing the way, leaving every inch of it free—and stared. And the woman in red, like Roger Hartland that first day, was thrilled and entertained. What a rough, crude place. A hole. A vivid flash of lightning bared the white shoulders of Old Baldy and the circling peaks. Then the darkness, bitter black, leaped in and the world seemed to rock in the resulting crash of thunder.

The woman had stopped. Now she plunged forward, grasping Joe's left arm, startled, but not terrified. For a few moments her face was chiseled marble.

"Almost there," Joe panted, his monocle shooting the length of its string. "Across the bridge."

They beat their way against the wind to the lower edge of the park. Above, the windows of Hartland's bungalow shot their gleams of light as beacons in the darkness. A *hissing* in the upper cañon grew into a roar and the rain came down in a solid sheet. Staggering, stumbling, buffeted by wind and rain, they struggled up the slope and reached the steps.

Joe was behind now. The woman was up the steps before him. She burst in the door and was fairly hurled against the table in the living room where Hartland was reading. He leaped to his feet. Papers flew about, swirling into the face of Fredricks who was entering from the dining room. He, too, stopped aghast, forgetting the door.

Monocle Joe trudged in and deposited the bag on the floor with a quick, rain-fogged glance around.

"Rose!"

He heard Hartland shout the name as he backed out the door and pulled it shut against the thundering blast of the storm.

"I'm glad you still know me, Roger," she said in the cool, confident, tantalizing voice she had so often used effectively.

He was around the table in two bounds, grasping her by the wrist. "Where did you come from?" he demanded, his face white.

"You're hurting me," she said calmly. Then, as he released his hold: "From New York, of course . . . and where else would I be apt to come from?" The fine brows arched.

"How did you know I was here?" He put the question almost in a shout. "Who told you. How . . . ?"

"Roger, Roger . . . Roger!" Her tone was urgent, commanding. "Don't you see that I am soaking wet from that terrible rain? I must have a drink and then change, and . . . oh, how I want a bath. We can talk later to your dear little heart's content."

Hartland bit his lip. His face still was white. "Fredricks, take Miss Raymond's bag to my room where she can change and use the bath. But you better bring a drink first."

Fredricks whirled as if on a pivot, his chin averted several degrees above normal. That woman! He returned in an incredibly short time bearing a tray upon which were decanter, glasses, and water. They still stood as he had left them.

"No ice?" murmured Rose absently.

"You'll find the water cold enough," Hartland growled.

"You seem rather cold yourself tonight, Roger," she observed, pouring out a drink. "Going to join me?"

"No." The word fairly crackled in the room.

"Oh, well." Rose raised her glass and drained it. "That's twice I've known a drink to hit the spot," she commented. "The other time was when you pulled me out of the ocean at Southampton. It's a long time between spots, Roger. And now, while I bathe and change, perhaps Fredricks, here, will start the ball rolling in the direction of the good old hot eats."

Fredricks took her bag and led the way into Hartland's bedroom. She threw Hartland a toss of the head and a wink as she followed, leaving him standing with both hands on the table staring down unseeingly at the oriental pattern of the runner.

In the meantime, Monocle Joe battled his way through the storm toward town. Rain fell in a torrent, subsided while the wind shrieked and raged, fell in again to do its part with a deluge like a solid wall. And Joe ran, ran as never before in his life. The world exploded in blue and red flame in front of him and he reeled backward with every nerve tingling painfully. Lightning had struck a tall fir between two widely separated buildings. That must have been the bolt intended for him, he thought, and fled down the street.

The rain dropped in a cloudburst after the strike. The middle of the street became a running rivulet. He splashed across to the post office and dashed in, drenched and streaming. He tipped his hat and the water poured off the brim. A pool formed beneath him on the floor.

"Where'd it hit?" someone asked.

"Tree up the street," Joe replied. "Was 'most under it."

"Who was that red woman, Monocle?" called another.

"Dunno," he answered laconically. But in that same instant Joe knew that from then on until doomsday the visitor who Hartland had called Rose would be known as "that red woman" in the camp.

Quite a few caught on that side of the street had taken refuge from the storm in the post office and curious eyes regarded Joe as he went about his business. The mail was sorted so he presented his order at the window. The paper was sodden but the writing upon it was legible.

"There's a registered letter," said the clerk, bringing a bulky envelope from the Yellow Jacket box. "You'll have to sign for it."

Monocle Joe signed and stuck the envelope in his inside coat pocket. He went to the door and surveyed the storm. It had abated some after the terrific downpour following the bolt that had struck the tree. Joe saw two or three men up the street and others were across the way. He wanted to finish his errand as quickly as possible. He stepped out into the rain and started up the street, but, as soon as he was clear of the post office, he took the registered envelope from his coat pocket and stuffed it in his shirt. He was nearly exhausted from the run down but he walked smartly.

The forms ahead disappeared in the darkness. Monocle Joe carried on with difficulty after he left the sidewalk. He waded through a veritable stream where the overflow from the creek came down and at length found the bridge. He had the advantage now of the lights shining from Hartland's windows. As he stepped off the bridge, two forms came hurtling at him.

Joe had no time to draw his gun but he cried out lustily as the men bore him down. His head was pressed into the mud, smothering his cries, but he squirmed and writhed like a snake while the butt or barrel of a gun *thudded* near his head several times as blows missed their aim.

Hands were about him, tearing open his pocket, grasping at his shirt. As it gave from top to bottom, he heard a fearful cry. Hoarse and weird it cut through the air—like the angry snarl of a wild animal. Suddenly the hands were no longer at his shirt; his throat was free.

He raised himself on an elbow. The sight he saw caused his jaw to drop with wonder. An ape-like man was holding two others by their necks, lifting them from the ground, bearing them toward the bridge, their arms flailing about futilely, croaking gutturals coming from their throats. It was Creeps Hallow dealing with Joe's attackers.

Joe saw Hallow drag the men on the bridge and hurl them one after the other over the rail into the raging stream. Then he came crouching back and lifted Joe to his feet. With a thrill, Joe felt within his torn shirt and found the envelope still there.

"We'll go up to the house," Hallow grunted.

"Gorblimey, yes!" Joe exclaimed.

They went up the slope into the park proper and hurried to the house. Joe rapped smartly. Hartland opened the door and, when he saw who it was, invited Joe in. Then, as Joe entered, he saw Creeps Hallow behind him. The gorilla man was staring past Hartland's shoulder at Rose Raymond, who had bathed and changed and was smoking a cigarette by the table. Hallow's eyes were like fiery pinpoints as he looked closer at the woman he had seen Joe bring to the bungalow.

"What is it, Hallow?" Hartland asked sharply.

"Allen's men were after him," came the hoarse reply, and Hallow faded into the night and the rain.

Hartland closed the door. He looked at Joe's

muddy and blood-streaked face, his torn clothing, and took the proffered envelope. "Tried to get it, eh? he said. "Well, you better clean up and get something to drink and eat. You'll stay here, tonight, Joe."

As Joe went toward the kitchen, Rose Raymond waved her cigarette holder so that a wreath of smoke floated upward. "Is all this part of the entertainment, Roger?" she asked languidly. "I'm not used to having an animal like that one in the door flirt with me."

Hartland did not reply.

Chapter Twenty-three

Oblivious to the downpour, his woolen garments soaked but retaining the heat of his great, ungainly body, Creeps Hallow crouched beneath a partly opened window of the bungalow's living room and listened. For within a human storm was raging.

For some time Hartland stood drumming on the table with his fingertips while Rose Raymond looked on idly. In the quality of her gaze curiosity, commiseration, amusement, and cold calculation were commingled. She wondered, of course, why Hartland had come to this god-forsaken place and finally was satisfied with the thought that he had fled to the wilderness to avoid temptation, quit the drink, and get physically fit. Yet why had he been so perturbed at seeing her? Her eyes took on a look of shrewdness. He wasn't merely angry because she had followed him; he was disconcerted, upset, flustered in a degree that showed plainly that her coming had plunged into disorder some carefully arranged plan of considerable moment. A girl? She put this aside lightly. She knew Hartland, she told herself.

Fredricks entered. "Dinner is served."

"Go ahead, Rose, I'm sure you're hungry," said Hartland irritably, leaning back from the table.

The woman's fine brows lifted. "Alone?" The brows arched higher at Hartland's nod. "That wouldn't be taking any firsts for hospitality, Roger. You'll have a cup of tea with me, of course."

But Hartland shook his head and pointed to the bulky envelope on the table. "I have business to attend to," he said curtly. "I'll look into it while you're eating, and then we can talk."

Rose Raymond saw a lurking look of determination—a firmness—in his eyes that she never had seen there before. Business! Roger Hartland having business! "I suppose you have some kind of interests here," she remarked as a feeler.

"Two mines," he retorted sharply. Then, taking up the envelope, he went to his desk. "You had better eat your dinner, Rose."

"That's good advice, anyway," said Rose, nettled, as she passed Fredricks and went into the dining room. She felt rather much at home with the fine china, glass, silverware, and Fredricks's excellent service. She was glad she had come.

Hartland opened the envelope, found the Huntley papers from Wright & Harris within, filed them in a pigeonhole of the desk. He considered briefly the attack on Monocle Joe. It would have availed Mann and Gordon nothing to have obtained the papers, or anyone else. He decided that the men who had attacked the cockney had seen him get the envelope at the post office and had assumed it contained money. Their motive had been robbery. He dismissed the matter with that.

But Rose Raymond! There was a problem. Not so much a riddle as to her purpose in coming. She wanted money, of course. That part of it would be easy. But to explain who she was, why she had visited him, and why she should leave so suddenly— that was a problem. The camp would talk, jeer, laugh in its sleeve, wink, and nod. She had been so conspicuous. That red costume! She had made the play purposely, of course. The more sensation, the higher the price. But Margaret Cram would hear, and it would not be so easy explaining matters to the mountain girl. Hartland swore. For by now he had decided he wanted to make as good an impression on Margaret as possible. He wanted to marry her. He wanted a home and an heir. What better combination could he ask than that of his own Eastern semi-aristocratic lineage and the pure Western stock that Margaret represented. Besides, he believed he was in love with her. She was so frank and fresh and true-blue that she was novel. But it wasn't this novelty that appealed to Hartland, nor was it her beautiful face and figure. It was some intangible quality in the girl herself that convinced him she would be loyal. Loyalty. That was the word. Hartland's fine eyes sparkled with a fire of satisfaction and enthusiasm. Now he knew why he wanted Margaret Cram for his wife!

He turned to the telephone to call the hotel. But the telephone office had closed for the night. He considered sending Monocle Joe to town to make arrangements for Rose Raymond's accommodation. Then it suddenly occurred to Hartland that Rose could not start away on the following morning. It would look worse for her to come, remain but a night, and leave, than if she stayed, say, a week. Once more he was confronted by the problem caused by the woman's appearance. These were thinking days—and nights—for Hartland.

Rose Raymond came in from dinner.

Funny there had never been anything about this woman to stir his passions. She was undoubtedly beautiful, even if there was an evasive coldness to her beauty; she was perfectly formed and she had an air suggesting voluptuousness that would have appealed to most men. He could have had her, all of her, at the snap of his fingers, but it had never occurred to him to make the gesture, and it did not occur to him now. "You had a pleasant journey?" he asked, biting off the end of a cigar.

Her brows arched quizzically. "Roger, you're no more interested in what kind of a journey I had than I'm interested in these funny mines of yours," she drawled. "You're cursing the ill luck that my train didn't fall through a bridge or miss a tunnel, and wondering how I found out you were here and why I've come." She took a sip of the coffee Fredricks had brought.

"Well, let's have it," he said dryly, touching a light to his cigar.

"I made a few discreet inquiries of the hall porters in your apartment house." She smiled. "They seemed to get more satisfaction out of telling me you were so far away and in such a terribly wild place, as they think, than they did out of their tips." She laughed softly, while Hartland resolved that the employees involved would be looking for new jobs within a fortnight.

"And I'm here because the last time I saw you, you said you wanted something new," she went on. "I had no idea what you were up to out here, but I thought it might give you something of a thrill if I walked in on you, bag and baggage. I've noticed that you've received a jolt. Why, Roger, old dear, at times you appear positively crestfallen."

"Not crestfallen," said Hartland grimly, rising and pacing the floor. He stopped, towering over her. "Rose, I'm angry. You have no right to take advantage of me. You've never been anything to me but a casual companion at public places of alleged entertainment. Your place in my life of the past year always reeked with champagne fumes and jazz. You were part of the tinsel, that's all." He noted that her eyes hardened. "Oh, this may sound rude, but it isn't. I'm merely telling you what you know to be the truth. I was your meal ticket. Perhaps you were foolish enough to think you could fasten onto me for life, or something like that. Well, you can't. We might as well understand each other before we, or you, open negotiations."

"Negotiations?" She spoke the word with a purring sound. "That smacks of business, Roger, and I sure didn't come here on business."

"Oh, don't beat about the bush," said Hartland sharply, drawing back to the table. "You came out here thinking your presence might embarrass me in some way, and, in any event, to bleed me for money. The way you entered town, for one thing, shows it. Decked out in that damned red thing as if you were a. . . ."

"Don't say it!" she interrupted. "Red becomes me, and that is why I wear it occasionally."

"No doubt," he said dryly. "But red has another meaning in these wild camps out here, and the meaning wouldn't be exactly flattering to you."

Rose Raymond's eyes narrowed. "I don't know what you're talking about," she said coldly, "but I do know something is wrong with you. You've never objected these last fifteen months or so to my being around. You've kept my telephone hot on more than one occasion, and now you're putting on the high brow and handing out veiled insults. What's the big idea, Roger, dear?"

Hartland was white. "What's your price?" he demanded hotly. "What do you want?"

"Well, for one thing, Roger," she replied languidly, "I want some of this delicious mountain air. I can smell it even if it is raining, and I've heard it is very stimulating . . . good for the nerves and all that. And you have such a cozy place here. . . ."

"Eh?" he interrupted, his eyes widening. "Do you expect to stay here . . . here?"

"Why, where else would I stay?" Rose simulated innocence admirably. "I'm your guest for the time being, am I not?"

Hartland laughed harshly. "Just as soon as this downpour lets up a bit, or before, if necessary, you're going down to our one and only hotel . . . two floors and two baths," he said, relishing the woman's shocked reception of this news. "I couldn't put you up here if I wanted to," he added, relenting. "My only spare room is occupied by an employee of mine who got shot the other day acting in my behalf. The hotel offers the only other accommodations. They are, possibly, a little different from those to which you have been accustomed. If you want to leave in the morning"—he had had a sudden inspiration—"I'll let it be known that you were a friend of mine who thought this was a resort and was tricked into coming as a joke, or something like that. But if you intend making a stay, the hotel will have to do."

Rose Raymond's expression was new to him. If it were not for Margaret, he would send her packing with just enough to get home, or throw her on the camp. But Margaret. . . .

As a matter of fact, Rose Raymond was just now realizing for the first time that there was a girl involved. She could see it in his eyes. In this moment she hated him. She forgot the entertainment and luxuries she had enjoyed by his bounty. She forgot the snug sums she had managed to bank. She forgot that she had absolutely no hold whatsoever on him. She forgot everything in a surging feeling of rage and jealousy. She would make him pay!

"Roger, dear, your new personality is an open book to me. What is she like, dear?"

Hartland's brain flamed, and then, in a moment, he was cool and collected. He walked over to her, put a hand under her chin, raised her face gently so her eyes looked fully in his own. "I see you've guessed it," he said softly. "I might know you would. She is very sweet, Rose, and the beautiful part of it all is that I love her." Hartland called Fredricks. "Scout around and see if you can scare up a suitable raincoat and boots," he instructed. "Better make it a hat, too. As soon as the rain slackens, or before twelve, I am taking Miss Raymond to the hotel."

Fredricks bowed profoundly.

Chapter Twenty-four

The rain continued. It beat down incessantly upon the bungalow roof, a peaceful sound in a soft rhythm soothing to the nerves. The log in the fireplace smoldered above red coals. Hartland and Rose Raymond were silent. Perhaps both were thinking of the same thing—of how fine it was to be inside, sheltered and warm, listening to the beating of the rain and the occasional song of the wind in the grass and trees.

Rose Raymond felt something well up within her, choking her. She stifled an impulse to sob. Here all was snug and homelike, and Hartland was going to take her to some old hotel. She shuddered in an effort to imagine what it would be like. Certainly it would not be like any of the hotels she had ever been in before. And through the rain. But her situation was of her own making. She could have written Hartland after learning where he was, and he would have sent her money to keep away. This realization again made her hate him.

"Roger, you're not going to send me to any shabby hotel on a night like this," she said suddenly with more or less indignation.

"Then where will I send you?" he asked quietly.

"Why . . . why I can stay here," she said, raising her voice. "I can sleep right here on this divan. I've slept on divans before, so it won't be a novelty or a hardship."

"I'd thought of that," he conceded. "For that matter you could sleep in my bed and I could sleep on the divan. But it wouldn't do." He shook his head.

"Wouldn't do?" Rose looked at him strangely. "Don't be silly. Why wouldn't it do?"

"It would cause talk," he replied, flecking the ash from his cigar in a graceful arc. "Can't have that."

She gave him an incredulous stare. "Roger, your love affair has softened your brains. Cause talk when there are three or four men around, and it's raining blue blazes, and I didn't get in until after dark? Cause talk in a dump like this where I'll bet there aren't enough morals to string a ten-cent necklace?"

"I'm supposed to have 'em," he said. "Anyway, I have many enemies here and they'd lose no time gossiping about your having stayed up here tonight. Next to rumor, a mining camp loves scandal. I have to watch my step here."

"I don't see why you should have any enemies," she said scornfully. "You never hurt anything but taxi drivers, and you always paid them so well afterward that they hung around hoping to get another beating."

"I've killed a man since I've been here," he said, unruffled.

Rose Raymond put down her cigarette. "All right, my bold buckaroo," she said sweetly, "let's have the Western heroics. What did you do . . . shock him to death with a loud suit?"

"Shot him," said Hartland laconically. "Had to do it or he would have got me. Lucky to hit him. The sheriff was up and knows it was self-defense. Big fight between my Yellow Jacket miners and the

Huntley miners started over it and a dozen of my men were badly hurt. Then Anderson in the spare room came in for a bullet, and tonight a couple of the rival outfit tackled Joe. This isn't a tame country, Rose."

"I heard somewhere that the West was wild," she said dryly, plainly disbelieving him. "Still, I wouldn't think it would be so bad since they've started wearing monocles." She laughed.

"Which reminds me," said Hartland. "Fredricks! Tell Joe to come in here."

Joe came, the single glass gleaming in his right eye. Fredricks had patched him up where he was cut, and, what with his diminutive stature, he made a rather ludicrous appearance. Rose suppressed a desire to laugh with difficulty.

"Tell me what happened tonight, Joe," said Hartland.

In the rich cockney into which he lapsed when excited—as he was now by the presence of the strange lady—Joe described his trip to town, even to the lightning bolt striking the pine tree, and the attack on the return, with Creeps Hallow coming to his rescue and throwing his assailants into the swollen stream.

"Oh, we needn't worry about them," said Hartland. "They got out . . . or, if they didn't, so much the better."

"I didn't have a chance to use my gun, sir," said Joe in a tone of apology. "It . . . with the storm an' everything, I just wasn't expecting trouble."

"You did all right," said Hartland. "Fredricks got you bunked? Good. Then you better tear off a night's sleep for a change." He looked at Rose Raymond. "If you think there's any joking about these things, you'll soon learn differently, if you stay around. Now you better get your bag packed. We're going to town."

"After that?" cried Rose. "Why, those same men or some others might attack us. I guess that blooming cockney was telling the truth, all right. He had his face to back him up. Not for me, Roger Hartland. No town for me tonight, unless you take me by force, and then I'd kick up a row. Here I stay, if I have to sleep on the floor, and your virtuous reputation can be torn into shreds and hung on the back fence for all I care." Her eyes were flashing with determination.

Hartland read the signals, but it was all as he had expected. He knew even Anderson had heard her stormy outburst, and Anderson's word would carry where Joe's word wouldn't. "Very well," he acquiesced. "You can take my room for tonight. I'll have Fredricks fix me up on the divan. And . . . we go to bed rather early here in the mountains compared to New York."

Later, when he was alone, Hartland considered the new slant he had obtained on Rose Raymond's character. In New York, like scores of other good-looking women possessed of good manners and the knack of choosing and wearing clothes properly, she had been a social parasite, not a gold-digger, exactly, as the term is accepted, but so close to the line that only she herself knew how precarious was her footing. Removed from her natural environment, with the bounds of restraint loosened, she might revert— and unintentionally—to a type that made Hartland's lip curl and, in the case of Rose, caused him to shudder. For women who live off the bounty of men who are not their husbands are sisters under the skin. So Hartland firmly believed.

But his thoughts might have been warped by his constant comparison of Margaret Cram with women of the type of Rose. He took this into consideration and tried to do her justice, but it galled him to know that she had followed him West to bleed him, and that she might try to attach added value to his feeling for the mountain girl. It was purely and simply a detestable form of blackmail. The more Hartland thought about it, the more incensed he became. He couldn't sleep, and he rose unrefreshed and in bad humor.

Meanwhile, Rose Raymond had succeeded in working herself into such a state of irritability that she also lay awake into the wee hours of the morning. Hartland's aristocratic air of superiority over her was nearly maddening. She had never seen him utterly normal, and this air was his heritage, as she confessed to herself. But this only made her angrier with him. Nor did it help any for her to realize that she had made a fool of herself. She was in a quandary. Plainly she should take a stake, as Hartland called it (some more of his affected Westernisms) and clear out. Without seeing the girl? Never! Her curiosity would bring her back afoot if need be.

Thus it was not a bright pair that entered the dining room for breakfast. It still was raining. Rose looked out the windows at the steady, sweeping sheets of moisture, the wet grass and trees, the wisps of fog that hung low about the drab peaks. The prospect, in her eyes, was cheerless, gloomy, dismal, dull. What could a person do to amuse himself in such a place on such a day—on any day? How long would the rain keep up? What . . . what . . . ?

"Doesn't look very cheery today, does it," Hartland ventured. "A steady rain like this may last a week or two."

"I hope not," said Rose crossly. "I want to see the country with the sun shining on it." That would let him know she had no intention of going at once.

"You'll find it quite as comfortable at the hotel as you could expect in a mining camp like this," he said easily. "Doubtless there is a livery where you can rent a horse to ride. I suppose you brought along riding things. There's no golf or bathing. I know no women in town, but you have a knack of getting acquainted."

Rose looked at him questioningly. "Why I thought . . . I thought. . . ."

"She doesn't live in town," Hartland explained calmly. "You'd hardly get to know her if she did. Not that I care. You see, Rose, I have a mine here called the Yellow Jacket and I've just taken over another, the Huntley. These are the largest properties in this district. I intend to make them both pay. The two crews are at odds and there may be some trouble, but it will have to be overcome. So, you see, I have something of a job on my hands. I have no time to entertain."

"Oh, I can take a rest cure," said Rose lightly.

"And fish," he suggested.

She could have killed him for that. And his next remark caused her to put down her egg spoon in a fury.

"Of course you understand, Rose, it would hardly do for any of your bills to be sent to me," he remarked.

She struggled to control herself. Then the light in her eyes was that of a tigress. If he saw, he made no sign. She had half expected him to make a definite offer of money this morning. No such offer was forthcoming; no such thought seemed in his brain. He was wearing corduroys and high mountain shoes, a soft gray flannel shirt, and a wide blue four-in-hand. This attire suited him, she had to confess. Again there was that annoying lump in her throat. Had she been in love with him without knowing it? Or was it the change in him?

"You can at least be decent in this thing, Roger," she complained.

"But do you think you've been quite decent?" he countered. "Do you think you've played the game in following me out here? I've been very decent to you when it comes down to brass tacks."

"I . . . I didn't know," she explained lamely.

"There's a train out today," he suggested.

There it was again! He wanted to get rid of her as quickly as he could. She had been good enough as a companion in the dizzy night clubs, but here she was excess baggage. Again she forgot his benefactions, forgot the amounts she had wheedled out of him, and—yes, stolen. Her hatred flamed anew.

"I'm not going today," she announced firmly. "Nor tomorrow, either . . . nor the next day."

"Just as you say, Rose," he said in a matter-of-fact tone, "but watch your step. If you try to make trouble for me with your tongue or by your actions, I'll throw you on the camp."

Her eyes widened. "What does that mean?" she demanded.

"You'll have to find out," he said grimly, rising.

Fredricks provided a raincoat, boots, and a big hat for her after breakfast. She packed her bag, refusing to speak to anyone, and they started. She walked at

Hartland's side and Monocle Joe brought up the rear, carrying the bag. She looked back at him in disgust. Why, the bag was almost as big as he was. He had to lean. And that monocle. What a positively ridiculous procession, she thought, striving to gather the fragments of her shattered dignity. They practically slid down the slippery grass of the meadow. When they reached the place where the bridge should have been, there was no bridge.

"It must have washed away," said Hartland in a wisp of a voice, staring at the raging, swollen waters of the creek that attested to a cloudburst in the cañon above.

"Perhaps it just dived under," Rose snapped out. Monocle Joe had the audacity to snicker.

"Oh, well," said Hartland cheerfully, "we'll go around. The upper bridge ought to be all right, hadn't it, Joe?"

"Ought to be quite all right, sir," came the answer.

They turned back up the meadow, but before they reached the bungalow, they veered across to the trail leading through the bull pines. On this trail they walked single file. Rose was boiling mad. The stiff slicker kept rubbing her knees, which were wet. The boots were miles too large. And Hartland's broad shoulders mocked her at every step. But she kept doggedly on, and on—and on, and on, and on! Was this some kind of a joke?

But at last they came out of the pines on a muddy road. They turned to the left and went down this road. In time they came to a large, stout bridge, and here they crossed the stream. Hartland had taken the bag from Joe. It was too much to expect the little fellow to carry it all the distance. They turned on the road toward town. A man in a spring wagon caught up with them and halted his team. It was John Cram. Hartland quickly explained about the bridge and helped Rose up to the seat.

"Miss Raymond, this is Mister Cram," he said simply.

John Cram nodded and took the information for granted. Hartland and Joe climbed in, and they drove down to the street and the hotel. Here Joe again took charge of the bag.

Hartland speedily made arrangements for Rose Raymond's accommodations. Owing to the congestion he could only get a room near the bath. He took it. Next he gave orders for Rose's luggage to be brought from the station. He explained curtly that she had come thinking Silver City was in the nature of a mountain resort and would have to stay for a rest before doing further traveling.

He went up with Rose and found her room to be the large, airy, corner room he had occupied when he had first arrived in town.

"Same room I had," he explained. "Not much in the way of decoration, but good bed, good chairs, big closet, and two windows affording an excellent view. If you persist in staying, Rose, this is the best I can do for you right now."

"I think it's perfectly lovely," she lied, forcing a smile, and stepping to a window. "It's so novel."

"It's all of that," he agreed, "and now, if there's nothing else, I'll be attending to business. I'll tell them downstairs to do everything they can to make you comfortable."

"That'll be a bottle of Scotch," she said flippantly.

"I'll attend to it," he promised, "and later in the day I'll have Fredricks send down some things for you. If you have any suggestions, there's a telephone downstairs."

When he had gone, she turned swiftly from the window and stared at the closed door. Almost any other woman of her calling, if it could be designated as such, caught in a similar predicament, would have burst into bitter tears. But Rose Raymond's eyes merely burned with a slow fire of resentment, anger, and malicious determination.

Chapter Twenty-five

Hartland saw John Cram's team and spring wagon in front of the bank as he left the hotel after giving his instructions to the clerk. As his next business was with Alex Gordon and Herbert Mann, he crossed over and entered the bank in his customary casual manner. The clerk caught sight of him at once and bowed respectfully.

Hartland started at a leisurely pace along the outside of the cage toward Gordon's private office. As he did so, a voice was suddenly raised to a pitch that made it audible to all in the front room. It came from the office in the rear.

"But I tell you I've got to have powder! How'm I going to get out enough ore to meet that note if I haven't got what I need to work with? You won't renew and you won't help me to get your money for you. Now what's the idea?"

It was John Cram speaking in the heat of high

passion. Hartland paused and the clerk came hurrying to the counter nearest him. "I'll tell Mister Gordon you're here," he said.

"Never mind." Hartland held up a hand and gave the man a look that held him motionless. Then Hartland strolled to the front door and stood looking out into the drizzling rain.

Powder—ore—note—won't renew. The words ran through his brain in a tangle and gradually, although nothing more was heard from the private office in the rear, he pieced the words together and made sense of them. He was helped by the fact that Cram's voice had betrayed great anger. Evidently he was trying to get enough ore out of his mine to pay off a note that the bank refused to renew. Mine mortgaged probably. Hartland whistled a popular air softly and moved out to the front step. In a short time John Cram came out. He paused by Hartland's side and strove to conceal the fact that he was very much agitated.

"I'll be going back in half or three-quarters of an hour, Mister Hartland," he said, "in case you might want a lift as far as the upper bridge."

"I was just waiting to put that proposition up to you." Hartland smiled. "I'll look for your team along the street." Cram clambered into his seat on the spring wagon and drove off as Hartland turned back into the bank.

Hartland strode to the door of the rear office and entered unannounced. As he had expected, he found Mann there as well as Gordon. He acknowledged their somewhat effusive greetings with a curt nod and pulled up a chair beside the desk. He sat down and took some papers from an inside pocket.

"Here are the . . . releases, I suppose you'd call

them," he said briefly. "Anyway, you both sign those two papers on the line marked with the little cross." He put the papers before Gordon, pointing to the lines that required his signature. Gordon signed without question.

"Call both those clerks to witness these," Hartland instructed, and Gordon opened the door leading into the cage and beckoned to the clerks.

"Now, it's your turn," said Hartland, spreading the papers before Mann. "I suppose it won't be hard for you since you must be getting plenty of practice signing your name to stock certificates." His smile was anything but pleasant.

Mann appeared rather white this morning. He signed as directed and the two clerks entered and affixed their names as witnesses.

"Now I'll take the paper you have in your vault, Gordon, as per instruction number two from Wright and Harris," said Hartland, very business-like. "Then we'll attend to the money end of it and our present dealings will be completed."

Gordon drew the paper—the original option, in fact—from a drawer of his desk and handed it over. Both he and Mann obeyed Hartland's orders like automatons this morning. And both gave the impression of being nervous and worried. Hartland examined the instrument, nodded in satisfaction, and pocketed the papers.

"Now we'll transfer fifty thousand dollars from the Yellow Jacket account into a private account of my own," Hartland said to Gordon. "Bring me a checkbook. I suppose I can draw a Yellow Jacket check?"

"Oh, yes, yes," said Gordon hastily. "I was going to suggest such a move after you gave me the ten-thousand-dollar check. I'll open an account for you."

He was filling out a blank. "That's on the Yellow Jacket account for fifty thousand," he said, pushing the check across for Hartland's signature. "I'll credit it to your personal account. I'll make out the deposit slip. And here is the signature card . . . please fill it out . . . and here's a checkbook. Sorry I haven't any of the good leather-cover checkbooks, Mister Hartland."

Hartland filled out the signature card, initialed the deposit slip, signed the Yellow Jacket check, and drew a personal check. This last he tendered to Gordon.

"Here's my check for twenty-five thousand to cover your first payment on the option," he said slowly. "I want this check, and the other check for ten thousand, duly canceled and marked paid with the date plainly stamped, and I want them at once."

Gordon looked nervously into the cool, gray eyes across the desk from him. What kind of a game was this? But Hartland's look brooked no delay. "Why, yes, of course," said the banker hastily. He rose and went into the cage where he attended to the matter personally.

When he returned with the cancelled checks, Hartland put them in his pocket and drew out another slip of paper. "Here's still another check," he said easily. "Quite a business we're doing this morning, Gordon. This is on one of my New York bank for one hundred thousand dollars and it's to be placed to the credit of the Yellow Jacket account. I hardly think I'd get that in cash, Gordon."

"Oh, it won't be necessary," said Gordon, his eyes bright. What a standing his bank would be getting! "You've endorsed it for deposit? Yes, I see. Very well, Mister Hartland."

Hartland was leaning with his elbows on the table. There was a faint, hard smile on his lips. "You know I've been thinking, Gordon," he said slowly, "just thinking, you know, that there might be an opportunity here for another bank if this boom you and Mann are engineering materializes. I've always had a sly hankering to be a banker." There was a look of positive fright in Gordon's eyes. "But I wouldn't think of it, or allow any one else to think of it, as long as our dealings are satisfactory." He drew out the last words and let them sink in.

Gordon sighed with relief. It was a threat, but it left him an out. "Any time I can be of any service, I am at your disposal, Mister Hartland," he said in a tone of respect. "You are . . . this bank's backbone, one might say. That is . . . I mean. . . ."

But Hartland, having driven in his point, was not listening. He picked up the telephone and called the Yellow Jacket. "Give me Miller," he said crisply into the transmitter when he had his number. The two other men looked at him more or less awestruck. Was this the same Hartland who had so recently come to Silver City? This the tailor's model and the man with the cane?—as he had been derisively called. Gordon's nervousness increased, but Mann's blustering look and important manner came back to him. Anything Hartland might do in the way of business—of development—was bound to be to the benefit of the Consolidated. Let Hartland start major operations and the camp and the Consolidated were made.

"Oh, Miller"—it was Hartland speaking again— "go over and have a chin-chin with Fred Crawford, the Huntley manager. That his name? All right. The Huntley deal is all closed. You're general manager.

Tell Crawford to notify his men that the Huntley will close down at midnight, Sunday, this June Thirtieth, and will resume operations at midnight, July Fourth. Got that? No, that's all. Those are my instructions and I want them carried out to the letter. Good bye."

Hartland rose. "Good morning, gentlemen," he said pleasantly. He went out, leaving Gordon and Mann wetting their lips and staring one at the other as if neither had ever seen the other before.

As Hartland's footsteps died away, Mann leaped to his feet. "Whatever it is," he exclaimed, bringing his fist down with a bang on the desk, "it's some kind of a damn' bluff!" He looked steadily at Gordon and both knew he lied.

Hartland walked across the street in the rain. He felt Rose Raymond's eyes on him from the window of her room that looked out up the street. He was filled with a growing resentment. Their situation was ridiculous. He had given the hotel clerk the excuse that she had come there thinking it was a resort and that she was a friend of his. This would be noised about the camp and the first part of it would be scoffed at. He knew as much. Had he found himself in the position of one of the townsmen, he would have scorned the explanation himself. Yet he could not afford to ignore her, for such an attitude would be set down as unfair and mean. Never would he be able to convince these men that he had not sent for her, brought her there. It was so preposterous—a woman coming all the way from New York thinking that Silver City was a resort. His resentment kindled into downright anger. Here he was with the Huntley on his hands merely to satisfy a personal whim, to fire Butch Allen and show

Mann a thing or two. But he had it, and it had to be looked after. There would certainly be trouble and he might have to shut the mine down for good. Then there was Margaret Cram. Hartland realized he was hard hit in that direction. And into the midst of these troubles and complications, Rose Raymond had thrust herself. No wonder Hartland swore as he turned into the Silver King.

His entrance silenced the noisy crowd. There were smiles, however, and surreptitious winks. He surmised the chief topic had concerned the arrival of Rose, and, if he didn't know it was as "that red woman" that they knew her, it was in the very air, that feeling and opinion of the crowd—silent thunder that roared in his ears. He had to steel his nerves to avoid striking out right and left. He wanted to fight. But to take offence without palpable cause would be a confession of guilt. An open insult could be avenged, but not these sly, artful, knowing hints broadcast by eyes in which there was more amusement than suspicion. The men were rather given to accord him credit for what they considered his boldness.

Hartland saw Butch Allen in his customary place at the center of the bar. He strode forward, a way opened for him, and he touched Allen on the shoulder. Allen looked around without enthusiasm.

"You working for the Huntley?" Hartland asked.

"Nope," said Allen with a brazen look. "The Huntley's working for me. That is, the men are. I'm the foreman."

"You mean you *were* the foreman," said Hartland firmly. "You're fired. Go up there any time and get your belongings and after that don't trespass on the property."

He turned on his heel, expecting an outburst. But he had no intention of replying to anything Allen might say. However, there was no outburst. Allen merely grinned into his glass. Hartland moved out through the silence that pounded in his ears. Somehow he had not derived the measure of satisfaction he had anticipated in dismissing Allen. And—was Allen dismissed?

John Cram was coming out of a general store as Hartland walked up the street. The miner signified that he was ready to go and Hartland climbed into the seat. They drove up the road with Cram making casual remarks about the rain, the benefit to the crops, the cloudburst of the night previous far up the cañon—anything except mining. He studiously avoided that subject. Hartland remained silent until they reached the crossroads at the upper bridge. Then he spoke.

"Mister Cram, suppose we drive up to the trail to my place, tie the team, and go on to the bungalow for a spell," he suggested.

Cram readily agreed. He had mountain miner's native intuition. He realized that Hartland had something on his mind that had to come out. It was but natural that he should select an older man for a confidant. They hitched the team and walked through the dripping bull pines to the bungalow.

"Will you have a drink?" Hartland asked politely.

"I'm a little damp," said Cram with a smiling nod, "an' no hard-rock man will refuse to drink with a gentleman."

Fredricks served them. Hartland hardly touched his potion. Then: "Mister Cram, you're a quiet man. I expect the solitudes of the mountains make you fellows that way. I assume you're a good listener."

Cram drained his glass, accepted the cigar Hartland proffered, and nodded his head. "Let's have it," he said briefly.

Then, while the rain droned on the roof and the fire crackled lazily in the hearth, Roger Hartland told the older man something of his earlier days, considerable of his later life, and all about Rose Raymond.

Cram listened attentively, his eyes on the blazing log. He did not interrupt, and, when Hartland had finished, he did not look up.

"That's the story," said Hartland, throwing his cigar end into the fire. "Have another drink, Mister Cram." The old man helped himself. Hartland had asked for no advice, had given not the slightest indication that he wanted or expected any. He had merely unburdened himself of what was on his mind and that was the end of it. Cram liked him all the more because of this.

"There's just one thing," said Hartland in a casual tone. "You are not to tell your daughter any of this." He paused long enough to catch a look from Cram that assured him. "And now, Mister Cram, what was it that I heard you raising your voice about in Gordon's office when I came into the bank? Something about powder, and having to get out ore to pay a note that couldn't be renewed."

"I'd rather not talk about it," said Cram quietly. "You have trouble enough of your own."

"Well, I told you something of my difficulties," said Hartland, "and I'm particularly interested in anything which concerns that bank. Perhaps I should have this information."

Cram considered this. Then he explained about his note coming due the Fifteenth of July and Gordon's refusal to renew it.

"Wants to get his hooks on your place, too, eh?" observed Hartland. "I should say you need about five thousand." He rose, went to his desk, and drew out his checkbook.

John Cram advanced and put a hand on his shoulder. "I don't believe I'd do that," he faltered. "It . . . it looks as if I was asking you for it."

"Don't worry," said Hartland testily. "This is a business proposition. Your mine is good for five thousand or you wouldn't be working it. I'm not giving you this money. I'm letting you have it for a year at the legal rate of interest, which I believe is eight percent in this state. I expect you to make out a note and send it to me. Here's your check."

Cram took the check with a glad smile. "That makes it different," he said in a new voice. "I guess you're a thoroughbred. Your dad tried to stake me many a time but he never put it in just the right way. Come up an' have supper with us, an' I'll figure it's a good day's work."

It was Hartland's turn to smile. The old man was helping him out of that evening's difficulty. "All right," he said.

He watched John Cram stride with springy step toward the trail in the pines. He went inside feeling better. He had helped someone. It gave him a thrill. Margaret's father, too. Then his heart sank. What would she think? She would have to know, of course. John Cram would have to explain his sudden prosperity. He couldn't keep silent and he wouldn't lie. Would Margaret Cram think that Hartland had assisted her father to gain favor with her? However, Hartland nursed another problem by the fire while events shaped themselves and the silent thunder once more trembled in his ears.

Chapter Twenty-six

Silent thunder. What days these were for Silver City, with sensation following sensation like the links of a chain, while fate marshaled events and drove them onward toward the great climax in Roger Hartland's life. Gossip was rife with the prevalent note, one of criticism of his personality and respect for what was assumed to be business sagacity. Even taciturn tongues wagged vigorously. The incident of "that red woman" was overshadowed by Hartland's move in discharging Butch Allen. For everyone knew that Allen had virtually picked the men for the Huntley and that they would stand behind him as a unit. And when the men came off the 4:00 P.M. shift that afternoon with the news that the Huntley would close down for the first four days in July, speculation and conjecture knew no bounds, and rumors ran riot through the excited camp.

Meanwhile, men were pouring into Silver City. Herbert Mann's advertising was beginning to be felt. Most of the newcomers were the parasites that always feed off a boom. But there were miners, too, and prospectors. Men began going into the mountains in search of likely mineral sign that would warrant staking out claims. Big Mose had sent for lumber and carpenters and a big addition to the Silver King was to be started at once. Other resorts were perking up. Big business for the summer and fall was in progress. Whether the Consolidated's hopes materialized, or Hartland did anything or not, the resorts, eating places, hotel, and rooming houses were bound to flourish. Naturally the owners and employees of these places were boosting, predicting, giving inside information, and in all cases lying. An extra coach was added to the train. Buggies, buckboards, and spring wagons rolled in; many came on horseback. Abandoned cabins were rehabilitated. Tents began to dot the meadows and the creekbanks. Silver City promised to present the wonderful sight of a superficial boom.

In the vortex of this seething whirlpool of excitement, Roger Hartland loomed as the predominating spirit without his having said a word or raised a hand to signify that this position was proper and the hope and belief in him justified. At this moment, had he announced that he was leaving Silver City, his life would have been endangered. It would be necessary to spirit him out of the mountains at night under guard. But he was blithely inattentive to the extraordinary transformation that was being wrought about him. It had come about too subtly. Yet this very night he was to make a decision that would shake Silver City like the tremors of an earthquake, and change the tenor of his life and the lives of scores of others.

Herbert Mann remained closeted with Alex Gordon in the bank for nearly an hour. The Consolidated had been incorporated with Gordon, Mann, and five others as the incorporators. The five others were owners of mines or prospects whose options Gordon and Mann held. All options now were made over to the corporation. Only $5,000 in cash was involved, excepting the cost of incorporation. An office had been rented in Silver City, agents had been arranged for in towns in the lowlands, stock certificates were being printed. Soon the money would begin to roll in. But the prime movers in the project were inclined to caution. Hartland's telephone message to Miller had them guessing. For Gordon had noticed that under the terms of the option Wright & Harris had given to Hartland, he did not have to work the mine. The closing down of the Huntley for the first four days in July might forecast the shutting down of the mine altogether. This would put the Consolidated on the rocks almost instantly, for it would puncture the bubble of the boom.

Mann heard of Hartland's action in letting Allen go as soon as he reached the street. He hurried to the Silver King and found a peculiar condition of affairs. Butch Allen was not saying a thing, which was not like him. Moreover, the Huntley men who were in the place were quiet, too. He caught a gleam in Allen's eye and gave him the signal to follow him into a card room in the rear.

"Just heard Hartland has let you out," said Mann, impressed by the other's quiet, forbidding demeanor. "But don't let that worry you." It was Mann who had brought Allen to Silver City and put him in at the Huntley, and he felt responsible in the present emergency. "There'll be something just as good."

"It's not worrying me," said Butch Allen. His tone was too cheerful, under the circumstances, to be anything but ominous. "You haven't got a thing in the world to do with the Huntley now, have you?"

"Not a thing in the world, as you say," replied Mann. "But you're not . . . not planning to get even with Hartland in some . . . some way, are you?"

"No?" Allen's eyes flashed. "Do you think I'm going to let that tenderfoot get away with the stunts he's pulled an' this last one in particular? Calling me in front of the crowd! He'll look like the hole in a plugged nickel when I get through with him."

Mann shook his head. "It won't do," he said seriously.

"You think it won't," Allen scoffed. "I'll make it do an' then some."

"Allen," said Mann, raising his voice, "we . . . you can't afford to antagonize Hartland. He has too much behind him. He's our best bet right now. He's making the boom and the camp without knowing it. I don't know why he's shutting down the Huntley for a few days, but there's something behind it. Now you lay off of him and I'll take care of you. Don't have any doubts about that."

"Yeah?" Allen was openly sneering. "I wonder if there's anybody in here who knows just how big a bag of wind you are as well as I do."

Mann leaned forward with his hands on the card table between them. "You can lay to it that Hartland's no bag of wind," he said in a low voice. "Do you know that he deposited a check for one hundred and fifty thousand dollars in Gordon's bank the other day? No? Of course, you didn't know. But I knew. And Gordon's getting that money in cash. In cash, you understand?" He had lowered his voice and Allen was all attention, every nerve alert. "And he deposited another check this morning for a hundred thousand more," Mann finished in a hiss.

Allen's lips pursed for a whistle but no sound issued from them. He merely stared into Mann's eyes. And for a full minute they stood, gazes locked, steady, unwinking, reading each other's thoughts until their conclusions met on the mutual ground of understanding.

"Come have a drink," Butch Allen invited.

"That's more like it," said Herbert Mann.

Hartland talked with Anderson, who was now sitting up in bed, reading and eating and mending speedily. The doctor paid his daily visit and said the patient could go out into the living room the next day, and be transferred to his own quarters at the Yellow Jacket in three days more.

Fredricks made up a basket of certain delicacies, including some drinkables, and sent them by Monocle Joe to Rose Raymond. She did not telephone. Later in the afternoon, Hartland again talked to his brokers in New York. He also talked to Wright & Harris in Butte. Miller called up with the information that he had conferred with Fred Crawford of the Huntley and that the notice of suspension of work at midnight, June Thirtieth, had been duly posted. Hartland told him he had fired Butch Allen and would inspect both mines next day. Miller rang off in excitement.

Hartland looked forward eagerly to the breaking of the afternoon's monotony by the visit to the Cram place. He asked Monocle Joe if he knew the trail up there after it branched off from the road and Joe said he did. Then Hartland decided he would take Joe along, as it would be dark and his services as a guide might be valuable on the way back. He sent Joe to the livery in town to hire a horse.

It was just about dark when they started, and the wet, inky night had closed in when they finally saw the lights of Cram's cabin.

John Cram gave Hartland a hearty welcome, and then went out to show Joe where to put up the horses and to help him. Margaret took Hartland's hat and slicker. "These will go in the kitchen to dry," she said, favoring him with a smile. "I'm just getting supper."

Hartland followed her out into the kitchen. It was the first time he had seen her when she wasn't in riding clothes. She looked more beautiful and delightfully feminine in the light blue frock she wore and the neat, white apron. Her eyes seemed dancing with mischief. He had to struggle with the impulse to gather her in his arms and kiss her.

"Margaret, suppose I were to ask you to marry me . . . what would you think?"

She looked more desirable than ever as she turned a puzzled frown upon him. "I'd think you were crazy," she replied.

"I'm beginning to believe that's the exact status of my mental condition," he said, slapping a palm with his fist. "Mad! Absolutely mad. But if I did, and you didn't think me crazy, you'd want to look up my record, would you not?"

"Mister Hartland!" She noted his look of exasperation. "Well, Roger, then. You have the gift of light talk with a weighty edge and it's refreshing to meet you, but you mustn't spoil it by trying to be funny."

"Funny? Listen, Margaret, girl, if there's anything in the world I don't want to be, it's funny. And I'll tell you something else while I have the chance. If I should become convinced I'm in love with you, and want you, I'll get you. Don't think for a minute I won't."

Before she could reply, John Cram entered, followed by Joe. "Oh, ho! An' how about supper?" said the old man, looking from the girl's flushed face to Hartland's steady, gray eyes. "Come into the sitting room, Mister Hartland. Joe, here, says he won't move out of the kitchen, even to eat, so I guess we'll have to humor him. Marge, are you shaking it up?"

"Supper will soon be ready, Father," said the girl.

They sat down in easy chairs and John Cram told Hartland about his mine. Hartland hardly heard him. He was thinking of the alluring picture Margaret made standing by the stove in her white apron, her forearms bare. She had a keen mind, too, and was able at repartée. Then his eyes clouded as he remembered the visitor at the hotel. He thought of Rose Raymond as she had come into his house the night before with her red dress clinging to her body, an annoyed, supercilious look in her eyes, and, later, an air about her of being where she belonged. It was preposterous. He would have to pay the woman her price and get rid of her. But even as he thought in this vein, he was obsessed with the conviction that Margaret would have to see her, meet her, perhaps, and hear the story before she would believe in him. But John Cram was asking him a question.

"Has that half-witted fellow, Hallow, bothered you any?"

"He did at first, but I've given him a job," said Hartland. "He's my night watchman, you might say. And he's right on the job." He related the incident of the attempted robbery and the attack on Joe the night before.

"They thought it was money," said Cram. "Well, if Creeps is watching your place, he'll watch it. He helped me cart my stuff up here some years ago and stayed here. Marge was a little girl then, an' he worshipped her. He's sort of looked out for her ever since. I'm never afraid when she's out in the mountains west of here. Hallow keeps an eye on her wanderings. Marge told me about the day you two met him in Moon Valley. He didn't like it because you were with her. But now that he knows you are friends, he'll be all right. Don't flash a six-shooter around him, though, or he'll fly off the handle. He's been scared by a gun sometime, when he was young probably. I can do anything with him. He works for me now an' then when I need him an' earns his keep. But what you pay him in a month will come near keeping him a year."

Margaret came in and announced supper. He was not again alone with her until her father and Joe went out for the horses. He thought he caught a significant look from the old man as he left. Was Cram purposely giving them some time together? If so, he didn't propose to waste it.

"Margaret," he said seriously, "do I have to learn those three things about women you mentioned before I'll understand you?"

"But I'm not hard to understand," she parried.

"You are to me," he said, frowning slightly, "because you're a new kind of girl in my experience. You have an attraction aside from mental and physical, and it isn't just personality. I . . . I can't say just what it is yet."

"As I said before, Roger, your imagination is at work."

"I've been thinking over what you said about your price when we were talking that day. You said your price would be love. You love your father, do you not?"

"Why, of course!" She appeared surprised.

"And you love these mountains and the people in them, I take it?"

"Yes . . . ," she hesitated, "but why do you ask?"

"If this was to develop into a copper camp," he said, leaning forward in his chair, "it would benefit your father and all these people up here. Suppose I were to agree to sink a shaft . . . go 'way down . . . would you promise to marry me?"

She was silent for some time. Then: "Because you were going to sink on that account?" she said, raising her eyes. "No, I couldn't promise."

"Not even with the stipulation that I get the copper?" he persisted.

She shook her head. "That isn't the way I meant what I said," she said slowly. "It would be helping those I love, yes. In a way I would be selling myself for love, I suppose, but not in the way . . . oh, you don't understand. You mustn't trifle with such a subject, Roger. And we are . . . you might say strangers. It's just that I'm the only girl you know here, and I suppose you must have women."

He started. This had been his own thought of a day or two before. He leaned over and put his hand on hers. "I'm not sure but that I want you," he said. "Very soon you are going to hear some things about me. After that, I'll know."

He was lighting a cigarette and looking into her troubled eyes when John Cram entered to say the horses were ready.

Chapter Twenty-seven

John Cram rode with Hartland and Monocle Joe as far as the main road. Here he left them and they followed down the cañon, guided by the deeper shadow of the trees on either side of the road, walking their horses for there were many mud holes.

They rode single file into the narrow ribbon of path between the dripping pines. Here all they could do was to hold the reins loosely and let the horses pick their way. It was so dark neither could see a hand before his face. Joe's right hand gripped his automatic under his slicker. Suddenly both horses stopped.

"What is it?" Hartland called softly.

"Listen!" came Joe's excited answer.

Creeps Hallow's troubled soul was sobbing to the wild spirits of the stormy night.

The notes of the song drifted away and died. The rain drove against the pines with a softly *hissing* sound as of escaping steam. It beat a dull tattoo on the stiff, board-like sides of the slickers. The horses pawed impatiently.

"Go ahead, Joe, that's Hallow!" Hartland called. "If he starts again, give him a whistle to stop him, so he won't scare the horses."

Lights glimmered ahead. They rode out of the timber and galloped across the meadow to the verandah steps where Hartland dismounted and turned his horse over to Joe.

"You can take yours back to the livery in the

morning," he told Joe briefly. Then he went up the steps and into the house.

Fredricks came to the dining room door. "Will you have some coffee, sir?

"Yes," replied Hartland, handing over his hat and slicker. "Any telephone calls?"

Fredricks cleared his throat ever so slightly. "Ah . . . Miss Raymond called twice, sir. I told her you were out to dinner and for the evening."

"And what did she have to say to that?" Hartland inquired.

"*Ahem.*" Fredricks cleared his throat again. "Begging your pardon, sir, I think Miss Raymond was rather touched with liquor. She was quite emphatic, sir."

"Yes?" Hartland looked at his man with an amused expression. "In what way was she emphatic, Fredricks?"

"She told me she thought I was a damned liar, sir," said Fredricks with great dignity.

"Well, there have been times when I thought the same thing." Hartland chuckled. "Bring the coffee and we'll call it a day."

Hartland had just finished breakfast next morning when he had a visitor. "It's Mister Milton, sir," Fredricks announced.

Entering the dining room, Hartland saw a tall young man standing near the closed outer door. A closer look, as he approached Milton, disclosed the fact that the man wasn't as young as he thought. He looked into a pair of cool, gray eyes, noted the firm mouth and chin, the strong features, and a skin that retained the bronze of outdoor life despite work in the chill and dampness and darkness of the mine.

He saw the cartridge belt through the opened front of the man's slicker.

"So you're the new deputy," said Hartland, offering his hand. "Well, I think Miller made a good choice."

Ross Milton smiled, and with his smile his face was transformed. Once more it was young, almost boyish. "Thank you," he said simply. "I'll try to make good on the job. Miller said you intended to inspect the mines today and he sent me down to bring you up."

Hartland waved him to a chair with a frown. "Does Miller think I have to have an officer of the law with me to get about?" he complained.

"No, sir," said Milton," I don't think he has any such idea. But the storm knocked a tree down up the road and it's necessary to take a short cut . . . a side trail. He sent me because he could spare me. I'll have to show you the way. You'll want to ride up to the Yellow Jacket and to the Huntley and back."

"Something in that," Hartland confessed. "Are you going to try to hold your job at the mine and be deputy, too?

"No, I'm leaving the mine today," Milton answered.

As Hartland was lacing his boots, he wondered if he should call at the hotel first and see Rose Raymond. He did not doubt but that Fredricks's hint that she had been drinking the night before was warranted. She was alone, far from the hectic life to which she was accustomed. Very possibly she was homesick. But she could go back. It was her place to go back. And he knew she would hardly be up at that hour of the morning. He decided to see her late in the afternoon after he returned.

The rain was still falling. Everything was wet, soaking wet, and wisps of mist hung over the valley with fog shrouding the mountains. Joe brought Hartland's horse and he started off with Milton. He wasn't foolish enough to think that Miller had sent the deputy just by chance. His manager was doubtless prepared for any emergency. In half an hour they reached the mine.

Milton looked after the horses and Miller, who had been awaiting them, led Hartland into the offices where he shed his slicker and hat and donned a blue denim jumper and a cap with a miner's lamp attached in front. The top of the Yellow Jacket shaft was at the end of a tunnel that led straight into the heart of the mountain for more than a quarter of a mile. Ross Milton joined them as they entered the bore, and they walked along the tracks over which the ore cars were hauled. When they reached the top of the shaft, they lighted their lamps before entering the cage. They dropped to the 200-foot level.

Here was a tunnel and Miller showed Hartland where the ore had been stoped out. There was no one working on this level, or on the 300-foot level. The veins had petered out. But work was in progress on the lower levels and Hartland saw the gleaming veins of silver ore both above and in the face. The tunnels were untimbered, for they had been driven through solid rock and there was no danger of cave-ins.

At 500 feet Miller first called attention to the copper stain. It was pronounced at 600 feet—the depth of the mine—and here, Miller explained, the silver was rapidly thinning. They were finding patches or pockets of wire silver, however. That might mean anything. No one knew for sure what was beneath them. It might cost a lot of money to find out—and it might be worth it. He deluged Hartland with technical information that the latter did not in the least understand or care about. What were mining engineers for, he was asking himself. He had made his plans. The thing that impressed him most was the loyal attitude of the men. Most of them touched their caps as he passed or paused to watch them at work. They left the Yellow Jacket after about two hours.

A ride of half a mile or so through the timber brought them to the Huntley. Miller pointed out on the way where he intended to cut a road through from the Huntley to join the Yellow Jacket road. This was the right of way that he had refused to Gordon and Mann. In the Huntley offices, Hartland met Fred Crawford, a tall, spare, gray man of uncertain years but with piercing black eyes and an aggressive personality. He went into the mine with them and Hartland at once saw furtive looks of hostility on the faces of the men.

"We'll send Sandy Anderson over here as foreman," he told Miller, and the manager nodded his assent.

Ore was being taken out on only two of the three levels in the mine. Despite his inexperience in such matters, Hartland could see there was ample opportunity for development. Again he listened to Miller, and to Crawford, too, but vouchsafed no opinion.

When they returned to the Yellow Jacket, he was closeted with Miller in the latter's private office for half an hour. There was a gleam of triumph in Miller's eyes as he came out and beckoned to Milton to bring the horses.

"You're making no mistake," Miller said heartily as Hartland mounted.

"If I am, it won't be the first time," Hartland observed curtly. It was as if he felt disgusted with everything, and Miller watched him ride away with Ross Milton and wondered. The manager had heard about Rose Raymond.

Milton left Hartland when they reached town and the latter rode slowly up the street toward the road and home. Men looked after him from doorways and porches, and in the resorts tongues buzzed. For already it was known that Hartland had been inspecting his properties and this was accepted as a good sign. Mann smiled and Butch Allen sneered, and "that red woman" was no longer the chief topic of conversation. At the moment Hartland was thinking of nothing more important than that Miller had promised to have a crew building a new bridge across the creek at the upper end of the street as soon as the water went down.

Then he saw Margaret Cram's horse standing in front of a store. So she was in town, and she would talk with some of the women, of course, and she would learn the gossip that was going the rounds. Hartland spurred his horse cruelly with the silent thunder again ringing in his ears.

It was 2:30 P.M. when Hartland returned to the bungalow. Monocle Joe was not around, so he put up his horse himself. He was in an irritable frame of mind. The cheerless, dismal, rainy afternoon matched his mood. The warm lunch Fredricks had ready, the glowing fire, a fine cigar failed to improve the temper of his thoughts. For the time being, mine matters need not be reckoned with. He knew nothing of mining, was sensible enough to realize this deficiency, and had sufficient common sense to know that his part was to leave such business to experts. That

would be his policy. It would be much easier and
more business-like to make decisions from engineers' reports. The more he thought, the more sick
and disgusted he became with everything.

Anderson had been sitting in the living room
most of the day, Fredricks informed him. He went
in to tell the convalescent that he was slated to be
the next foreman of the Huntley.

"Don't do it," Anderson warned. "Better take one
from their own crowd. I wouldn't last long anyway."
He smiled wanly when he saw Hartland's look of
surprise. "They'll have dynamite planted on every
level where it'll do the most good," he explained.

This gave Hartland something more to think
about. It was quite possible that in event of dissen-
sion or serious trouble the Huntley crew, openly
loyal to Allen, might attempt to ruin the workings
of the mine. Hartland went back to the living room
fire and swore at himself for being a fool to become
involved in such a mess. And he had to visit Rose
Raymond, confound it! There was no way of getting
out of it. Perhaps it would be best to bring matters to
a showdown. He started with the potency of a new
idea. Suppose he were to leave?

It was nearing 4:00 P.M. when he decided to go
down to town. The rain had become a drizzle; the
mists were lifting. But the skies were lowering and
it promised to become dark early. He went out to get
his horse, but stopped dead in his tracks on the way
to the barn. Rose Raymond was riding across the
meadow from the trail through the pines.

"Couldn't stand it any longer in that dead hotel,"
she said lightly as she dismounted near him. "Good
thing I remembered this was the West and brought
riding togs along. Are we going to have tea?"

"Go into the house," Hartland ordered. He led her horse to the barn, frowning darkly. He was angry, tormented, disgusted—but he did not know what to do Fredricks was serving Rose with a highball when Hartland entered. The sight made Hartland furious. He strode toward Fredricks. "Take it away," he ordered in a voice Fredricks could not misunderstand. "Miss Raymond is having tea."

Fredricks retired hastily, taking tray, decanter, and glasses with him. Hartland turned to meet a snaky gleam in Rose Raymond's eyes. "You're not even as hospitable as you were before," she said. "Perhaps your dinner last night didn't agree with you."

"I don't thank you any for using insulting language to Fredricks over the telephone," he said sternly. "And you're not going to bring your drinking orgy up here and feed it at the expense of my peace of mind. I won't have it, and that's final. The thing for you to do is to clear out of town, and you know it. If you don't go, I'll go. And if the camp finds out, or suspects that you were responsible for my going, you're liable to ride out sitting backwards on a horse instead of in a train." Hartland was altogether too thoroughly angry to talk reasonably.

Rose Raymond's eyes were flashing; her face had gone deadly pale. "You wouldn't dare!" she cried, her nerves a-tingle from the effects of her indulgence of the night before. "You can send me away properly when the time comes, and you'll know best when that time arrives."

"I wouldn't dare?" Hartland forced an uproarious laugh. "My girl, for once you've picked the wrong game. I'm going to. . . ."

He ceased speaking as he heard footfalls on the verandah. He hurried to open the door and there stood Margaret Cram. Her eyes held his for a space of several moments. Then he stepped outside and closed the door.

"Father sent me to deliver this envelope," she said, holding out the missive. Her voice had something dead and gone and chilling in it. The eyes were painfully accusing.

He took the envelope, stuffed it into a pocket. "Margaret, I want you to come inside," he said thickly. Then, as her brows went up and she started to shake her head, he grasped her by the arm. "You must," he said tremulously. "You must do this for me, Margaret. It's only fair to me and later you will learn why. I want you to meet Rose Raymond from New York."

He drew her toward the door and her astonishment and curiosity made her efforts at resistance feeble. He opened the door and led her inside, closing the door after them.

"Margaret, this is Miss Raymond, of New York," said Hartland in introduction. "Miss Raymond, this is Miss Margaret Cram."

"Oh, why not just Margaret?" said Rose, holding out a slim, drooping hand. "I have a horror of last names."

Margaret took the hand gingerly and removed her fingers at once. Not for an instant had her eyes left Rose Raymond's. So this was the woman she had heard about in town. This was the woman who had come two days before, dressed all in red, holding her head high, sneering at the simple folk she met, who had stayed the night in Roger Hartland's bungalow, who had swore at the maid in the hotel the night before because there was no ice water. Rumors concerning her were flying thick and fast in town, and, although Margaret discounted them, there was something in Rose Raymond's cool, tolerant, appraising gaze that overcame the girl with revulsion. She could think of nothing to say.

"You'll stay to tea, of course," Hartland was saying. "I'll put your horse in the barn so your saddle won't get soaking wet."

Before she could protest, he was out the door and she was alone with the notorious visitor.

"You're a pretty girl," Rose condescended. "I understand Roger has taken a fancy to you. He has an eye for a pretty face and a neat form." She waved her cigarette holder and smiled knowingly. "You seem to be the only thing presentable hereabouts," she said languidly," and, if you play your cards right, he *might* marry you."

Margaret was struck cold by the brazen nature of this casual remark. It was like a slap in the face—an insult. Yet this Raymond woman did not appear to intend it as such. Margaret's cheeks flamed. "Such a thing never entered my head!" she flared excitedly.

"No?" Rose smiled again. "Well, girlie, let it enter it now. You've got Roger off by himself, alone. Hook him while the hooking is good. I guess he rather expects some such thing and doesn't care a whoop. Cinch him while he's got his head down, as they say. Don't forget, child, he's worth a pile of money."

Margaret's face was white and her lips trembled. But when she spoke her voice was firm. "I don't know who you are," she said, holding the other's eyes with her own, "save for the name Mister Hartland has given me, but I believe I know something of what breed you are. You can't be right or you wouldn't talk as you do. We're mostly right up here in these high, clean mountains, open and above board in our animosities, and right in our friendships.

You do not seem to fit in with our notion of things and I don't want those notions spoiled. I came in to meet you out of curiosity, and, now that it's satisfied, I'll be going."

Rose Raymond's cold, derisive laughter followed her out the door.

But Rose was white with fury. The girl had circumvented her, placed herself on a pedestal that was unassailable with one simple little speech—put her in her place. Rose all but gnashed her teeth. No plain, silly little mountain girl, this. And she was just the kind Roger Hartland would be liable to fall for. He was an ass, anyway. And she herself was a fool. The galling thing about it was that she knew it.

Margaret Cram ran through the drizzle toward the barn. Hartland caught her in the entrance and held her tightly by the arms. She looked over his shoulder, white-faced, cold as stone.

"Don't forget, I wanted you to meet her before she went away," he said, the words burning in her ear. "When you are ready, you can ask me why. I'm banking that you'll play the game."

He led out her horse. She mounted, and galloped away like mad without uttering a word.

As Hartland entered the living room, Rose Raymond held back the hot torrent that was on her lips. Something in Hartland's eyes stayed her tongue. His look was one of triumph. He sat down at his desk as Fredricks brought in the tea and lighted the lamp.

"Serve Miss Raymond, Fredricks," he said crisply.

"I don't want any," Rose snapped out with venom in her tone.

Hartland opened the envelope Margaret had

brought and found it contained John Cram's note for $5,000. He put it in a pigeonhole. Then he turned to Rose. He looked at her so steadily that she shifted her gaze.

"What is your price?" he asked mildly.

Rose tossed her head. "I wouldn't put it that way," she said, struggling to regain her old composure.

"What is your price?" The words cut the still air of the room like knife thrusts.

Rose Raymond saw him passing out of her life with that question. The mask fell from her face. She shed her shallow, artificial pose as she would throw off a wrap. "I don't know, Hartland," she said in a voice that was coldly insolent. "I'll have to think it over. Pure little buttercups come high." For the first time he saw her sneer, realized how many things might have happened in New York. Wrested from her natural environment, Rose Raymond had reverted to type.

"I should have said . . . what *was* your price?'" he observed grimly. "Think it over tonight, Rose. Meanwhile, I've made up my mind. I'll get your horse."

He left for the barn, and, when he returned with her mount, which looked like the same animal Monocle Joe had ridden the night before from the livery, he found her on the verandah, ready to go. She had to get away from there, had to get back to the hotel and get a drink and think. She might be losing Hartland, but she intended to get a receipt.

She mounted and leaned down from the saddle. "Have you told the little violet about the big city and your motor cars and Europe?" she said mockingly. "That line ought to be good for a successful summer." Her jeering laugh trailed back to him as she rode away in the gathering dusk.

At 9:00 P.M. he called the hotel to make sure that Rose Raymond had gotten back safely. He gave a startled exclamation when the clerk answered: "Miss Raymond has not returned."

Chapter Twenty-eight

Hartland hung up the telephone receiver and paced the room nervously. Could Rose Raymond have lost her way? It had not been dark when she started, and, in any event, the horse would certainly know its way home. He called the livery. He learned from the man in charge that Rose had hired a horse there that afternoon and that it hadn't been returned. No, she hadn't mentioned any places where she intended going. Yes, it was the same horse Monocle Joe had had the night before.

Hartland next called the Silver King resort and asked for Joe. After an interval Joe answered. Hartland instructed him to scout about town and look for signs of Rose or the horse. Joe knew the horse, and, if he should see it anywhere on the street, it would indicate the whereabouts of Rose. When he was ready to report, he was to hire a mount and ride to the bungalow, if the telephone exchange was closed. Otherwise, he was to telephone for further orders.

An hour passed with Hartland moving about the house, sitting down before the fire, getting up to walk around again. He didn't know whether to be worried or not. Had Rose picked up an acquaintance or two? If she had become lost, and anything should happen to her, Hartland knew he would be in for harsh censure from the camp. Moreover, he would blame himself.

He went out on the verandah. The drizzle had stopped and a cold wind was blowing. Here and there a star peeped bravely through the scuttling clouds. The rain was flying away on the wings of the wild, weird night. There seemed to be a throbbing in the air, as if it were shaking off the dampness. Hartland went down the steps and walked a few paces out into the meadow. He whistled three times—sharp, imperative calls.

From the shadow of a clump of poplars another shadow disengaged itself. Hartland instinctively took a step backward as it glided toward him. He swore lightly under his breath. It was Creeps Hallow, of course. It was almost uncanny how the fellow kept watch on the house.

Hallow straightened unexpectedly as he reached Hartland and seemed to tower above him. "What is it?" he hissed hoarsely. He kept peering about in a disconcerting manner.

"Have you seen any riders tonight?" Hartland asked irritably. He would not have been surprised if the gorilla man had shrieked or ran or sprang at his throat because of the loud voice.

"No," replied Hallow. "You look for somebody?"

"Not exactly," said Hartland. "Joe may be along, though. You haven't seen a woman rider . . . a woman, Hallow?"

"No. You look for woman rider?"

Hartland realized with disgust that it was useless to ask the half-wit questions and it would be best not to stir him up. He must have seen Rose

Raymond the night she arrived and came to the bungalow with Joe. He started to ask him if he had seen her, decided nothing would be gained thereby, and desisted.

"That's all," he said instead, and went back into the house.

It was after 11:00 P.M. when Monocle Joe arrived. Hartland let him in and saw at once by the expression on the cockney's face that he had learned nothing of Rose Raymond's whereabouts.

"Nothing doing, eh?" he said, frowning.

"Not a thing," Joe answered. "I combed the town, sir, an' couldn't find a trace. She hasn't showed up at the hotel an' her horse is still out. They think down at the hotel that she's up here."

"I wonder if she could have ridden up to the Crams' place?" said Hartland, half to himself. "But she doesn't know where they live, and, if she did, she couldn't find the place in the dark and wouldn't be fool enough to try it. Joe, is Allen down town?"

"I didn't see 'im," said Joe. "But I was playin' cards in the back of the Silver King an' he might have been in one of the other rooms, sir. I didn't see 'im anywhere else, either."

"Something's wrong!" Hartland exclaimed with conviction. "Joe, go saddle my horse."

When the cockney had left, Hartland went to his room and buckled on his cartridge belt. He examined his six-shooter to make sure it was loaded and slid it into its holster. His face was gray and grim.

"Anyway, whatever has happened will teach her a lesson," he muttered. "She'll be ready and willing to go now . . . if she's alive." He hadn't known until this day that she could ride and he was considering the possibility of her horse having bolted, thrown her off, and run into the mountains. These Western horses, he understood, had a way of making off for their old range the first chance that offered after they were taken away from it. The mount Rose had might be a new horse here. He would have to find out. Meanwhile, he proposed to start a search with Monocle Joe. No use rousing the Yellow Jacket or the camp as yet. He hoped he would be able to find Rose without the business becoming public property.

They took a lantern, and, when they were half-way along the trail Rose had taken through the bull pines, Hartland called a halt. He dismounted, and, while Joe held the horses, he lighted the lantern and examined the trail. But he could make out nothing. Rain had fallen after Rose must have passed along it, and Joe's horse's tracks were the only ones that bore the appearance of having been recently made.

Hartland put out the light in the lantern and they rode on to where the trail left the pines and joined with the west road. Here they made another examination with the same result. The only new factor was the sign left by a horse coming down from the west ridge, and those tracks doubtless were made by Creeps Hallow's mount when he had ridden down to take up his nocturnal vigil at the bungalow.

"We'll ride up to the Crams' place," Hartland decided.

The wind had swept most of the clouds from the sky and the stars were shining brightly. They rode fast, keeping a sharp look-out along the road. At the point where the trail branched off to the Cram cabin, they again examined the ground. This trail was not so muddy and they made out clearly the tracks of a horse that had come out from the cabin and gone back. These would be the tracks of Margaret Cram's horse, made when she went to town, and Hartland's place, and returned. They rode on far enough to see that the Cram cabin was dark.

Then Hartland, thoroughly alarmed, turned about and they galloped down the road to town.

Rose Raymond had not returned to the hotel. They went to the livery and ascertained that the horse she had ridden away had been there for a long time and was not an animal that would bolt, unless greatly frightened, even though an inexperienced rider might be in the saddle. Hartland was stumped. He looked at his watch and found it was going on 2:00 A.M. There no longer existed in his mind any fragment of doubt but that disaster had overtaken Rose. What to do next?

Monocle Joe read his thoughts. "We can't do anything tonight, sir," he pointed out. "We've got to 'ave daylight an' we've got to 'ave men. The only thing to do is to wait till morning an' start a big search."

"I guess you're right," grumbled Hartland. "Well, I'll go back home and you round up Squint Evans . . . he ought to be a good trailer . . . and rout Miller out at daybreak, and get Ross Milton on the job, too. And see if you can get a line on where Butch Allen has been tonight. I'll tell you frankly, Joe, I wouldn't put it past him to kidnap Miss Raymond, thinking he could get a bunch of money out of me. But keep that to yourself. It wouldn't do any good for me to start prowling around the Silver King and the other places that are open. It would only start a lot of talk. There's no use stirring up this beehive till it's necessary. If she should show up, or you should get word of her, get the news to me . . . and me only . . . as quickly as you can."

Hartland harnessed the liveryman's tongue with a gold piece. He passed a yellow-backed bill to Joe and told him to attend to the hotel clerk. But he was not figuring on the surest and swiftest means of sly communication in such a place as Silver City, especially where a strange woman was concerned. The chambermaids and kitchen girls had gone forth, after their day's work, with choice new bits of gossip. The strange tale had found its way into the ears of waitresses and had been passed across tables and lunch counters for the edification of sundry and diverse masculine patrons. Then it had spread like wildfire through the camp.

As he started for home, Hartland saw the light streaming from the windows and wide entrance of the Silver King. He checked his horse to a walk. He was worried and irritable. He hated the thought of going to the bungalow and sitting idly by the fire waiting for daylight. He knew he could not sleep. He wanted a drink. He felt he had to have a drink. The beams of light beckoned. Inside the Silver King there was life, movement, diversion. He might learn something there. He could talk with Big Mose. He could listen and keep his eyes open. He should be in town in the morning, anyway, shouldn't he?

He turned in at the hitching rail in front of a store just above the resort, dismounted, and tied his horse. He sauntered back in the cool night air to the Silver King. Despite the lateness, or earliness, of the hour the place was thronged. Hartland remembered that the day before had been Saturday and this was Sunday morning. He assumed that all the men who did not have to work that day were making a night of it. Joe could have told him it was thus every day. He stepped to the head of the bar where Big Mose was keeping an eye on the activities of his three bartenders. Two men moved aside to make a place for him. He had come in quietly, with merely a casual glance around. But two pairs of keen eyes had observed him instantly. Butch Allen's face hardened; his black eyes gleamed with a vicious light of malice. It would not be policy, because of his and Mann's schemes, to interfere with the Huntley yet. But a personal altercation was different. He had a score to settle along that line. Squint Evans, who also had spotted Hartland the moment he entered, stood at the end of a roulette table where his fishy, faded blue eyes could survey both Hartland and Allen.

Hartland ordered whiskey and Big Mose went into his office for his private bottle while the gleam in Butch Allen's eyes leaped into fire. The group about him had ceased speaking and fingered their glasses in expectancy. Allen had been making talk this night. He had not been drinking to any degree of excess, and he had been doing a great deal of thinking. His very soul rankled with Hartland's curt dismissal, the Yellow Jacket owner's open contempt and disdain, his fearlessness. It was a moneyed man's bluff.

Allen put down his glass with a sharp rap. Men forgot their conversation and peered along the bar at him. Squint Evans was cashing in his checks.

"I hear you've lost your red woman, Hartland!"

Hartland met the challenge calmly. He put down his glass with its contents untasted, drew his gun, and slid it across the bar to Big Mose. None could ignore or misunderstand this action. He stepped back and strode toward Butch Allen. Outwardly he was cool, collected, although a bit white; his jaw was shut firmly, his eyes narrowed. But inwardly he was glowing with a fierce, burning joy. Here was the outlet he needed to ease his troubled mind and relieve the tension of his nerves.

The men about Allen stepped aside. A figure streaked through the crowd. Allen leaped back from the bar too late. Squint Evans had his gun. Then the big man was whirled in a grasp of steel. He came up on his toes, snarling, his face purple with diabolical rage. His hands came up instinctively, through no apparent effort of his own. He might as well have tried to ward off the punishment with a wave of a silk handkerchief.

Hartland's right shot fully and truly to the gunman's jaw and landed flushly with a *crack* that broke the sudden silence of the room like the report of a pistol. Allen was sent backward as if hurled from a catapult. His great body crashed against several who were behind him and knocked them sideways, backward, and to the floor. Allen went down on his knees, his head wagging groggily.

"Give 'em room!" It was Squint Evans, no longer the meek, watery-eyed gambler, but a man who seemed to have suddenly grown taller, whose eyes flashed with a green light, and who stood on the edge of the crowding semicircle of spectators with legs well apart and a gun in each hand. "I'll drop the first man that butts in, an' that goes for you, too, Mose!" He waved a threatening pistol at the Silver King proprietor who had climbed on top of the bar and was shouting incoherently.

There was an uproar as tables were overturned, chairs kicked aside, chips flung this way and that to the *jingling* ring of silver. Men stood the tables up and climbed upon them for points of vantage. Others stood on chairs, were pulled down by others anxious to see. Curses and cheers rang in the place. Allen's friends and followers did not dare interfere since they were in the minority. Also they were caught unawares by the suddenness of it.

Butch Allen leaned forward on his hands, gave a final shake of his head, came to his feet with a bound. Hartland's left came curving with sledge-hammer force and caught the big man behind the right ear. Allen spun clearly around and then met another straight left on the jaw that Hartland sent with every iota of strength in his body behind it. Allen went down in a heap, blood oozing from his bitten tongue.

The newcomers cheered lustily, although they didn't know what it was all about. They knew good work with a pair of fists when they saw it, and they had heard about Hartland and the red woman, had heard Allen's jeering challenge. Big Mose was waving the gun Hartland had pushed across to him. But Squint was watching him. The green fire from his eyes shot in all directions. No one could mistake that message.

Allen stirred, licked the blood from his lips, rose on an elbow, and looked up at Hartland out of blazing eyes that were pinpoints of liquid fire between the narrowed lids. Now Hartland spoke for the first time.

"You can get up on your knees and say you were mistaken, Allen, or you can get up on your feet and take some more of what you've been needing for a long time. But whichever you want to do, you'll say you were mistaken or I'll prove it to the crowd by knocking you cold and turning you over and spanking you!"

Hartland might have been more alert to his own

words than to Allen's position, for the latter suddenly twisted like a snake, caught Hartland's ankles, and tripped him. They were down together with Allen reaching for his enemy's throat. Hartland caught his wrist in both hands and twisted it until he cried out in pain. Allen rolled over, sinking his teeth into Hartland's upper arm.

This foul fighting drove Hartland into a frenzy. He released his adversary's wrist, rolled upon him, and before Allen knew what was happening a strong right thumb and forefinger were inside his lips, pushing them wide until they drew back white against his teeth. He clutched for that right wrist, but Hartland's left hand was at his throat. He tried to clasp that. Wider and wider his lips drew apart across his face—wider and wider. He squirmed and twisted and clutched to no avail.

"Nod your head that you're through and was mistaken, and I'll let you up," Hartland panted hoarsely. "Nod, or I'll split your mouth from ear to ear!"

Allen nodded his head as best he could.

Hartland released him and rose to his feet. "You can have more of that kind of fighting any time you want it," he said to the man on the floor. "And now there's some more of the other kind coming to you if you've got nerve enough to get up."

Allen got to his knees as Hartland backed away to give him room. He was beaten—beaten for the first time in his life. Beaten! The word surged through his brain on a rush of blood. He leaped to his feet and lunged at Hartland. The vicious blow missed and his jaw cracked upward as it met Hartland's wicked left. He swung aimlessly—then came night.

He groped his way through dazzling mists and came out of them with his face on the dank floor. All

the strength seemed to have gone out of him. There
was a strange silence everywhere. Someone was
shaking him, turning him over; cold water splashed
in his face. He saw the eyes of a friend.

"Snap out of it," said a rough, familiar voice in his
ear. "You'll have to get out of here."

He permitted two men to help him up and lead
him to a back room where he slumped into a chair,
dazed. "They got my gun," he muttered. For the
twentieth time since he had passed his insulting
challenge to Hartland, his right hand dropped to his
holster. Then he started, and stared straight ahead,
licking his blood-stained lips. His gun was there.

Hartland stepped to the bar and took his weapon
from Big Mose. He turned on the crowd, spoke
slowly, evenly, in a tone that signified good faith. "It
is true, gentlemen, that Miss Raymond, who is visit-
ing me a few days, is missing. She has either had an
accident with her horse or has lost her way in the
mountains. I'm starting a search in the morning and
any who wish to join one of the parties will be welcome." With this brief explanatory speech he was
gone.

There was a full minute of silence. Then Squint
Evans walked to the head of the bar. "Well, boys, we
gave him a square deal," he said, "an' I reckon it's up
to us to help him find this dame. I'm one that's going along."

He downed the drink Hartland had left untouched.
And within two minutes fifty others had volunteered
to ride forth at dawn to aid in the search.

Chapter Twenty-nine

With the first glimmer of the dawning day on that Sunday morning—the Sunday before the scheduled temporary shut-down of the Huntley—Silver City witnessed a sight that is not uncommon in the high mountains: the grim, thorough preparations for a search for someone lost in the mountain fastnesses.

Ross Milton had taken charge of everything. Monocle Joe had found him within an hour after leaving Hartland and the young deputy had lost no time. He had visited the Silver King shortly after Hartland's departure, heard the story of the unmerciful beating the Yellow Jacket owner had given Butch Allen, nodded his approval, and accepted the offer of scores of men to aid in the search. Practically every man in town who had a horse volunteered his services. Even Allen's cronies came forward to save their face. But Allen had disappeared.

Milton didn't wait until morning dawned to notify Miller. He routed the mine manager out and got the names of every Yellow Jacket man who owned a horse. Then he sent word to those on the list who were in the mine and to the others at their quarters and about town to be ready to take the saddle at daylight. He had a talk with Squint Evans, who was notorious as a reader of sign on the trail or off (knowledge that was reported to have stood him in good stead when evading more than one posse), and it was agreed that Squint should have charge of the party that went west. Milton was going south, and

Miller was taking a third party north. Each party would consist of thirty or more men.

Hartland had ridden home feeling better. He had driven the silent thunder from his ears, had effectively closed Allen's mouth. For no one would listen to the gunman after his ignominious defeat that night. Why, he hadn't landed a single blow. Nor had Hartland intended that he should land one. This had not required as much skill as Hartland could boast, but then Allen was more of a rough-and-tumble wrestler, an unfair fighter at best. He depended on a formidable reputation and his gun, and would use his fists only when caught unawares. And Hartland had not forgotten Squint Evans's quick move in disarming Allen. The wise little gunfighter had seen what was coming. Probably Allen didn't know who had taken his weapon and then slipped it back into his holster when he was knocked out. So much the better, and, if his cronies told him, what did it matter? But Hartland was not discounting Allen's cunning, his uncanny skill with his gun, and the powerful determination for revenge that would burn in his brain. The desire to get even with Hartland would be his religion until. . . .

Hartland called for coffee when he entered the bungalow. He would have welcomed a talk with Sandy Anderson, but did not want to wake him. So he sat by the fire, drank coffee, and smoked until the early dawn brought Monocle Joe with the news that the searching parties were forming in town.

Hartland rode into town with Joe to find the street swarming with horsemen. They had hardly joined Miller, Ross Milton, and Squint Evans in the center of the milling riders when the liveryman came running up the street, waving his arms.

"The horse!" he shouted. "Her horse is back!"

They moved in a body to the livery, surrounded it, and found what the liveryman had said was true. The horse Rose Raymond had ridden the afternoon before had returned. The animal had arrived unnoticed, while practically the entire population of the town was giving its attention to the preparations for the search. No one knew from what direction it had come. Thus it was out of question to backtrack its wanderings. It was saddled but the bridle was missing.

"Might have snapped somewheres with the horse stepping on the loose reins," said the liveryman. "Might have caught on something an' been jerked off."

This explanation was received skeptically. It was more probable that someone had removed the bridle to facilitate the animal's return. The missing bridle strengthened Hartland's conviction that Rose had been kidnapped, and he confided as much to Miller and the other leaders. But they dismissed the theory. Then Hartland wondered for the first time if this could not be some kind of a new game on the part of Rose. He had no time to consider this at any length, for the horsemen were again moving into the upper street and the leaders were dividing the riders into three parties.

They rode uptown and on to the upper bridge. There they waited while Squint Evans and Ross Milton examined the trail that led through the bull pines to the bungalow. The only sign discovered were footprints, but these were found to be identical with Hartland's and were undoubtedly made by him when he had examined the trail by lantern light the night before.

Both Evans and Milton shook their heads and gave it up. Here was mystery, but everything pointed to Rose having made the main road. In such event, there were only two directions in which she could ride of her own free will, or be taken against it, and those directions were up the cañon to southward, or down past town. Ross Milton, almost as good a trailer as Squint Evans, announced that he would go south. It was left to Miller's party to search below town and up the draws above the Yellow Jacket road. The third party, led by Evans, was to go west into and up Moon Valley, and up the high ridges west, south, and north of it. All the riders were to return at dark unless trace of Rose Raymond had been found, in which case the riders finding the trace should camp in the mountains for the night.

Hartland choose to go west. He rode with Squint Evans at the head of thirty men. They crossed over the low ridge and rode down into Moon Valley. Here Evans divided the party into three groups of ten men each. One party was sent to the upper end of the valley with instructions to climb to the summit of the west ridge there and work back along the crest; the second party was sent down the valley to where the east ridge fell away and the stream flowed north of town, and there to climb the west ridge and work back. The third party, with Squint and Hartland, was to follow the trail over the west ridge and on to the ranges beyond.

Before taking the trail, Squint and Hartland rode up to the cabin of Creeps Hallow. They found the door open and Hallow asleep in the single bunk. Hartland had explained that the halfwit had been up all night watching his place and therefore they were not surprised to find him in bed. But Squint woke him.

"Have you seen a rider up this way?" he asked as Hallow peered up at him out of small, beady, animal-like eyes. "Anybody on a horse or afoot?"

Hallow shook his head and transferred his gaze to Hartland.

"Oh, it's no use asking him," said Hartland. "I tried to question him last night. He got down after Miss Raymond disappeared."

"Well, we haven't lost anything by it, anyway," Squint Evans grumbled, and they went back to their horses.

As they rode down to join the others of the party, Creeps Hallow threw off the covers and bounded lightly to the floor. He was in his stocking feet but fully dressed. He stole to the north window and looked down the narrow valley after his two early visitors. His facial muscles were working and he was muttering to himself. He watched until he saw the searching party going up the west ridge trail. Then he took a small telescope from a shelf and focused it on the crest of the ridge where the trail crossed it to descend the other side. He kept his glass glued to his eye until the party had crossed the ridge. Then he pocketed the glass, pulled on his boots, put on his hat. He reached under the bunk and drew out a good-size pack. With this under his arm he hurried to the lean-to behind the cabin that served as a barn. He saddled and bridled the horse that was there, secured the pack to the rear of the saddle, mounted, and rode across the valley to the shelter of the pines along the west slope. Here he turned north down the valley, following along the slope, passed the trail, and vanished in the trees.

The sun climbed steadily to the zenith and started on its long glide into the west. The searchers led by Squint Evans and Hartland wound along tortuous trails up into the higher mountains, spread out fanwise in the narrow valleys, ravines, and meadows, and climbed and climbed until, in the late afternoon, Squint Evans called a halt.

"We're wasting our time going up here any farther," he said. "Look at those steep slopes, look at the shale rock. Anyone who came up here would have to take this trail. But we haven't seen a sign of a track. Anyway, that horse couldn't have got back so soon from here. We're out of luck in this direction."

Hartland and the others could not but agree. They turned back, knowing it would be after dark when they reached town.

Rose Raymond rode away from Hartland's bungalow with rage swelling within her until it almost choked her. She realized that in some way Hartland had scored in introducing her to Margaret Cram, but just how the meeting had reacted in his favor she did not know, nor could she fathom his purpose in bringing her face to face with the girl and permitting them to be alone together so that she could say whatever she wished.

So intent was she upon her resentful thoughts that she hardly realized where she was until it began to grow dark. Then she found herself on the thin trail that led through the dripping pines. The stand of timber on either side—so close that she could reach out and touch the branches—was filled with sinister shadows and vague, disturbing whisperings. Although she was warmly clad, she shivered. There was no sunset, for there was no sun, only the gray, darkening sky above her, and she could see but a thin ribbon of that through the trees. She began to peer about her and to look behind. A darker mass of clouds drifted overhead and it became almost as black as night. She leaned forward to pass under a projecting limb that appeared low, and the next moment something tightened about her shoulders and she was lifted from the saddle. A wild scream sounded hollow and dull in the forest and died in her throat as she fainted on the ground where she had fallen.

When she opened her eyes, she saw a lone star that seemed to be hanging high above her. Gradually she recovered her senses and could think in orderly fashion. She must have struck that low branch and been swept from her horse to the trail. She was lying on her back with her head upon something. She raised herself on an elbow and looked about. It was still light enough to distinguish objects near at hand. There were the trees—but what was this? She wasn't on the trail, but in what appeared to be a small patch of gravel. The stones were hard, some of them sharp beneath her. Then a shadow loomed over her and her blood seemed to freeze in her veins. Two glittering, beady, animal-like eyes regarded her, two long arms and hairy hands of atrocious size hung just above her, two rows of teeth that were more like fangs were bared below the eyes, above the arms. The rest of this monster's body was like some great, unwieldy shadow, half man and half ape.

She tried to scream, but no sound passed her lips. Then she trembled violently and struggled to ward off another fainting spell.

"Don't shout!" The warning came in a hoarse,

guttural voice. The immense, hairy hands brushed her face; the small eyes gleamed, sparkled with red and green points of fire.

Rose Raymond went cold all over. She recognized the horrible creature who had looked at her over Monocle Joe's shoulder the night she had arrived and he had come bursting into the bungalow after having been attacked. She could remember what the man was called: Creeps, Hartland and Joe had both mentioned him. The name seemed appropriate.

"Get up!" One of the hairy hands slid under her shoulders and raised her to her feet as if she had been a sack of fluff.

She stood, wavering. Her horse was tied to a tree. There was another horse behind Creeps. He was coiling a rope. It fascinated her, that rope. He had—what did they call it?—lassoed her. What did he want? Suddenly she stiffened with an illuminating thought. This creature was in Hartland's employ and was obeying his orders! He didn't intend to buy her off; he proposed to frighten her away. This conviction gave her courage.

"What do you want with me?" she asked boldly.

A long arm shot out and a great hand crushed over her mouth. She thought he would push in her teeth so great was the pressure.

"You keep still?" The voice was accompanied by a hot breath in her ear. "You keep still?"

She nodded as best she could, and, when he released her, she felt limp and faint again. She knew it would not do to speak. Did Hartland think he had absolute control over this beast? Had he considered what might happen if this human gorilla were given charge of a woman in these lonely mountains? She shuddered and grew sick with fear.

"Come!" The hand left her face, gripped her firmly by the arm, led her to the horse that was not tied. Before she realized what was happening, she had been swung into the saddle, the man had mounted behind her, and they were making their way through the trees, following no trail in particular, as she could see, climbing—climbing.

They came to a swollen brook and splashed up its bed for a long distance. The pines were thinning. They came out upon a bare slope of shale. They were very high now, almost to the top of the western ridge. Clouds were racing in the sky under a few brave stars. A cold wind drove across the rocky ramparts. Rose shivered with cold and fear.

They were on a table of rock at the side of the steep slope of shale. The bed of the brook and the rocky trail below would leave no tracks to follow. She was as completely isolated with this man-beast as if they had been in an open boat in mid-ocean.

He got off the horse and lifted her down. He dropped the noose of the rope over her shoulders, tightened it about her waist.

"You walk behind me . . . close," he said in that terrible voice. "One slip an' you go"—he pointed down the long slope of treacherous shale to the rocks below—"an', if the rope don't hold, or I slip, we both go. I don't care. Maybe I hope it will."

He stepped out on an almost indistinguishable path—an old game trail leading across the shale. He held the coiled end of the rope in his hands. Rose followed closely behind him, her heart pounding in her throat. If she could only close her eyes. But she didn't dare. Did he, after all, intend to kill her?

The horse was left behind as they crossed the shale. On the farther side they turned up again and climbed. There was no trail, just natural steps formed by boulders and blocks of granite. When the steps were too high for Rose, Creeps Hallow pulled her up with the rope. Her hands were cut and bleeding through her thin gloves; she skinned her legs, bumped her knees, tore her clothes. They seemed to be climbing to a solid wall of rock, but when they got up there, a jagged opening showed. The entrance to a wide fissure in the rock was like a false front; it could not be seen from below or above. He led her into the defile and a natural cave opened. He pushed her into utter darkness.

After a time a match flared into flame, then a lantern was lighted. She saw some rough stuff like burlap on the rock floor of the small cave. The lantern hung from a sharp spike of rock. There was a rude bunk made with saplings, covered with pine boughs over which were some blankets. There was a crude, high stool on which was a pail of water. A package beside it looked as though it might contain food. But the thing that held Rose Raymond's attention longest was a square door fashioned of saplings nailed close together so that only very narrow slits remained. Had it been steel, it might have been the door of a cell.

Creeps Hallow was fixing her with that terrifying stare out of his glittering animal eyes. "This is the Moon Ridge Fault," he said with a hissing inflexion in his voice. "The fault in the rock only I know. Nobody find you here, nobody know how to get up here. You be good an' you be all right, an' we go sometime. They look for you tomorrow but they won't find. Nobody know this fault but me."

"Did . . . did Hartland tell you . . . to bring me here?" she asked in a faint, faltering voice.

"Not!" His eyes glistened with triumph. "He doesn't know. But he will be glad. When the rain fall the night you come, I listen outside the window an' hear what you say an' what he say. You no good! You come to make bother for him an' Margie. Now I take you away so you do no bother. You want a drink?"

He took a pint bottle half full of whiskey from a pocket and put it down by the lantern and the package. "It keep out the cold an' you like drink. So you no good. I go back now."

She watched, numb with horror, struggling with the impulse to cry out in protest as he took the door, and, keeping on the outside, drew it snugly against the rock on either side of the opening of the cave. It overlapped the entrance on the inside. Two bits of steel cable tightened on either side as he secured the loops to rock outcroppings on the outside. Thus it could be opened from without, but not from within. Creeps Hallow was the only living being who knew where she was and could come to open that door.

She heard the dull echoes of his cat-like tread die away as he walked along the narrow defile to the top of those dangerous steps. Then something snapped in her brain. She leaped to the door and pounded upon it and shrieked. The rock walls without took up her cries and flung them in reverberating echoes. The shrieks became wails and blubbering moans. She staggered to the bunk and fell upon it.

The lantern filled the place with its yellow light, but Rose Raymond was in darkness.

Chapter Thirty

Rose came to, stiff with cold. Her scratched hands, legs, and knees smarted and burned; her head ached; her feet were sore. Her tense nerves tingled and she felt very weak. Her throat seemed raw from shouting. She sat up and stared at the lighted lamp, the pail of water, the small package, and the bottle half filled with amber liquor. She swung off the bunk, took a cup of water, and followed it with a drink from the bottle. The whiskey sent a warm glow through her, soothed her twitching nerves. She took off her riding boots, poured water on her handkerchief, and bathed her cuts and scratches. Then she removed her riding jacket, took a cigarette case and holder from a pocket, put it on the foot of the bunk. She lighted a cigarette from the lamp, got between the blankets, and tried to consider her desperate situation in the cold light of reason.

First of all, escape that night was out of the question and there was no use in thinking about it. To shout and scream, even if she were not too hoarse to do so, would be futile for no one could hear her. She must wait until Creeps Hallow returned; she must trick him in some way. If he had told the truth and Hartland knew nothing of her predicament, Hartland would doubtlessly start a search as soon as he learned she was missing. But he might not learn of her disappearance until late the next day. This thought made her very uneasy. What had Creeps meant when he had said they would go away after the search was abandoned? She had read too often of people being given up as lost in the mountains. Would it not be possible for Hartland and the townspeople to accept this explanation in her case? In fact, might not Hartland welcome such a turn in their affairs? Her uneasiness increased until she was again frightened. No, she couldn't be cool and calm under such circumstances. Had she been in danger in New York, she would have known what to do. Here in the wild, wind-swept desolation of the mountains it was different. And suppose something were to happen to Creeps Hallow and he wouldn't be able to come back? Suppose those men he had routed when Monocle Joe was attacked should kill him?

All the stories she had ever heard of bears, wildcats, and other dangerous animals came crowding into her memory. A bear might have cunning enough to loosen the cable loops that held the door on the outside. Then came the sharp barking of dogs. She did not know it was a lone coyote. The sounds heartened her. Could they be looking for her already—with dogs? She thought of bloodhounds. But the barking went the way of the wind, then the wind came again—then the long, wailing cry like a baby in distress.

She longed for daylight and looked at her wrist watch. It was only 10:30 P.M. She lay back and drew the covers over her head to shut out the alarming voices of the mountain night. She was terribly tired; she yawned and dozed, and awoke with a start. What was that? Something—someone tapping at the door.

Again she sat upright, her heart pounding, every

nerve quivering. The soft tapping seemed to come from the bottom of the door where there was a narrow open space its whole width. Suddenly a dark object streaked across the floor of the cave and through the open space. Her body went dead cold and her heart seemed to stop. A monstrous rat!

She shook until the bunk rattled its legs on the hard rock. This was the greatest shock of all. She became numb with fear for she didn't know it was a pack rat and that they never attacked a human. Suppose it were to attack her? She looked wildly at the lantern, wondering how much oil it contained, wondering if there was enough oil to burn all night. She was afraid to take it up and shake it to make sure. It might go out and she had no matches. And what good would it do? There was no more oil to put in it. She looked at her watch again. Only 11:00 P.M.

The tapping had ceased. She was too shaken, too tired to sit up. Her brain and her muscles were weary. She lay on her side so she could see the floor. Once more she dozed and this time body and mind claimed its rest and she slept the deep, dreamless sleep of utter exhaustion.

She was awake before she opened her eyes, awake to the innumerable aches and pains of her body, and to a sickening, sinking feeling in the pit of her stomach, awake to renewed fears. She was afraid to open her eyes at first. She seemed conscious of a presence. Was someone there? Finally the lids fluttered, she sat up, wincing with a stab of pain in her back, looked about.

The light in the lantern was still burning. The amber liquor in the bottle mocked her, nauseated her. What time could it be? Midnight? Later in the morning? Never had she so dreaded the night; another like it, and she would surely go mad. She mustered the courage to look at her watch—stared at it in surprise and disbelief. The hands indicated 7:00 A.M.

She threw off the blanket and sat on the edge of the bunk. Her feet were so swollen that she could not pull on her boots. She donned her jacket against the chill. The burlap was cold against the rock floor of the cave as she walked upon it gingerly. She flung the bottle into a corner where it was smashed to bits, its contents forming a little pool that she covered with a piece of the burlap. Then, being ravishingly hungry, she undid the package by the water pail and found sandwiches—meat sandwiches. She ate one and drank copiously of the water. This strengthened her.

A cigarette followed her scanty breakfast and she turned the wick in the lantern as low as it would go and still burn. She had to conserve the flame by which she could light her cigarettes. Even this trifling detail seemed a hardship in her dire predicament.

She peered through the cracks in the door but could see nothing but the sunlight flooding the rock walls of the defile. There must be some kind of an opening or fissure in the wall to the right—the east side—that let in the sun. She thought she could see the place, at the end of the rock passage, where the steps led downward. It had been so steep there that Creeps Hallow had had to pull her up by means of the rope. She could feel the soreness where it had cut in under her arms. The recollection of that precipitous trail gave her an idea. If she could get outside with Creeps Hallow when he came, on the pretext of wishing to walk back and forth in the passage for exercise, and could entice him to the top of those steps, she might be able to push him over so he would fall headlong on the rocks below. At last she had it, that was the trick!

She laved her feet with the cold water, massaged her ankles, worked until, after an hour or more, she succeeded in getting her boots on. They hurt terribly, but she walked about the confines of the cave until they became easier. She ate another sandwich, drank more water. Slowly a measure of confidence returned to her. Creeps Hallow would not dare to harm her. He had kidnapped her because he thought she was interfering with Hartland's love affair with Margaret Cram. Of course all these people in these mountains would be overjoyed to see Margaret catch the big prize. They would all expect to live off him, one way or another.

"The poor fool!" she exclaimed, her lips curling.

She wondered if Hartland had discovered she was missing. She could not know that three searching parties were scouring the mountains for her at that very minute, that one party was coming along the crest of Moon Ridge and would pass above her. But members of this party could look down over the sheer rock wall and see nothing.

10:00 A.M. came. This was late in the morning for those who lived and worked in the mountains, early for those who gambled and frolicked away the nights. But it was Sunday, and this gave Rose more cause for doubt. She was sitting on the edge of the bunk, thinking of her plan for escape. When she had thrown Hallow down on the rocks—where he would surely break his head or neck, or something—she could make a rope of the blankets and let herself down the steep upper pitch. Then she could slide—anything to reach the bottom of that treacherous trail and liberty.

A shadow darkened the slits of sunlight in the door. There was a rasp of the left cable loop on the rocks outside. The door moved inward in the grip of a great, hairy hand. Rose Raymond's heart leaped into her throat. Creeps Hallow stood before her, his enormous, awkward body framed against the dazzling light of the defile, his eyes gleaming and glittering, his lips drawn back against his yellow teeth in a gruesome, twisted smile.

"You all right?" The voice seemed normal. He did not wait for an answer, but stepped inside. He had a package—a rather large pack—under an arm. This he tossed upon the bunk and then, to her horror, he sat down beside her—close to her. She gave him a single, fleeting glance, and her confidence ebbed.

His furrowed brow under the shaggy hair was damp and streaked with sweat. He had a reddish growth of beard in which his wide mouth showed like an ugly gash. But it was the eyes that held her, frightened her. They were not natural—that was it. They were not animal eyes, either. Then the first terrifying suspicion gripped her, left her body cold and clammy, her brain numbed. She shook it off. It couldn't be. But she dared not look again.

Hallow took up the pack and opened it. He put an orange in Rose's lap. Then he blew out the light in the lantern, put it on the floor, and piled eatables in its place.

"You want more to drink?" he asked, grinning.

"No!" The question made Rose angry. If she had had a gun, she would have willingly, gladly have shot him in the back. She looked to see any signs of a weapon on him that she could snatch and use, but apparently there was none. "How long am I supposed to stay here?" she demanded, her eyes flashing and her cheeks flushing.

The grin widened and the small, black beads of eyes snapped. "Maybe tomorrow we go," he croaked.

"Tomorrow?" she ejaculated. "Another night here? I can't stay here another night. And where do you think we're going?"

"I show you." His great head nodded violently. "I got a horse for you. Your horse go back this morning."

"Did you send it back?" she asked quickly.

"He go back by himself," was the answer. "They won't know where he come from. See? They're out looking for you now, but they won't find you. Only I know this place." He seemed proud.

"What do you think Mister Hartland will do when he finds out what you've done?" she said in as stern a voice as she could muster.

Creeps Hallow laughed and his laugh had a queer ring to it that forced her to look at him again. What she saw caused her to turn her head away quickly.

"He maybe no find out," said Hallow. "He maybe no care. You come to make the bother." His eyes glittered with red fire. "You want the money, then you want the man. I hear an' I see . . . through the window in the rain. You think you're smart, eh? You're a fool. I stop you. You get no money, you get no man. Only me. I take you across the mountains an' up to where the rivers end. An' there you stay an' no bother the man or Margie."

This was the longest, most coherent speech he had made, and Rose caught its ominous significance.

He was not threatening her; he was merely stating in a cool manner what was to happen.

Her heart was in her throat again. She got up from the bunk and he did the same, rising to his full height, towering above her.

"I . . . I want to walk back and forth out there in the sun," she said, her face very white. "I need exercise. I'm sore and cramped. Let me walk out there."

"Yes," he assented, "you walk."

He ambled along ahead of her to the end of the defile and stood there, looking down at the piles of rock and slopes of shale above the line of trees. He was at the top of the trail, above the perilous steps, on the edge. Her heart beat wildly and she shook and trembled as she came up behind him. He was looking off across the valley now, apparently oblivious to her presence. The time had come to put her plan into effect. He was so close to the edge! A single push, and. . . .

She took a long breath to steady her nerves, drew back a pace, and threw herself against him.

Creeps Hallow didn't move a fraction of an inch. Rose gasped in chagrin and astonishment. A huge, hairy hand swept around and caught her about the arm. He swung her around in front of him and held her out over the edge of the cliff, his face leaning forward close to her own. She could feel his hot breath, see the gleaming lights in his eyes. She tried to scream, but it was only a queer, squeaking sound in her throat. Then she went limp, and closed her eyes.

He pulled her into his arms and carried her along the passage to the cave. There he put her on the bunk. Then she felt a wet cloth on her face and brow. He was muttering incoherently to himself and the sounds made the chills run up and down her spine. She dared not open her eyes for fear of meeting his. She had read the dreadful truth in them when he had held her over the cliff. He might be a brute and a beast, but what made it so awful was the fact that he was not responsible. Creeps Hallow was mad!

"You better?"

The words stabbed into her tortured brain and try as she would she could not avoid opening her eyes. He was leaning over her with a damp hand-kerchief in his hand. He nodded and grinned.

"I know you want to push me off the rocks an' kill me, but you can't do it." His eyes clouded darkly. "You be good!" The words rang sharply in the cave.

"Why can't we start now, if we're going away?" she asked faintly. Anything to get out of that place. She felt that she was suffocating with horror and dread.

"No." He frowned heavily. "You be good. You no stay alone tonight. I come. You 'fraid of me?"

"No, Creeps." She managed the words although they trembled on her lips. It would be best to humor him. It might be fatal to show how terrified she was. "But I think we ought to start right away."

"I come tonight, an' tomorrow we go." His tone was final. He got up and started for the door. "I come back after sunset," he flung back at her.

"Leave me some matches to light cigarettes," she pleaded.

He hesitated. Then he drew some loose matches from a pocket and threw them on the bunk. He went out, pulling the door after him, and securing it with the cable loops. She heard his footsteps die away in the passage. Once more she was alone. But she drew a long, quivering breath of relief. For the time being she was safe.

Chapter Thirty-one

It was midnight. Rose Raymond was sitting on the bunk. The oil in the lantern had given out, but she had found some candles among the things Creeps Hallow had brought and one was burning on the high stool. Its flame flickered in the breath of air that stirred in the cave. Fantastic shadows danced on the rock walls. Outside, in the defile and about the higher rocks, the winds made carnival. She had been listening for more than an hour to these winds, now faint, murmuring, singing, and again harsh and roaring, shrieking, and dying away to a whimper as they fled over the ridge to the wild freedom of the peaks. At times they were hideous with sound multiplied tenfold by the acoustic properties of the peculiar rock formations.

She had eaten the food and oranges Hallow had brought, and refreshed herself with a bottle of milk he had been thoughtful enough to include. She had given up trying to fabricate a plan of escape. Her fears had reached a climax and given way to resigned waiting. She was powerless. Only the intervention of a kindly providence could save her. She had forgotten to wind her watch and it had stopped. What of it! Time meant nothing to her. The thought that always nearly drove her frantic was that she was so close to safety—only the short distance from the bungalow in the park below to her rock prison— yet she was beyond all help. Once she had thought wildly of breaking the milk bottle and cutting her wrists with a piece of glass that she might bleed to death. Then she had laughed, and lit a cigarette. Her luck would be sure to come to her rescue. Like all habitués of New York night life, she was superstitious. And Hartland would pay for this!

She found solace in that thought. She had heard a maid speaking in the hall outside her room in the hotel. She had heard herself called "that red woman." Very well, she would be a red woman and extort her blood money. She could live comfortably in France on a small fortune. Her luck had brought her into touch with Hartland; it had kept her in luxury for more than a year; it had indulged in the ironical whim of setting her down in this mess—now it would pull her out. So she had thought, but in this midnight hour she sat hopelessly and dejectedly without even the solace of tears.

She hardly looked up when she heard Creeps Hallow's footfalls in the passage. The left cable loop was loosened, and he swung the door inward, letting it hang askew by the other loop. He looked at her out of greenish eyes and licked his thick lips.

"You all right?" He stooped and peered at her searchingly. "Yes . . . you all right. That's good. They look for you but no find." His maniacal laughter filled the cave, sounding horribly harsh above the rioting winds. "They go back to town . . . all of them. Hartland, too. I don't guess he care. You eat?" He looked about and saw that she had eaten. "That's good," he said, sitting down beside her. "I get your horse down below. Tomorrow we go. You bad girl, an' they say me bad man." He nodded and grimaced. "So we go together, like we belong . . . an' leave no bother."

"When do we start?" she asked dully.

"After you have some sleep," he said. "You feel sleepy now?"

She shuddered at the tone of his voice, which he meant to be solicitous. "I slept some this afternoon and some tonight," she answered. "Why can't we start now?"

"You want to go quick?"

His hot breath was on her neck and in her hair. She risked a look at him. Then she screamed, struck him in the face, raked his swarthy cheek with fingernails. Next her hands were caught as if in bands of steel. He leaped to his feet and jerked her up.

"You fight?" he cried hoarsely. "You want fight?" He lifted her in his enormous, hairy hands and flung her on the bunk. "You try to push me over the rock an' now you want fight!" The fingers of his right hand closed on her throat, closed just tightly enough to let her know they were there. "You be good. You do as I tell. Then you be all right. I keep you all safe an' feed you good. I give you little love, maybe, eh?" He leaned over her, and she fainted.

Strange music came to her ears as if from afar. It was like the sighing of waves, the wind in the trees, the tortured symphony of a soul in distress; it rose and fell in lulling and stirring cadences. She was conscious that she was listening, that the music was soothing. Her eyelids fluttered and opened. She looked out the entrance of the cave and saw the silvery moonlight flooding the defile. The dark form of Creeps Hallow loomed at the farther end. He was standing, hatless and motionless, and he was singing.

Despite herself, Rose Raymond was thrilled by his voice. It rose and fell in perfect harmony with every note clear and true. The extraordinary performance was so out of keeping with this monstrous man, the glorious tenor so different from the lunatic she felt him to be, that she was awed. She sat up and swung about on the edge of the bunk. Then he saw her. The song ceased abruptly. He came striding to the entrance of the cave, stepped inside, and took her by the arm. "Come an' look!"

It was a command and she had no alternative but to obey. He led her to the opening above the steps and pointed out over the shadowy valley with its silver ribbon of stream, to the east range and the gleaming summit of Old Baldy, bathed in moonlight.

"This is half the world," he said in a softer voice than she could have imagined he possessed. "Tomorrow, I show you the other half behind our backs. Then I take you where you can see all of it . . . the whole world. And there we stay."

She looked at the silent majesty of the mighty panorama spread out before her, and she knew why the loneliness of the mountains made men different, drove them mad.

"Go back!"

She went back to the bunk without hesitation, lit a cigarette. Creeps Hallow sang and the wind caught up the strains and carried them away. The words were unintelligible, but she would not have heard them for the soothing, soul-inspiring sobbing of that voice.

He was walking slowly back and forth now, his face held up to the wind and stars. The fierce, terrifying look in his eyes was subdued. Rose forgot her cigarette as she listened. She had a feeling as of one lost, as if she were floating out of life. Then heaven granted her the blessing of a woman's tears.

When Hartland and the others returned to town about 9:00 P.M. that Sunday evening, they found Miller and Ross Milton also arriving with their searching parties. No trace of Rose Raymond had been found. Milton was very much perturbed and said he would have to telephone Sheriff Currie about Rose Raymond's disappearance and the unsuccessful search. Miller frankly said he didn't know what to think. But there was something in the attitude of the two men that drew Hartland's attention. He tried to fathom what lay behind their manner toward him and it was not until he was on the way home with Monocle Joe that he sensed the possibility of his being under suspicion. Could it be that they suspected him of having spirited Rose away— of hiding her in the mountains, or of something worse?

This thought left him in wretched humor for dinner, although he was very hungry. He ate hurriedly, his mind in turmoil, and paced the living room afterward, smoking a cigar and trying to think. What had become of her? What—what—what? Over and over again the simple questioning word asserted itself. He could get no further. He was worn and worried and bewildered. Finally, around midnight, he sought the cool air outdoors, and walked in the park.

A full moon was climbing the sky above the eastern range, trailing a white mantle of silver light over the shoulders of Old Baldy. The wind ran wild and free, and Hartland felt its stimulus. He listened to it singing in the pines on the slopes of Moon Ridge.

But suddenly he stopped walking and strained his ears. Was that the wind singing up there?

He looked about him across the moonlit meadow to the shadows of the trees, eyes and ears and every nerve in his body alert. He whistled three times. The wind took up the echoes of the sharp, commanding signal and bore them down the sleeping valley. There was no response. Again he whistled with the same result.

Thus Hartland knew it was not the singing of the pines he heard, but the tenor voice of Creeps Hallow, coming to him from somewhere on the ridge. He remembered the effect the storm had had on the half-wit. But it was not a chant he was singing this night; it was a wildly weird and sweet symphony, the notes of which were exultant and embraced everything—the night, the velvet sky, the moon and stars, the shadowy ranges, the gleaming peaks, the streams and trees and flowers—the universe. That was it—a soul soaring in the freedom of the universe.

But why should Creeps Hallow be high on that ridge? The question answered itself in Hartland's mind. The crazy fellow had seen Rose Raymond arrive at the bungalow with Monocle Joe; he had looked at her over Joe's shoulder that night; he had most likely spied on them; he was jealous of her because she had come to Hartland, who was Margaret Cram's friend; he had decided she didn't belong there; he had resolved to carry her away so she could not cause trouble; he might be holding her a prisoner in some secret place on the ridge, and his joy in having taken her away without leaving a trace, his tumultuous thoughts now that he had her were finding expression in this wild song.

Hartland ran for the bungalow, telling himself he was a fool for not having thought of this before. He found Monocle Joe taking tea with Fredricks in the kitchen and in short, crisp sentences told him what he had heard, what he suspected, and ordered him to get the horses.

"We'll need fresh mounts," he said, "and we'll ride up to Cram's place for them. Cram will have them. Then we'll make for the top of the ridge. Hallow may keep on singing for a long time if that twisted brain of his keeps bothering him. That'll guide us, or we may see him when daylight comes. A gun will make him talk."

Within a few minutes they were riding through the pines on their way to the road up the cañon. Hartland had stood outside the barn waiting while Joe saddled the horses, listening to the faint notes of the song that came down to him from the high ridge. Only one thing could he determine. The singing came from some point north of the pass by which the trail crossed the ridge. But this was enough to start on.

When they reached the Cram place, they found the cabin dark as they had expected. Hartland knocked loudly on the door. In a short time a light showed in the front window, then a bolt was drawn, and John Cram opened the door. His right hand was behind the door but Hartland knew it held a gun.

Hartland stated briefly what he wanted and why. He could not see Margaret but he could almost feel her presence. He knew she was in the darkened dining room, listening. John Cram invited him in, saying he would get busy at once with Monocle Joe to help him, get the horses from his upper meadow, and saddle them. He insisted on going along as he knew the trail along the ridge. But Hartland didn't go in.

Cram came out fully dressed in a few minutes, and they made their way to the upper meadow where Cram caught the horses. Soon they were in the saddle and galloping down the road. They didn't ease their pace until they came to the trail up the first, low ridge and down into Moon Valley. Here they halted and listened. There was no sound save the hurrying winds in the trees along Moon Brook.

But Hartland was certain the song had come from high on the ridge to northward and they pushed on across the narrow valley and up the ridge with the moonlight flooding the trail and landscape until it was almost as light as day. They swung off on a side trail, with John Cram in the lead, and avoided the pass, climbing to the crest of the northern end of the ridge above it. Here they stopped again and were rewarded by the telltale notes of Creeps Hallow's song borne up to them on the freakish winds from somewhere beyond and below.

"That's him," said John Cram softly, and led on along the rock-ribbed spine of the ridge.

Soon the three of them checked their horses as of one accord, for the swelling notes came up to them from directly below and very close. There was a precipice here, where the rock fell away sharply. They dismounted and Hartland whispered excitedly in John Cram's ear.

"You and Joe hold on to my ankles while I lean over and take a look down there."

Then, while they held him securely, Hartland crawled forward, wriggled on his stomach until his head and shoulders were over the edge of the precipice. His heart leaped into his throat with excitement as he saw the dark, bulky form of Creeps Hallow moving back and forth in the narrow defile, a scant fifty feet below. He had stopped singing. Hartland saw the light from the candle shining from the entrance to the cave that was concealed from above. There was no longer any doubt as to the whereabouts of Rose Raymond.

He wriggled back, aided by Cram and Joe, drew them away from the edge of the rock, and told them what he had seen.

"I brought a sixty-foot rope, thinking it might come in handy," said Cram. "You two can hold it and let me down there." He went to his saddle and took off the rope.

"I'll go down myself," Hartland insisted. "There's no danger. Hallow doesn't carry a gun and I have one. Anyway, I believe he'll listen to me. You can let me down easy, and, when the rope slackens, you'll know I've hit bottom. If I shout up to you, stop lowering. If I shout again, pull up."

John Cram wanted to go down himself because he knew Hallow so well, but in the end Hartland had his way. They secured the rope snugly under his arms, found a rounded, smooth indentation in the edge of the rock over which he slipped, and then they began to lower him.

Hartland had his gun in his right hand. He was halfway down when Creeps Hallow, turning in the light that shone from the cage, looked up. A hoarse, wild, inarticulate cry came from the man's throat and he bounded to the spot just under Hartland. He recognized Hartland, who was covering him with the gun.

"Get back, Hallow, or I'll shoot!" came Hartland's ringing command.

Hallow cringed under the gun and backed to the edge of the entrance to the defile, above the steps. Rose Raymond came running out of the cave, queer sounds like hysterical sobs issuing from her lips. She recognized Hartland's voice; she saw him at the end of the rope.

"Roger, Roger . . . kill him!" she shrieked as she got her voice.

"Go back!" Hartland shouted.

But Rose was in a frenzy of hope, relief, overpowering joy at the unexpected prospect of being freed. She plunged at Hallow just as Hartland's boots came down on the rocky floor of the defile. Hallow was standing limply, unprepared for the onslaught, staring with terrified, bulging eyes at the gun. Rose Raymond's body struck him on the left side. He toppled, slipped, and went over the edge of the rock. A piercing shriek came up to them from the void below.

Chapter Thirty-two

Roger Hartland and Rose Raymond stood alone on the flat shelf of rock that jutted out over the boulders and steep trail above the shale slope. No sound came up to them from below save the soft plaint of the winds in the flowing stands of pine.

Rose Raymond's face was as white as the dazzling moonlight. She had nearly gone over with Creeps Hallow, so vicious had been her plunge. Now she stood, breathing in short gasps, her hands on her breast, looking at Hartland with an awed, terrified light in her wide eyes. She had killed Hallow when there was no need for it. She saw the accusation and contempt in Hartland's steady gaze and it shamed her. There was a weight about her heart. If he would only speak, swear at her, abuse her—anything.

But Hartland did not speak. He untied the rope from under his arms, pulled sharply three times by its end. He heard John Cram's voice from above: "Are you all right, Hartland?"

"All right!" Hartland called.

"Keep an eye out!" came the answer. "I'm coming down!"

Cram had heard Hartland's command to Creeps Hallow, had heard the wild shriek of the doomed man as he fell into space. He had felt the loosening of the rope as Hartland had landed. Then he had jerked the rope from Monocle Joe's hands, secured its end to the horn of his saddle. As luck had it, he had ridden the one horse he owned broken to work cattle: cut out, rope, and throw. He pulled on the rope and the animal braced itself against the pressure. Then, after he had called down to Hartland, Cram told Joe he would shout instructions up to him. He lowered himself over the precipice and went down the rope hand over hand, his horse bracing itself and pulling slightly.

John Cram came down near Hartland and Rose and looked questioningly at the two of them. Then he looked about for Creeps Hallow. But Hartland shook his head and pointed over the edge of the rock.

"He jumped off?" said Cram. "Or . . . ?"

"I pushed him off!" cried Rose impulsively. "I thought he would attack Roger and get his gun. Oh, I was so excited! I didn't mean to do it!"

"How did you get up here?" Cram asked.

"He brought me . . . night before last. Up a terrible trail. There are big rocks down there that he used for steps and dragged me up after him. He was going to take me somewhere in the top of the mountains and keep me there. He was crazy! Crazy, I tell you! I nearly went mad with the long night and with him. He said he had horses down there. He set my horse loose. We were to start at daybreak. He would have killed me in the end."

"Maybe so," said Cram. "The poor fellow wasn't quite right." He shouted up to Joe to loosen the rope from the saddle horn and throw it down, and to take the horses back the way they had come into Moon Valley and wait there.

Then he and Hartland looked over the edge of the rock, and, aided by the rope, which they secured about a rock outcropping, Hartland went down the first pitch. Rose had entered the cave and put out the candle. She had her jacket on and had merely to put on her hat. When she came out, Cram tied the rope about her and lowered her. He followed, using the rope as a stay. Step by step they made their way downward until they reached the smooth, steep trail at the upper end of the shale slope. Here they came upon Creeps Hallow.

He lay on his side, his face twisted up to the stars. The hair, the brows, the beard were sticky with blood. The eyes were closed.

Hartland bent over him, opening his shirt. He was breathing and the heart was beating faintly. "He isn't dead," Hartland muttered," but he must be broken to pieces. We'll have to carry him out."

Rose Raymond knew nothing about the way they had come, when they asked her, except that they had crossed the shale on a path as thin as a knife blade and had come up from the valley through the trees. But John Cram knew the path she mentioned was a game trail and that it must lead down to water, probably down into Moon Valley. Hallow hadn't come up by way of Moon Valley with Rose because he would have had to leave tracks in the road over the low ridge, through the valley, and part way up the upper trail. But he had doubtless come the easier way this night.

Cram made an examination and found both the path leading south through the trees and the two horses that Hallow had intended for himself and Rose and a pack animal, heavily loaded. They put Rose on one of the horses, and then Cram and Hartland picked Hallow up and carried him down to the starting point as gently as possible. Neither expected the man to live until they reached Moon Valley.

They put the injured man on the ground and John Cram went swiftly to work. He took the axe, which was twisted in the rope holding the pack on the pack horse, and cut down four young pines of the lodgepole variety, tall and slim, and trimmed them. Next he undid the pack, cut the rope into two pieces of equal length, and tied the saplings at each end so there was a space of about a foot between them. He folded the tarpaulin in which the pack had been wrapped and put it on the saplings, thus improvising a stretcher. They lifted Hallow to the stretcher, raised it by the two outside poles, and so were able to carry the unconscious form along the path, with the saddle horse and pack horse following, and Rose Raymond bringing up the rear on the other mount.

There were frequent stops for rest as Hallow was heavy, and the trail rough and narrow. Finally they emerged upon the main trail and with sighs of relief turned down toward Moon Valley. It was daybreak when they reached the brook in the valley and found Monocle Joe awaiting them.

Hartland dispatched Joe to town at once for the doctor and told Rose Raymond she might as well ride in with him.

"What will I say if anyone wants to know where I've been?" she asked.

"Say anything you like," Hartland retorted in disgust. Then he instructed Joe to notify Ross Milton and Miller. "We'll take Creeps to his cabin," he finished.

When the two had left, Hartland and John Cram carried their burden up to the cabin on the east slope. They took off Hallow's clothes and found his body a mass of bruises and cuts. There was an ugly gash in the back of his head, another on the lower left side of his face. A broken shoulder blade protruded through the skin. They heated water, washed and bandaged him as well as possible, and put him beneath the covers in the bunk. Then they went out into the brightness and the freshness of the early morning.

"I shall bring Marge up to do what she can," said John Cram.

Hartland nodded.

After that they sat in silence, waiting for the doctor.

When the doctor came at last, Creeps Hallow was muttering in delirium. The physician made an examination and worked over the injured man for more than an hour. Meanwhile, Deputy Ross Milton and Miller arrived with Joe. The latter told Hartland that Rose had gone to the hotel and he had put the horse she had ridden in the livery.

Ross Milton asked for an explanation and Hartland told him everything in the presence of John Cram and Miller, everything except the real reason for Rose Raymond's arrival in Silver City and the exact way in which Creeps Hallow came to be injured. "He slipped and fell over the edge of the rock," he finished. "He was deathly afraid of the gun I held, and crazed with excitement."

Milton had kept his steady gaze on Hartland's eyes. Now he turned to John Cram. "Is this the way of it?" he asked quietly.

"I heard Mister Hartland shout to Hallow to go back or he would shoot," said Cram. "Then I heard the terrible scream Hallow gave as he fell over. Hartland had the rope around him and could not have taken a step after touching the rock down there without my knowing it. He took the rope off and gave the signal that he was free. Then I took a hitch or two around my saddle horn and went down the rope. I found Hartland and the woman standing as if turned to stone. We got down an' out of there, an' sent Miss Raymond into town, an' brought Hallow here."

"Then it was an accident and I'll have to report it as such," said Milton, looking straight into Hartland's eyes.

Hartland knew the deputy had scented a flaw in the story, but with the circumstances so overwhelmingly against Hallow he would ignore it.

The doctor came out. His face was grave and he was shaking his head. "He recovered consciousness a few moments under a stimulant," said the man of medicine. "But he is paralyzed. His back is broken and his skull must be fractured. He won't live through the night."

John Cram left for home, announcing that he

would return with Margaret. Ross Milton rode away to telephone to the sheriff from Hartland's bungalow. Joe accompanied him to bring back some food for Hartland.

"If it would be possible, or do any good, we could move Hallow to my place," Hartland told the doctor. "Anderson has been taken to his quarters at the mine."

"It would be senseless," said the doctor, going inside.

Hartland and Miller walked slowly about the sloping meadow in front of the cabin. Luscious green grass and wild flowers bent under their tread. A golden sun swam in a sea of turquoise. The pines were waves of beryl on the slopes of the ridges that marched up to the gleaming peaks. It was a world of sweet scents, soft breezes, and inspiring beauty, such a day as Nature should send to mark the passing of one of her wild spirits from an earthly to a celestial sphere.

Hartland stopped and spoke in a low, earnest voice. "Miller, there is something in all this." He waved an arm in a gesture that seemed to encompass the universe. "Something has been brought home to me with a bang. It is *life* . . . I've been living in an empty tin."

He fell silent, and Miller made no comment. He sensed the troubled thoughts with which Hartland was struggling. He saw in the other's eyes the birth of an understanding—and he was content.

John Cram arrived with Margaret. The girl looked at Hartland out of large, solemn eyes. Then she held out a hand, and, as Hartland grasped it, said: "I'm sorry." She went into the cabin.

Joe returned with food, and Hartland ate in the

shade of the poplars down by the brook. Ross Milton came back, saying the sheriff did not think it necessary to come up that day. They talked idly in the cool of the trees. Afternoon came, and the day wore on. John Cram, the doctor, and Margaret remained inside.

It was nearing sunset when the doctor came to the door of the cabin and beckoned to them. They found Creeps Hallow conscious. His face was white and softened, no longer hideous or grotesque.

"He's been talking some," the doctor whispered. "Telling Margaret and her father why . . . all about . . . everything. His mind seems clearer than I've ever known it. Must have been the blow on the head. But he's going fast. This is the final rally."

Hallow saw Hartland and his lips trembled. He could not move a muscle of his body otherwise. He mumbled something and Hartland bent over him. But whatever it was that the dying man wished to say, he never said it.

The look of intelligence in his eyes clouded, then they flamed forth, wildly brilliant.

"I'll be a wind, that's what." The lips twisted in a frothy smile. "I'll be a wind an' race down the valley an' over the mountain tops, an' you'll hear me." A sublime joy seemed to rest on his face as those by the bedside watched. Another flicker of sanity, and, in the brief lucid interval: "Margie can have my mine." Then the eyes closed.

Creeps Hallow's spirit winged forth on its quest at sunset.

Chapter Thirty-three

Hartland rode back to his bungalow in the gathering dusk. There Fredricks prepared a hot supper with coffee, and Hartland ate abstractedly. Monocle Joe had gone to find Squint Evans and the pair was to sit up with Creeps Hallow's body that night. John Cram and Margaret had gone home. Miller and Ross Milton would leave when Joe and Evans took up their vigil. Hallow was to be buried the next afternoon on the hillside near his cabin.

When he had finished his supper, Hartland busied himself at his desk. He drew a check and placed a number of bills with the check in a pocket of his wallet. Then he got his horse and rode down to the hotel. He was able this night to ford the stream as the water had gone down almost as suddenly as it had risen. Miller had mentioned that the men would start a newer, stronger bridge on the morrow.

Hartland's entry into the lobby of the hotel was the signal for silence and curious looks. Many of these looks were friendly and sympathetic. The clerk was obsequiously polite.

"She's in her room, sir," he said in answer to Hartland's question. "Shall I tell her you're here?"

Hartland nodded, and stood by the desk until the clerk returned with the message that he was to go upstairs.

He found Rose Raymond's door open. She was sitting by the table near one of the windows, looking fresh and beautiful in a mauve morning gown.

Her eyes were bright and defiant, but a question glimmered in their depths.

"Well, Rose," said Hartland easily," your work here is finished." He sat down on a chair across from her.

"Is he . . . is he . . . ?" Rose found herself unable to ask what was on her tongue.

"He's dead," said Hartland bluntly, noting the flush leave her cheeks. "But I didn't so much refer to Creeps Hallow. You can have *that* memory to last you the rest of your life, and I guess it'll be enough. You'll not be inconvenienced in any way, because in the circumstances you could not be blamed. Don't think that I'm blaming you, Rose, for I'm not. In fact, I feel rather sorry that your . . . your association, we'll say, with me brought you this trouble. We'll pass over your motive in coming out here in the first place. In a way, I feel actually indebted to you." He surveyed her critically.

"In what way? Because I've given you a new thrill?" she asked sarcastically.

"I felt the thrill before you came," he said complacently. "But you've opened my eyes to some things and I'm not going to explain them. You probably wouldn't understand, anyway. You're thinking of leaving on the morning train?"

"I suppose it would be best," she said, the dark light of defeat and anger again shining in her eyes.

"Under the circumstances, I believe it would," Hartland remarked dryly. "However, the fact that Creeps Hallow was not mentally sound has long been known hereabouts. The report has gone forth that he abducted you when in the throes of a particularly bad spell, for it was only at such times that he was known to sing. His song was responsible for your discovery . . . or for us discovering you. He slipped and fell in the excitement. The sheriff has accepted that version, with John Cram, Joe, and myself to back it up." He paused for a space while he lighted a cigarette. Rose was already smoking. "You can have one of the maids here help you pack. Joe will look after your luggage before train time."

"You seem to have everything planned," she said. "I suppose you'll see me off . . . if I go."

"For the sake of appearances, I will," said Hartland. He took out his wallet, removed the slender packet of bills and the folded check. These he placed on the table before her. Then he rose.

"There's something like five hundred in cash there," he said, "and a check on a New York bank for one thousand dollars."

Her eyes widened and a sneer curled on her lips.

"Oh, it's not as much as you expected or wanted, or intended to demand," he said lightly, "but it's the exact amount I intended to give you from the start . . . out of pity. Remember that, while you're spending it, my dear. But since I first fixed the amount, I do not believe it is a charitable donation. I'm getting my money's worth. I'll see you off in the morning, as you suggested."

He left the room, closing the door after him, leaving her sitting at the table, idly flicking the ashes from her cigarette on the bills and the folded check in front of her.

Meanwhile, Margaret Cram's feelings toward Rose Raymond had been directly opposite to those of Hartland's. Margaret felt only compassion for Rose. She felt guilty, too, in a sense. For hadn't she been indirectly responsible? Creeps Hallow had told what he had heard through the open window of

Hartland's living room the night of Rose Raymond's arrival. He had told why he had taken Rose to the mountain cave. He had explained everything with the simplicity of a child making a confession. So Margaret saw matters in a different light, learned something of the wiles and chicanery of that outside world of which she knew nothing except that Roger Hartland had come out of it to shape the first great climax in her life. Of Hartland she could not think intelligently. He had three personalities in her eyes: the man of the world, the man of promise, and. . . . She put aside the recurring thought of that other personality time after time for it was the personality that she loved. She lay awake most of the night and could not get to sleep until she had decided to visit Rose Raymond in the morning.

When her father left for Creeps Hallow's cabin after breakfast, Margaret saddled her horse and rode down to the hotel. She asked to see Rose.

"Miss Raymond left for New York on the morning train," the clerk informed her.

Silver City scented a fresh sensation during this last week in June. The town was crowded, overflowing its original boundaries as new arrivals flocked to the new boom camp created through the efforts of Herbert Mann. Although Mann bustled about, mysteriously important, arranging for the opening of the Consolidated office the next Monday, there was a furtive look of worry in his eyes. Alex Gordon, too, appeared nervous. Only Butch Allen was calm and unperturbed, cheerful, in fact. He was known as one of the big three, which included Mann, Gordon, and himself. His importance had lost much of its glamour after the beating he had received from

Hartland, and the newcomers took little stock in the reports circulated concerning him, but the men of the Huntley, who he had carefully picked, were with him, and half a dozen cronies—rough, dangerous men—were ever within hailing distance.

He and Mann held many secret conferences in the latter's private office that had already been fitted up in the rear of the building the Consolidated had rented. There was a back door to this room that opened on an alley that ran parallel with the main street behind the stores, two resorts, the post office, and the bank on the opposite side from the Silver King, the hotel, the largest store, and two cafés.

Allen entered the office by this door on Tuesday morning. He found Mann in a state of some excitement.

"I have a brand new, sure-fire idea," said the Consolidated promoter. "When we open the sale of stock, I'm going to tell 'em we intend to sink a shaft to tap the big copper deposits these yaps think are under their feet. That'll bring every one of 'em in with the last dollar he's got. We ought to take in better than fifty thousand the first three days."

Allen shrugged. "The bank will take in a lot of cash on the third an' fourth," he said. "You better make your end of it snappy for I'm calling the men out at midnight of the Fourth."

"Maybe we better wait a while longer," Mann said nervously.

"An' let Gordon have time to get cold feet about having so much cash on hand?" Allen sneered. "What's more, we've got to work fast. You can't blow up a big soap-bubble boom like you've started here an' get away smooth as gravy when it comes to the bust. An' there's something else. My men have noticed some keen gents in town . . . if you know what I mean. Let some of those *hombres* get it into their heads that Gordon has a vault feathered with yellow-backs, an' you've got a safe in the same enticing condition . . . which you will have soon . . . an' our little job will be done for us. Ever think of that?"

Mann's face clouded again. "There's a big risk," he said, shaking his head. "We'll lose by waiting, but I guess you're right. You're sure of your men? I mean the men for the big job?"

Allen laughed. "Don't ask me that damn' fool question again. An' you know they buried that lunatic Hallow yesterday."

Mann nodded, but appeared puzzled.

Allen leaned on the table. "That means that Hartland has no watchman up there to start a fuss if anybody was to come around," he said softly.

"But you're not thinking of going after Hartland, are you?" Mann demanded angrily. "I told you he's dynamite an' to lay off of him. Now that's cold turkey, an' I mean it."

"Don't get excited," said Allen coolly. "I'm not going after Hartland." He swore under his breath. "The man I am going after is the bowlegged little runt who grabbed my gun the night of the fight. He. . . ."

"Maybe it's a good thing he did grab it," Mann interrupted. "If you had shot Hartland, things would have gone to pieces right there."

Allen shook his head impatiently and his eyes snapped. "Mann, will you keep your mouth shut when I'm talking? What I'm trying to get at is . . . Hartland may have a bunch of cash up there. He'll be gone when the big fracas is on an' there's no sense in leaving any loose ends."

Mann shook his head. "If you think Hartland is

that big a fool, you're mistaken. We'll have enough
to attend to as it is. An' I wouldn't trust you in shooting range of Hartland with your gun handy. An'
that little runt you're talking about is a gunman an'
a killer, an' don't you forget it. I've heard a dozen
who know the signs when they see them say so. Big
Mose said so himself."

"All the better!" exclaimed Allen viciously. "That
gives me an out."

"I should think you'd have sense enough to forget
these little personal differences," Mann complained.
"With big game in sight, you'd frighten it away by
shooting at a rabbit."

"What you think an' what I do, or intend to do, are
two different things," said Allen grimly. "Now go
ahead an' tell 'em you're going to put down a shaft . . .
tell 'em anything. But get the money."

He went out, and Mann began puttering about
his desk. He was mad clear through, and he was
beginning to have his first serious doubts. But he
had gone too far in the project he had in hand with
Butch Allen to back out. If he did back out, he would
have to leave Silver City, anyway—and penniless.

On Wednesday, Silver City's regulars and those
who were interested in the Consolidated in particular received something of a shock. In every post-
office box an envelope, properly addressed, was
found, and, when opened, yielded a small printed
circular that read:

To Whom It May Concern:
   Rumors have been spread in Silver City to the
effect that the undersigned paid a large sum of money
for the working option on the Huntley property.

These rumors are unfounded and misleading. The amount paid to Messrs. Mann and Gordon was twenty-five thousand dollars ($25,000). That was the refund of the amount they had paid on their option, and ten thousand dollars ($10,000) to be divided between the said Mann and Gordon equally as a bonus. These amounts were paid by checks and the cancelled checks can be seen by any who are interested by applying at the offices of the Yellow Jacket Mine. The undersigned wishes it understood that no extensive development was contemplated at the time and none is contemplated now. Any statement connecting the undersigned, or any property in which the undersigned is interested, with any company or corporation now existent, or being promoted, is false. Rumors in circulation have compelled the undersigned to issue this statement in his behalf, and for the information of those who may feel inclined to place credence in unauthorized reports.

(Signed)Roger Hartland

The effect of this notice was electric. The circulars were passed from hand to hand, and the chief reaction was one of resentment and anger toward Hartland. Mann, dismayed and enraged at first, took immediate advantage of the opportunity to spread the report that it was the first move on the part of Hartland to fight the Consolidated because he could not get control of it for himself. He implied insidiously that the temporary cessation of work at the Huntley might be the forerunner of a complete shut down, that Hartland wanted to ruin the camp and buy the Consolidated holdings at a song. He declared as much to the miners and prospectors who had given him options on their claims or mines when they visited him in a body on Wednesday afternoon.

These men, and their sympathizers, collected in a large crowd in the middle of the street. They were in a languorous mood, fired by Mann's vituperations directed at Hartland, and angry at the thought that Hartland's statement might frustrate their efforts to sell their holdings at a good figure or to receive nice blocks of stock in the Consolidated in exchange for them. They talked and milled about until Butch Allen plunged into their midst, waving his arms for silence. They quieted down and listened.

"Why don't you go to this Hartland an' ask him what he's tryin' to do?" Allen shouted. "He's playin' you for a bunch of pinheaded saps an' you're letting him get away with it! Make him come clean! He's tryin' to bust the Consolidated with his Eastern methods, without giving it a chance to make good. Is that a square deal? Put it up to him so he'll know you mean business before it's too late. Maybe he's left town by now! Maybe . . . !"

Allen's words were drowned in a roar of angry voices. "Let's go!" came the cry. Then the crowd, which had become a seething mob, started up the street on the way to Hartland's bungalow.

Monocle Joe, who had hovered on the edge of the throng, both in the big, vacant front room that was to be the Consolidated's main office, and in the street, now shuffled into the Silver King and winked a signal to Squint Evans, who was playing cards.

Squint joined him shortly behind the resort and they made their way along the trees on the bank of the stream, Joe talking while they hurried on. When they reached the ford where the bridge had been, they found themselves ahead of the approaching mob. They waded through the water and hastened up to the bungalow.

Hartland, who had been sitting in a chair on the verandah, rose as they hurried to the steps.

"Inside," said Joe sharply, climbing the steps and walking quickly into the living room with Squint Evans following.

Hartland entered after them and his puzzled expression gave way to a look of grim satisfaction as Joe explained what he had heard Mann say to the crowd, and how Butch Allen had stirred them up and spurred them on.

"They're pushing things to a showdown quicker than I expected," he said when Joe had finished. "It's the old story about giving a man enough rope. . . ." He turned on Evans. "Squint, would you be willing to draw with this Allen?" he asked quietly.

"Yes." The answer came in a lisp.

Sounds of a commotion came to them from the lower side of the park. Hartland looked out the door and saw the mob splashing across the stream. The ringleaders must have decided it was too much of a walk to go around by the upper bridge. The original delegation of two score or so, which had visited Mann, had swelled to 200 as other scores had joined out of curiosity or because of sympathetic leanings.

"Stay here," Hartland told Monocle Joe and Evans. Then he went out on the verandah to the top of the steps and waited.

The crowd formed a semicircle about the front of the verandah and packed the little park nearly down to the stream. A large, florid man stepped out as spokesman. His coat sleeves were tight about his great muscles; his gnarled hands were hooked, as if more accustomed to gripping a drill and hammer than to hanging idly at his sides; his face was scarred, and he wore a thick stubble of black beard, but his hard, level gaze was honest enough as he looked straight into Hartland's eyes.

"Mister Hartland, we're here to find out a few things," he said. "We represent the bunch that's given options to the Consolidated an' we have as big an interest in the camp as you have . . . more, maybe, because we're poor men and not millionaires. We want to know. . . ."

He paused as Hartland held up a hand. The crowd pressed forward, very still, ready to listen now that they were actually confronted by the man they held responsible for Silver City's destiny.

"I know what you want to know," said Hartland in a ringing voice that carried to every ear. "Mann's speech to you and what Allen had to say has been reported to me. You want a showdown and you're going to get it."

He paused while his eyes searched the sea of faces. Then, at the edge of the crowd, down the slope near the stream, he saw Allen and Mann. At once he began speaking again, and his words carried fire to the ears of his listeners.

"It was the notice I issued this morning that started you on this rampage. That is just as well. I know all about the hints, the false reports, and the veiled innuendoes directly, or indirectly, circulated by word of mouth, by looks, by sly winks, by mysterious suggestions to the effect that I paid a huge sum for the Huntley lease and option, and that I planned extensive developments. It was Herbert Mann and his gunman, Butch Allen, who did this work. I had to spike these false reports because when the Consolidated bubble burst, it would be me who would be blamed. Now I have two things to tell you. I don't have to tell you anything. I am not the guardian of you or this camp. I didn't induce you to put your names on any dotted lines. If I was playing you for a bunch of pinheaded saps, as Allen would have you believe, I wouldn't have said a word . . . wouldn't be talking to you now. It's because I want to be fair that I'm going to tell you why I took over the Huntley."

Hartland could see Mann holding Butch Allen by the arm. The others were pressing forward behind their leader, their eyes fixed on Hartland's face, their ears alert to his every word.

"When I came here, Mann asked me to put in with the Consolidated, which was then a private enterprise between himself and Alex Gordon. I refused and he tried to bulldoze me into it. He failed in that. Then an attack was made upon me and on the Yellow Jacket miners and property. This move was engineered by Butch Allen, and I took over the Huntley for the one and simple reason that I wanted to get him out of it and prevent further trouble. I had no thought of any big development in that mine, but I did not intend, and do not intend now, to shut down the mine indefinitely unless I'm compelled to do so. But it is evident that I haven't stopped the trouble. Allen sent you up here. Now I ask . . . what is he doing for the camp? Who does he represent? What is his position here?"

Hartland was looking over the heads of the throng to where Mann and some others were struggling with Allen, holding him back. The crowd craned their necks in that direction but Hartland claimed their attention immediately.

"Allen has made this a personal issue," he sang out. "He has slandered me, turned your attention to me for some secret purpose of his own . . . even if that purpose is merely to try to get even with me for defying him. He wants revenge for his injured reputation as a badman. I gave him fists, but he wants guns. I'm not a gunman, but I have a man in my employ who can handle a six-shooter fairly well. Allen is in hearing distance. If he must have gun play, he can have it now with a man who is, at least, a match for him. Squint, come here!"

The crowd held its breath as a diminutive figure slipped out the door behind Hartland and stole with cat-like tread to the grass below the steps. It was the mild, little gambler they had known as Smith. But these men were from mountains and plains; they knew the half crouch, the narrowed lids, the tight lips, the blue-green flame of the eyes of the natural-born gunfighter. They saw one before them, and then they all turned and looked behind toward the spot where Butch Allen stood, black-faced, eyes flaming, hesitating. . . .

Suddenly someone in the crowd laughed, and that laugh drove Allen away with Mann and his cronies pulling him along.

"Now the other thing!"

Hartland was smiling, holding up his hand. Squint Evans was sitting down leisurely on the bottom step.

"I am closing down the Huntley for a few days for a reorganization and an expert inspection of the mine," said Hartland, his eyes sparkling with satisfaction and excitement. "I am not a mining man, nor will I take the word of any one man who is an expert, even though it be my manager, Jim Miller, who many of you must know. I have sent for engineers who are this minute on their way to Silver City. If these engineers ... men of international reputation ... report favorably on the Yellow Jacket, I'll sink! That's all!"

The breathless silence that followed this announcement suddenly exploded in a mighty cheer. Hats went sailing in the air, men pounded each other on the back, tears came into the eyes of old prospectors who had never lost faith. Silver City was to have its chance. At last they would know if their convictions were well founded. Money was nothing to Hartland; Hartland was everything to them. They crowded in a dense jam in front of the bungalow, cheering and cheering. Strangers and old-timers alike caught the inspiration. Hartland waved a hand and went into the house.

Then the mad rush into town began.

Chapter Thirty-four

The crowd surged into the Silver King and found Herbert Mann and Butch Allen already there, surrounded by half a dozen of the latter's cronies. Allen was grim and glowering, but Mann's eyes were sparkling. All trace of worry, of furtiveness was gone. His eyes sparkled. He rapped sharply on the bar with a $20 gold piece.

"Boys," he cried in his old, loud, blustering voice, "the promoter of the Consolidated is buying a drink for the house if it takes every cent of the five-thousand-dollar bonus Hartland says I got for selling the Huntley option! Step up an' take 'em fast an' make room for the next man. Then I'm going to tell you something that'll be just as interesting as what Hartland said."

The crowd was in a happy mood, although many of the strangers did not quite understand it all. They jostled about the bar, taking their drinks on Mann, thinking to themselves that here was real boom-town spirit.

Mann did not wait until all had been served. He climbed on a table and waved his hands for silence. His face was flushed with excitement. Hartland's speech had given him the greatest inspiration of his life. It had done more. He was beginning to believe in the company's venture. He realized his golden opportunity. He had, for the time being, forgotten that other project that Butch Allen represented.

"You all heard what Hartland said, boys," he roared when his audience was at attention. "It hardly seems necessary for me to say anything, but I'm going to talk for the benefit of those who do not understand conditions. Gordon and I gave up the Huntley for the money he says he paid us because we wanted that money . . . needed it . . . to get the Consolidated started right. Our properties are ten times as large as Hartland's. He told you he wanted the Huntley because he wanted to discharge my foreman, Allen. Do you believe that? Of course you don't. Now he announces that he has sent for mining engineers an' that, if their report is favorable, he'll sink. He says he'll sink in the Yellow Jacket. You bet he'll sink in the Yellow Jacket. He intended to do that from the first. Do you suppose he'd be sending for high-priced engineers if the Yellow Jacket's showing didn't warrant it? Not on your life! I tell you, boys, the Yellow Jacket has got the goods. They're going down for the copper an' they know they're going to get it! The ore indications and stains probably show that the Huntley has it, too, for the Huntley adjoins the Yellow Jacket. That's why he wanted the Huntley. An' that's another reason why we let him have it. So he would go ahead an' sink, because every dollar he spends in development will go to prove the value of the Consolidated holdings. Every word Hartland spoke this afternoon . . . an' he spoke a mouthful . . . went to show that the Consolidated is not a bubble, that Silver City's boom isn't hot air, an', if Consolidated stock, which goes on sale next Monday, isn't worth five times, or ten times what it cost within a year, I'll blow my brains out in the middle of the street an' you can throw what's left of me to the coyotes!"

He finished, hoarse and perspiring, got down from the table with good-natured cheers ringing in his ears. None there but felt that there was logic in what he had said. Only Butch Allen remained passive, his darting glances roving over the crowd. Now and then he spoke to some of his companions. Gradually it became noised about that it was Mann who had prevented him from meeting Hartland's gunman openly before the crowd because Mann thought it would give the camp a black eye. It was whispered that Allen was eagerly awaiting an opportunity to draw against the mild little gambler they had known as Smith. Any day now might witness the spectacle of two killers going for their guns. It was the old, thrilling stuff a boom camp loves.

Hartland stood by the table in his living room until the crowd had gone. The smile of satisfaction on his face gave way to a frown. He had, so he thought, pricked the Consolidated bubble, but, at the same time, he had placed himself in a position where he was responsible for the future of the camp. The decision he had made the night he took supper with the Crams had now made him the instigator of a boom. The very fact that he was bringing in experts showed, at least, that he contemplated development, and he had told them as much. He had acknowledged that he would sink if the engineers' reports were favorable. As he thought of this, he suddenly realized that this announcement would act as a stimulus for Consolidated promotion. Prospective investors might wait until after the engineers' reports became known. There would be no keeping the nature of these reports secret, for the activities at the mine would tell the story. If he sank, Consolidated stock would sell and soar. He saw then that it was inevitable that he would have to take control of the Consolidated for he knew Mann's stamp of promoter, knew he would wreck the company he headed and make trouble. Yes, Hartland was involved in the network of Silver City's destinies to such an extent that he could not extricate himself by the easy method of merely leaving the camp to itself. He could not do so and retain his self-respect; he could not do so and be true to that motive within him that had prompted his actions of late.

He went into the kitchen expecting to find Monocle Joe and Squint Evans there. It was nearly 5:00 P.M.

and he knew Joe and Fredricks were in the habit of taking tea at that hour. But neither man he sought was there. Fredricks, pale and nervous, hadn't seen them.

Hartland stamped through the house to the verandah. At the top of the steps his whole manner changed. His face softened and lightened, his eyes brightened and shone. He had not seen Margaret Cram save for during the brief ceremony of burying Creeps Hallow since the Sunday when she had attended the dying man. Now she was dismounting by the steps.

He hurried down and took her horse. "I'll lead him around into the shade," he said. "Sit down on the divan, Margaret."

When he returned, he sat down beside her. Never had she looked so beautiful as in the late afternoon, he thought. Sunshine, green trees and grass, kindly skies, the sweet scent of countless blossoms—June, the month love claimed as its own. Her hands were in her lap and he put his own upon them.

"What did you come to tell me?" he asked.

"That I'm an eavesdropper," she answered lightly, withdrawing her hands. "I was riding into town and saw the crowd. I edged over by the creek and heard every word you said. Then I galloped back around by the upper bridge and came to tell you how proud I am of you. Why did you do it, Roger?"

"Because of you," he replied bluntly. "I made up my mind the night I had supper at your house."

"Oh!" Her eyes were wide, swimming with mysterious lights. "You decided to buy me . . . *that* way?"

Exactly." His voice was precise. "But now I feel differently. I don't want to buy you that way, or any other way save by paying the price you mentioned.

You said your price was love. You have mine. And the wonderful part of it all is, that I have yours."

"What . . . what are you saying?" Her hands came up to her breast and she looked at him wide-eyed, startled.

"Didn't you know it?" he said softly, putting his arms about her. "Perhaps you suspected it, but wouldn't confess it even to yourself. Anyway, it's true. And I've learned two of the things I think you had in mind when you said there were three things I had to learn about women. First, I had to learn really to love one for her own sweet, dear self. Then I had to experience the thrill of knowing that she loved me. That thrill is mine this minute. I suppose the third thing to learn is the love of a home and children, and the joy of making the woman of my choice happy . . . and keeping her happy. That thrill, too, is going to be mine." He raised her face, kissed her lips. Her arm stole about his neck for a few moments, then she drew away from his embrace.

"Roger, you don't know what you're saying!" She flushed, then grew pale. There were deep, gleaming lights of passion in her eyes. "It's your imagination running free again. It's the subtle, hypnotic spell of the mountains. It's . . . it's. . . ."

"It's you," he interposed. "To put it rudely, I've got wise to myself . . . and to life. This mining business means nothing to me . . . I'll be frank. These mountains mean something, I guess, but you mean everything." He took her in his arms again. "Kiss me, Margaret!" It was an authoritative command, rather than a request.

That side of his personality that she loved was dominant. She surrendered and gave him her lips. "I was sorry for you," she whispered.

"Sorry?" He drew back. "Don't you know if there's anything a man, who is a man, hates and abhors it is having a person feel sorry for him?" He was almost angry.

"And I was sorry for Miss Raymond," she said softly. "I went down to see her the morning after . . . after the funeral. But she had gone. She might have loved you, Roger . . . who knows? But I don't blame you."

"Don't blame me?" He rose and stood above her. "Margaret, you don't think . . . you don't think . . . ?"

"I don't allow myself to think," the girl said firmly. "I only know what Creeps Hallow told me, and what my father told me when Creeps made him break his trust not to tell. I only know the impression she made upon me. And I don't care. You understand, Roger? You were right. I *do* love you . . . and I don't care."

"Great God!" Hartland's exclamation was reverent rather than otherwise. His face was white, drawn. Then suddenly he smiled. He sat down again, close to her, took her hands. "I can't expect everything," he said slowly. "I never thought until recently that it might be in the cards for me to be genuinely and thoroughly happy . . . to love life for itself. When you forget what you say you won't think about, and believe in me, that time will come. It's said that the eyes are the mirrors of a man's soul. Look into mine."

Margaret locked her troubled gaze with his. What was this she had done? What was this different phase of his nature? Did she love him? Or were the restless spirits of the mountains playing with her imagination? Or did she know anything at all except that she was a silly, young girl. Her lips brushed his. "I'm going, Roger," she whispered. "When I come to you again, you will know."

Three of the engineers arrived on the night train. Miller met them and they went to the quarters that had been made ready for them in the best of the Yellow Jacket bunkhouses. These accommodations had been arranged fully as comfortable as any the hotels could offer. They began their inspection of the Yellow Jacket and the mineral showings and rock outcroppings in the vicinity. Hartland spent all of Thursday at the mine, and the next night Hale arrived from New York. Hale was one of the three most famous mining experts with an international record of achievement. He became a guest at Hartland's bungalow.

It was an exciting end to the month of June. Silver City seethed with speculation and rumor—and held its breath. Not a word of what the engineers said or thought leaked out, but the fact that they were there and were doing their work thoroughly was enough. Hale's name was magic; it was whispered in reverence by the old-timers, spoken always in a tone of respect by others. It became known that the temporary shut down of the Huntley at midnight Sunday was to presage the examination of that mine.

Butch Allen and the few closest to him played cards incessantly in the rear rooms of the booming resorts. Alex Gordon was feverishly excited and a bit bewildered by the sudden prosperity of the camp. He had to send for another experienced teller for his bank. Herbert Mann had supervised the furnishing of the Consolidated office, and by Sunday everything was in readiness for the launching of the stock sale.

He was pacing his private office, Sunday night, in the last glimmer of the dusk, when there was a knock on the rear door, and he opened it stealthily to admit Butch Allen.

The gunman looked at him searchingly. He had seen little of Mann since the day the crowd had gone to Hartland's place. As he inspected him now, he noted a change in the promoter's look and manner. "Light the lamp," he ordered, "so I can see you better."

"Not so loud," Mann admonished, glancing at the open window. He lighted the lamp and met Allen's gaze with a question in his eyes.

The gunman did not appear altogether satisfied with what he saw. "Look here, Mann," he gritted through his teeth suddenly, "you're gettin' mighty well worked up about this Consolidated business, eh? Think it's going over big?"

"That's just what I'm thinking," Mann confessed. "In fact, I know it's going over big. Butch, I think there's something in this scheme, after all. At last Hartland is really interested and going ahead. What's more, I think I've guessed the reason, an' if I have . . . well, he'll never back out."

"Yeah?" sneered Allen. "An' what's his reason?"

"Margaret Cram," Mann whispered. "He's taken a shine to her. He's been seen with her several times since he came here, had her up to his place for lunch, an' one thing an' another, introduced that red woman to her, an' now Gordon tells me he's let her father have five thousand dollars to take up his notes an' go ahead with his development. I'll bet she got him to do what he's doing."

"An' what's that got to do with us?" Allen demanded harshly.

"Not much, maybe, but then again. . . ." Mann paused, undecided.

Allen leaned in the back of a chair and looked straight into Mann's troubled eyes. "Tell me," he said in a voice that struck a chill to his listener's nerves, "are you getting cold feet?"

"Of course not," Mann protested nervously. Then he gathered himself together with a shrug. "But I can't help thinking that there might be something bigger in this Consolidated business, as you call it, than we ever suspected. Maybe we're going off half-cocked."

"Listen to me." Allen's eyes were gleaming between the narrowed lids. The words cut the stillness of the room like a razor-edged blade. "I've taken about everything this Eastern snob of a tenderfoot you call Hartland had to offer. I don't know as he'll ever find out how lucky he's been. It galls me to think that. An' I've kept off that little runt of a would-be gunfighter of his so far because, if I shot him to pieces, it might interfere with our plans. He'll get his later. But I want you to know that, if you even look as if you're gettin' cold feet, or even think of double-crossing me, I'll send you to hell with your toes kickin' if I have to fight my way past the devil himself."

Mann was staring, terror-struck, his face blanching to a sickly greenish-white.

Allen was satisfied with the effect he thought his threat had had on the promoter. He turned without noting that Mann was staring past him at the window where he had seen the flash of a narrow, bronzed face.

At the door, Allen spoke again in a soft, hissing voice. "At midnight on the Fourth, I'll tell you the hour." Then he went out.

A croaking gurgle came from Mann's throat as he listened for the shot. But no report of a gun broke on the night air. No shot. But Hartland's gunman had been out there, listening at the window. Did it mean there would be another with whom to divide the spoils? Mann dropped into a chair, limp and cold, yet perspiring. He mopped his brow and blubbered, watching the door—expecting a visitor who was not to come.

At midnight the shift went off at the Huntley and the men sought the bunkhouses for a good sleep in anticipation of a four-day celebration. There was no disorder.

Chapter Thirty-five

Herbert Mann was up and about at dawn Monday morning, the First of July. In the excitement and flurry of launching the Consolidated, he forgot the gnawing worry of the night when he had tossed and turned in his bed, seeing the burning eyes of Butch Allen and that pinched, narrow face at the window. The front of the office was hung with bunting; flags fluttered overhead. Others along the street caught the early spirit of the forthcoming holiday and soon most of the buildings were similarly decorated. Young firs were cut and brought in to stand at corners, be tied to posts, made into wreaths, adding a refreshing touch of green to the dusty street.

The sale of Consolidated stock was to open sharply at noon. Fifteen minutes before this hour the office was packed and the street jammed with an uproarious crowd. A board had been rigged on a wall in the Silver King where Consolidated and other stocks were to be listed and prices quoted. To all outward appearances, Silver City now was a genuine boom town.

The throng cheered enthusiastically as the postmaster was honored, on the stroke of twelve, by being allowed to purchase the first share. The official was followed by others, by scores of Huntley men who had been advised to buy, and then that strange, inexplicable force that is characteristic of a boom camp and is nothing more than an impulse of the moment swept the crowd off its feet in a wild rush to buy the only stock offered in the renewed diggings. The frenzy of speculation seized conservative and reckless souls alike. Stock certificates, already signed, could hardly be filled out fast enough by Mann and an assistant in the rear office. Money poured in, and, when the first sale of 100 shares in a lump was made, Mann came out into the main office, waving the certificate, and, jumping on a chair behind the counter, made a ringing speech that was cheered to the echo.

The gold-and-green edged certificates, with their red seals, seemed in an hour's time to endow the boom with the substantiality of permanent prosperity. No one would think of going about without at least one share of Consolidated. The very name of the company was a lure. And the money poured in. Mann could think of nothing now but stock and money.

All the Huntley men were on holiday, and all had half a month's wages or more in pocket. By sundown every resort was crowded. The addition to the Silver King had been rushed and, although the floor and walls were plain boards, it was being used.

More celebrants were coming up from the lowlands and prairie towns for the word had gone out that Silver City would be the place to spend the Fourth.

Mann had placed his safe in a prominent corner behind the counter of the front office. A lamp in a reflector bracket was left burning above it so that it could readily be seen through the front windows. But then, he reasoned, no one would suspect that he had a large sum in the safe. When he closed the office at 9:00 P.M., locked the doors, and left, he did not know how much he had taken in that day. His nerves were too frayed and he was too tired to figure up the stock sale. But he was jubilant, for it looked as though Consolidated was going over with a bang.

He went into the Silver King to get a drink before going to eat. And this was a night when he certainly needed sleep.

Allen sauntered up to him as he came out of the resort. Mann did not attempt to conceal the satisfaction in his eyes.

"It's a knockout," he said to Allen in a low voice. "If we didn't take in twenty, probably twenty-five thousand, I'm a liar. An' we've got three days or so to go yet."

"Go get some sleep," said Allen. "The boys an' myself will keep an eye on the diggings across the street."

Mann ate absently. Allen had meant the safe in the office, of course. They would keep an eye on it. Oh, the money would be safe enough until. . . . He put down his knife and fork suddenly and stared, unseeing, straight ahead. Allen and the men who were with him in the bank deal were watching the money. He was being watched himself undoubtedly.

For the first time he realized how completely he was in Allen's power. Suppose Allen was to have the same thought he had had himself—the thought that there were too many to go shares with? What was to stop Allen and his men from leaving him dead by the trail when they made their getaway? He might be able to do it in a way that would make it look as if Mann had been responsible for the whole business.

Mann half rose from his chair, then sat down suddenly. He had had no word from the gunman Hartland had called Squint. Yet he knew Squint was aware that something big was in the wind. Had he told Hartland? The sweat broke out on the promoter's brow. Why hadn't he told Allen? Allen would see that Squint was fixed mighty quickly. He would have to see Allen and tell him.

He left the table and went in search of the gunman, but everywhere he went he was immediately surrounded by a crowd and he had to give it up. Anyway, what difference would that night make? He yawned. The town was ablaze. It would be that way until after the Fourth. He went to the hotel, to his room, and to bed.

Tuesday was another banner day for Consolidated. Mann was again kept busy filling out certificates. But the demand for stock fell off in the afternoon and Alex Gordon came in.

"I thought you would want to make a deposit," he said pointedly. "You must have a big bunch of money here, Mann, and this isn't as safe a place for it as in the bank."

"That's right, that's right," said Mann hastily, fussing with the sheets of figures he had apparently been totaling. "Just as soon as I can get things straightened out, I'll be in. This has been a big rush an' it isn't over, Alex. I'll be in as soon as I can."

"Perhaps my new clerk can help you," Gordon suggested. "He is an experienced man in such things. I can take his place at the window for a while."

"No, it won't be necessary," Mann said irritably. "Just leave me alone an' I'll make out all right, Alex. We'll have to get together an' go over everything after this rush . . . after the Fourth. But we've got a winner. You can see how busy I am."

Gordon went out, but returned shortly with some stout canvas sacks such as are used by banks for holding cash. "If you want to put the money in these sacks for me to put in the vault, you can bring them in by five o'clock," he said, "and I wouldn't advise you to be counting large sums of money in here, either. You can do that later in the bank where it'll be safer."

Mann sat for some little time staring at the sacks on his desk. He hadn't liked Gordon's look or the tone of his voice, and what he had said last had conveyed the impression that he was giving a command rather than making a suggestion. Alex Gordon's office with the Consolidated was that of treasurer. Mann upbraided himself for a fool. Of course, he couldn't keep all that cash in the safe in the front office. It was but natural that Gordon should expect him to put it in the bank vault. That was where it belonged. It was common sense. And, since Allen and his bank bandits were going to blow the vault anyway, what difference would it make if the money was there or in the office safe? Allen should have thought of these things.

Gradually a great light dawned upon Herbert Mann. Allen *had* thought of this! He was playing for a come-on, letting him do the dirty work, as it were, and raise a big sum on Consolidated stock so that he and his gang could get away with it. He had no intention of splitting with him. Instead of Mann's double-crossing Allen, the gunman intended to double-cross Mann and kill him in the bargain. The more Mann thought along this line, the stronger became his conviction that Allen planned to make him his dupe. At heart Mann was a coward. Suppose he were to go through with Allen and the latter really intended to play square. How about the men with him? Mann didn't know one of them. There was a terrible risk. A slip could mean but one thing or the other: death or prison. Yet here he had manufactured a boom and had actually started the Consolidated. Why (it struck him with the suddenness of a lightning bolt) if Hartland did sink and get copper, the Consolidated was made—absolutely made! And the stockholders would have made a gilt-edged investment, and he would have a fortune made legitimately and above-board. It was taking a chance to hang on, but wasn't it worth it?

Mann paced his private office, stopping only when a clerk came in to get a stock certificate and pay in money. His face was set in thought—thoughts so daring and dangerous that he seemed to contemplate them as from a distance. At the end of an hour he mopped his damp brow with his handkerchief and looked about as if the room appeared strange to him. He had made his decision. He would deal Allen the double-cross instead of getting it himself, and bask in the brave light of heroism in the bargain.

He took the money from the drawer of his desk and from the safe and put it in three of the bags. He took these and walked boldly down to the bank. He found Gordon in his private office and tossed the sacks one by one onto the banker's desk.

"Put those in the vault, Alex," he said, "an' remember I don't know yet what's in them. I haven't checked over the amount."

"That's all right," said Gordon. "I'll seal them."

Mann left, conscious of Gordon's stare at his back.

He walked back to his office in an angry mood. He was annoyed at Gordon. The banker's look had been downright suspicious. He hated Allen! At best Allen was a ruffian, a bandit, a gunfighter, a crooked gambler, and a killer. He winced at the last word. But he had only to slip a word to Hartland and he would have the young millionaire behind him. What if this Squint had told Hartland anything? Nothing had been done as yet; there was no proof against him; he could say he had been stringing Allen along because the man had threatened him. After all, Squint had heard nothing except Allen's threat in event of Mann's double-crossing him, and Allen's vow he would get Squint himself. He had nothing to report. Mann was shrewd enough to suspect that it was Miller who had hired the gunman in the first place. Perhaps it would be well to see this Squint and have a confidential talk with him. But Mann knew it would be impossible to see anybody without the meeting, and perhaps the conversation, being reported to Allen. He was closely watched.

He hadn't been in his office ten minutes when Allen entered. Mann frowned when he saw him. Strange he should be cool before this man after the decision he had made. But his coolness gave him confidence.

"You shouldn't walk in here so openly during the day," he told Allen. "You know how things stand an' folks will be asking each other questions."

"I saw you goin' down to the bank, loaded," said Allen, ignoring the other's remark.

"Gordon was here," said Mann irritably. "Wanted to know when I was going to bank the money. Said it wasn't even safe to count it here. He acted an' talked like he was suspicious. An' he was right. We were fools to think we could stuff that dinky safe out there with yellow-backs an' not start Gordon thinking, an' maybe talking. He's treasurer of the company, you know."

Allen hadn't taken his eyes from Mann's. "So he is," he said at length. "Maybe we had the wrong hunch, eh?"

"Certainly we did," said Mann, looking down at his desk. Then he raised his eyes. He was a little pale, but he met the big man's gaze squarely. "There's only one way to work this thing an' that's for me to attend to my end, an' for you to attend to yours, an'. . . ."

"You mean for me to attend to the big end," Allen interrupted grimly. "An' what else did you have to say?"

"I was going to ask what difference it would make whether we copped the money here or in Gordon's vault," said Mann.

"Reckon it wouldn't make any difference a-tall," said Allen as the clerk came in to get a stock certificate.

When Mann had attended to the clerk, he looked up to find that Allen had gone. Then he remembered the peculiar tone of voice Allen had used when making his parting remark. The furtive, worried look came back into his eyes. Did they understand each other? His fingers trembled and his lips twitched with nervousness. Perhaps he had gotten himself in a hole he couldn't crawl out of as easily as he had thought. But he had two days left.

The engineers had inspected the Huntley during the first two days of July. Hale spent most of Tuesday in the Yellow Jacket. That night he handed his report to Hartland in the presence of the other engineers and Miller. The single typewritten line at the bottom of the report was what interested Hartland most. It read:

> *I recommend further prospecting below the 600-foot level for copper showings.*

The engineers left next morning. At noon on this day before the Fourth an envelope was delivered to Hartland at his bungalow. When Hartland opened it, he found it contained a notice to the effect that:

> *Unless R.T. (Butch) Allen is given back his place as foreman of the Huntley, we, the undersigned employees of that mine, will refuse to return to work at midnight, July 4th as requested.*

It was signed by more than 100 men and Hartland was told over the telephone shortly afterward by Monocle Joe that a duplicate of the notice had been posted on the board in the Silver King. He asked Joe to report at the bungalow and gave him a paper to be posted on the board. In less than an hour, Silver City was reading:

> *Notice*
> *Any man who refuses to report for work at the Huntley will not again be employed on my properties.*

Miners are wanted for the Huntley and the Yellow Jacket.

(Signed)Roger Hartland

Herbert Mann, white and furious, sputtered and fumed in his office and looked helplessly at the grave face of Alex Gordon. He hadn't known this thing was to be done. Allen was mad to lay half his cards on the table thirty-six hours ahead of time. Mann wanted to tell Gordon the truth, but his sense of caution kept whispering: *Not yet!*

He listened to Gordon's tirade with the instinctive feeling that other ears were listening, too. He knew he was a marked man. Finally he broke into the banker's outpouring.

"When you're through, get out!" he cried shrilly. "I have no more control over the Huntley men an' Allen than you have!"

Sheriff Robert Currie arrived in Silver City at daybreak.

Chapter Thirty-six

The morning of Independence Day was clear and bright, with golden sunshine flooding the green loveliness of the mountains and a mild breeze tempering the heat. Before the sun had climbed above the shoulders of Old Baldy, most of the town was astir. Everyone was on holiday save the few required to look after the mines, and they were working special short shifts. Buckboards and spring wagons climbed the road from the basin ranches and towns loaded with merry-makers. Silver City's dusty street was thronged; cafés, resorts, stores, refreshment stands were crowded. Bunting and flags waved and fluttered in the breeze. A band in gold and blue, imported from a town sixty miles away, played stirring airs. Everywhere the spirit of carnival was rampant.

Herbert Mann made his way across the street from the hotel to his offices, looking neither to the right or left, ignoring the friendly or hilarious salutations of celebrants who knew him, intent upon what he had come to believe was to be his fate this day. He had dreamed of shooting and blood—blood flowing red over yellow bills. An omen.

It was after 9:00 A.M. He nodded perfunctorily to the three clerks waiting for him, unlocked the front door, passed through the main office to his private room in the rear. There he hung up his hat, raised the window, and sat down at his desk to confront again the problem that had put fresh gray hairs in his head during the night.

Allen had said he would tell him the hour at midnight. So Allen expected him there at midnight. Where would he be an hour afterward? He shivered. His face was gray, his brow furrowed and sweating. A clerk came in and said men who had bought stock were asking what effect Hartland's notice concerning the men who refused to return to work in the Huntley would have on the Consolidated.

"Tell them it will not affect the company," said Mann wearily. "Tell them the Consolidated is not interested in the Huntley, and that Hartland's big development will be in the Yellow Jacket. Say that the Consolidated has a card up its sleeve and that I'll have a statement to make tomorrow. That'll stall them off until . . . until. . . ." He was mumbling thus to himself after the clerk went out.

There were no sales that morning. *Might as well close the office*, he thought. But what would Allen think—or do? And where was he to go? Why shouldn't he put it straight to Allen that Allen could go through with his plans alone? Or how could he get in touch with Hartland? The telephone. And everyone in the office listening? It would be a long explanation. Hartland could not be seen coming to the office, either. In his frenzy, Mann failed to see how he could get in touch with Hartland, failed to realize that it would take but a few words to give away the plot. His thoughts continually reverted to himself. It was the saving of his own skin that was uppermost in his mind.

A tall, soldierly figure loomed in the doorway and Mann looked about, startled, to see Sheriff Currie. His heart gave a bound. His chance! Instinctively he looked out the window. A man, no!—two men were lounging out there within hearing and seeing distance. Allen had his sentinels on guard.

"Howdy, Sheriff," Mann managed to say, summoning his old reserve of blustering cheerfulness. "Looks like Silver City's big day, doesn't it?"

"Everywhere except in here," said the official. "Your business seems pretty slack." He had been eyeing the promoter keenly. "You don't look any too pert yourself," he observed.

"Tired," said Mann with a frown. He was careful to speak loudly. "I've had a mighty busy three days.

I suppose you've heard how Hartland is going ahead up here? Of course you've talked with him. Well, I've put the Consolidated over an' we're going to do things."

"Yes, I understand Hartland received a favorable report from Hale and the other experts," said the sheriff. "That ought to help the Consolidated . . . if it's managed properly."

Mann's eyes had lighted with fierce interest when Currie mentioned the engineers' report. And he didn't mistake the meaning of the official's last statement. "You needn't worry," he said heartily, "the Consolidated will be managed by the most able men we can get."

"Do you need Butch Allen?" Currie asked sharply.

"I . . . I . . . why I might give him a job, if that's what you mean." Mann could not help stammering. He glanced out the window. The eavesdroppers were still there.

"Are you sure you know what you mean?" asked the sheriff.

"Oh, I know you're thinking about the Huntley walk out," said Mann. "I had nothing to do with that. It hasn't helped us any, as you can see. I'm not interested in the Huntley except that I'd like to see it worked. I hired Allen for a foreman because he could handle men. Hartland has ridden him to death, an' . . . but I have nothing to do with it. If the Huntley men want him back an' are ready to walk out thinking it'll get him back, I can't help it."

"Don't you think maybe Allen started all this?" the sheriff persisted.

"Maybe he did, for all I know," Mann retorted angrily. "If he did, I couldn't have stopped him. I have no control over him now."

Currie's eyes were gleaming; his face was set in stern lines. "It might be just as well if you closed your office for the day," he said. "Of course, that's just a suggestion." He turned on his heel and left.

A suggestion? Mann knew better. And the two eavesdroppers had heard. He looked quickly out the window and saw they had gone. He closed the offices at 1:00 P.M.

He crossed to the Silver King where a place was made for him at the bar. "Nothing to say," he told his eager questioners. "Tomorrow I'll tell you something. Tomorrow!" Then, to Big Mose, as the latter put out a bottle and glasses: "You can post it on your board that the report of Hartland's engineers was OK."

"So I heard," said Big Mose dryly.

Mann took several drinks and enjoyed the feeling of confidence that they restored to him. He ate a big meal, topped it with another drink, and went into a rear room of the Silver King where he got a seat in a stud poker game. There he would stay. Allen's men had doubtless reported to him what the sheriff had said. Allen would know, if he wanted him, he would have to look for him. Very well. Mann ordered another drink. If Allen wanted him, let him look.

Mann played and won, lost and won, won and lost—imbibed freely and let the world go hang. The lamps were lighted. He played on, eating sandwiches, drinking. Allen might come anytime now. Well, let him come. If he had to, he would go through with the thing. But his slightly befogged brain had given birth to an idea. Probably Allen didn't want him to go through with it. It would be easier to leave him behind than to take him along and kill him. He startled the other players with a laugh, and looked up just as the door opened.

In the open slit of doorway he saw the narrow, pinched face of the gunman, Squint. There was an imperative gesture with the snapping eyes. He was wanted. A sober chill swept over him. He automatically sized up his stacks of checks and cashed in. The fire of those eyes sobered him.

Squint took him by the arm in the narrow passageway between the rooms, led him to the rear door. As they passed out, two men followed closely behind. Squint pushed his charge headlong down the three steps and leaped to the ground. Two streaks of red fire spurted from his hip. Mann heard the sharp reports of the gun, saw two figures tumble down the steps. Then he ran for the trees behind the resort with Squint Evans at his side.

As they plunged into the dark shadow of the cottonwoods and alders, the earth trembled beneath their feet and the heavens seemed to explode with thunder.

"They've blown up the Huntley and Yellow Jacket powder houses!" cried Squint as they stopped in their tracks. "I might have known it!" Then he prodded Mann in the back with his gun. "Run, you chicken-livered four-flusher, run! Set those fat legs of yours twinkling or I'll speed you up with bullets, s'help me God!"

They weaved in and out among the trees and tents along the stream. From the street came a hoarse, roaring tumult of noise. Squint knew the sounds of the two shots behind the Silver King would be forgotten in the excitement, but it didn't matter. He prodded Mann with the gun until the promoter dropped, puffing and blowing and spent, on the new bridge that had been completed the day before.

Squint caught the gleam of the moonlight on Joe's monocle before he saw him running across the bridge.

"Get him to the house!" he yelled to Joe. "Hide him an' watch him! The sheriff's got to have him alive!"

Then Squint was off to town.

Silver City's celebration had reached its climax. Hundreds were in the street. "They've blown up the Huntley!" came the cry. "They've blown up the Yellow Jacket tunnel!" another shouted. Then the milling mob concentrated in a mighty rush for the Yellow Jacket road. Huntley and Yellow Jacket men in even numbers were in the lead. Gamblers, prospectors, cowpunchers, trades people—they started up the road. Flaming pine torches appeared as if by magic, for Allen's lieutenants had done their work well. Men who had celebrated too strenuously fell by the roadside. A torch was flung into a pile of dry brush. Instantly, almost, the flames leaped angrily against the black shadow of the trees. More shouts. Men coming on the run down the road. The mob paused, wavered between the mounting flames and the rush of men coming down the road. The rush stopped. The light from the mounting flames glinted on the barrels of rifles and six-shooters. A volley went whistling over the heads of the mob. It broke and ran pell-mell back down the road.

"Yellow Jacket men back to fight the fire!" came Miller's roaring voice.

There was confusion as the Yellow Jacket miners struggled out of the press of the crowd and started back up the road. They saw Hartland, Miller, Ross Milton, and a few others running down. All carried guns. "Stop that fire from eating up the hill!" Miller shouted as they passed. They literally mowed their way through the mob.

In the street below, nearly deserted save for groups of frightened, excited women and girls, shots sounded. Men were running about the bank. Squint Evans was entering the upper end of the street, reloading the two empty chambers of his gun as he ran. The tall figure of Sheriff Currie showed in front of the bank. Red flame streaked from his gun to the accompaniment of shattered glass and splinted wood as the bank doors gave way before his Yellow Jacket deputies, smashing their way in with a battering ram. A terrific explosion seemed to thrust out the whole front of the building. Men were thrown into the street. They raised to their knees and fired. Other shots—a fusillade—came from the rear.

Then from around the corner of the bank came the wild, plunging figure of Butch Allen, hatless, blood streaming from his face, his eyes blazing. He shot once at the men who were pushing into the bank, then darted up the street, keeping close to the buildings. Sheriff Currie saw him and started in pursuit. Squint saw him just as he crossed toward the bank. He fired twice, but the range was too great. Then he, too, ran after the gunman. But Squint was nearly winded and Allen was faster on his feet than either of his two pursuers. He gained.

Hartland, Miller, and the others came down the road into the street just behind Evans and the sheriff. They saw Butch Allen ahead and joined in the chase. The foremost of the mob behind followed, with stragglers bringing up the rear. As they reached the bridge and crossed, they came to a stop at the foot of the slope, looking up at the bungalow. In the light streaming from the open doorway was framed the slight figure of Monocle Joe, his single glass glistening. Behind him was John Cram and the frightened, twisted face of Fredricks. Butch Allen was stumbling toward the foot of the steps.

"Stop where you are or I'll drop you!" came Joe's high-pitched voice in sharp command.

For answer, Allen raised his gun.

Hartland started bounding up the slope before Miller could stop him.

"Turn around!"

It was not till then that the crowd, surging forward, saw the diminutive gunman, Squint Evans. The sheriff was some little distance behind him, having been outdistanced by Squint's final spurt.

Allen whirled. He appeared to see Hartland and Squint Evans at the same moment. He fired at Hartland and missed all in the twinkling of an eye. "Then you take it!" he cried hoarsely, whipping his gun on the leaping Squint.

Too late! Too slow! Evans had deliberately challenged Allen while his gun was still in its holster and Allen's was free! No one had seen him draw; no one remembered the flash at his hip as he had leaped. But Allen was staggering back, turning around, shooting aimlessly with the last strength left to him. He went down on the grass, tried to rise, sprawled his length with his face to the ground.

The crowd caught its breath and came up the slope in a surging wave. Sheriff Currie's tall, commanding figure confronted them. He held up a hand in a signal for silence.

"You Huntley men and others, go back to town.

What happened tonight, as well as the projected walk out, was engineered by this Allen and by Mann to make excitement and start you rampaging up the road while they and their gang looted the bank. They didn't get away with it. We've got Mann a prisoner and he's going to talk. Go back to town and we'll have news for you in the morning."

Slowly the crowd melted away, started down the slope, and across the bridge. Sheriff Currie turned to Squint Evans.

"I reckon we're even, Squint," he said.

"I was thinking the same," was Evan's remark.

Then, with Hartland, Miller and Milton, they went inside the house where Herbert Mann was cringing on the divan pleading with Fredricks for a drink.

Chapter Thirty-seven

Sunrise found Silver City's main street thronged again. Crowds were in front of the wrecked bank where the terrific blast had shattered the outer doors of the vault and virtually demolished the furnishings. Other crowds moved up and down in the dust of the street or gathered in front of the Consolidated offices.

The front office was locked, but there were several people in the rear room where a conference had been in progress for three hours. Roger Hartland and Sheriff Robert Currie were there; Miller and Ross Milton were there; Herbert Mann, white and shaking, helping himself at intervals to a stimulant, was present, and Alex Gordon, also shaken and nervous, was there. Gordon had been found under the débris in the bank's private office, gagged and bound. He had been in the bank when the bandits had entered, overpowered the two watchmen, and tried to compel him to open the vault. He had told Allen point-blank that, if the money in the vault was stolen, the bank and he himself would be ruined and he would have nothing to live for and he could shoot if he wished. Allen had seen the tired resignation in Gordon's eyes and had ordered him trussed up. They had been surprised to find him in the bank in the first place and had come prepared to blow open the vault.

It was Squint Evans's guarded phone message to Sheriff Currie that had brought the official. He had recruited his special deputies from among the Yellow Jacket men. Miller and Hartland were told and a guard posted at the mines and secreted near the bank. The Huntley powder house had been blown up, but it was not known how it had been done or by whom. Squint had been unable to learn the hour set for the attempt upon the bank, although by clever spying he had learned the bank vault was the objective. Sheriff Currie had ordered him to get Mann away and keep him safe. So far as they knew, every one of the Allen gang had been killed, wounded, or captured. Currie had lost two men. Five were wounded at the bank and two hurt fighting the fires near the road. The fire had been put out.

Both Hartland and Sheriff Currie felt a new respect for Alex Gordon, especially when the banker explained that he had gotten in so much cash because of the thrill it gave him to see it when he wanted to and to know his bank was so sound in this dawning era of prosperity. He told Hartland he had made up his mind to break with Mann and that he would have renewed John Cram's notes, but was afraid it would make Mann suspicious. He confessed that he had been overawed by Butch Allen—until it came to the point of parting with the money. Allen possibly had suspected something when he heard Sheriff Currie was in town. One of the prisoners had confessed that his chief had been suspicious of Mann, and that they really hadn't intended to take the promoter with them or divide with him. When Allen realized the game was lost, he leaped to the conclusion that Mann had betrayed him. Then he had started for the one place where he thought they would have Mann a captive.

Mann had sat on the divan in Hartland's living room and, between drinks, had told everything about the scheme, except that he didn't know about Allen's preparations to draw the crowds up the road. He tried to explain the fear that had prevented him from sending word somehow to Hartland, or telling the sheriff. Over and over again, he asserted that he had not intended to go through with the thing. He had intended to leave the card game and chance it on a run for the woods at midnight, but it had grown late before he realized it. He had been drinking.

Sheriff Currie showed his disgust and merely said that he could leave the country when certain papers were signed. There was, after all, no direct evidence against him for Butch Allen was dead.

Ross Milton took Mann to his room in the hotel soon after daybreak.

The others remained, discussing the affairs of the Consolidated. Already it was camp gossip that

Hartland had received a favorable report from his mining experts and the spirits of those who had bought Consolidated stock were high despite the present muddle. The Huntley miners were angry with the knowledge that Allen had used them as mere tools. They would have mobbed, and possibly have tried to lynch Herbert Mann if the former promoter had not been kept under heavy guard.

At 9:00 A.M. Hartland talked over the long distance telephone to Butte. Shortly afterward, he and Sheriff Currie went into the front office and opened the front door. They stepped out in front of the expectant crowd that quieted immediately. Hartland looked a bit pale and worn, but some of his best friends in the East would have thought he looked bored. His voice was steady and clear and carried up and down the street as he addressed the throng.

"I have taken over the control of the Consolidated in conjunction with Wright and Harris of Butte," he announced. "The company will be reorganized and no further stock will be offered at present. Any who may wish to do so, can cash their certificates at this office after noon today. Alex Gordon will be in charge."

Having spoken, he made his way through the crowd with the sheriff who accompanied him up the street until the way was clear. Not until the sheriff left him and turned back did the big throng break loose. Hartland smiled faintly at the cheering.

As Hartland climbed the steps to his verandah, a vision of loveliness was framed in the doorway. He took off his hat and managed a cheerful smile.

"You here, Margaret?" he said, noting the white apron over her pale blue frock, her sparkling eyes, the rosy cheeks, and soft hair. "Getting breakfast?"

She put her arm through his, led him inside to the big divan. There they sat down and she looked at him steadily for a few moments. "Fredricks isn't feeling too well," she said. "So I'm officiating. I was here last night, but took care that you didn't see me. You look tired."

"Do I?" he said foolishly. Then he kissed her. "I *am* tired," he confessed, fondling her hands. "I wasn't cut out for this sort of thing, Margaret. I've made a coup, I suppose, by getting Wright and Harris in and taking over the Consolidated. I'm the big man of the new-born camp with the making of it in my hands. But I don't get the thrill I expected. It doesn't seem to mean much to me. Maybe I'm just a misfit when it comes to doing things."

Her arms crept about his neck. "But you're not a misfit," she said stoutly, her lips brushing his. "You are doing things. And you'll do bigger things. Look into my eyes, Roger, and see that I believe in you."

He looked, and held her closely. "Then, if you believe in me, you'll marry me because I'm the one man you want," he said softly.

"Yes, Roger," she whispered. "And I want you for yourself, sweetheart. Just for . . . you."

One week later, Hartland went into the high mountains. With him were Monocle Joe and Fredricks. They had three pack horses in addition to their saddle animals, and Joe was to act as wrangler and packer, while Fredricks was to officiate as cook and learn something, as Joe put it.

They went over the range and down into the Smith River country, and on into the Big Belt mountains, camping where sunset overtook them, fishing for trout and grayling, taking it easy. They turned northwest into the Rockies, went on to Swan Lake, up into Gordon Gulch, down the South Fork of the Flathead. July, August, and September slipped away. Hartland luxuriated in a new peace and happiness that was, nevertheless, suspicious and disquieting when he thought about it. He made friends with forest rangers, fireguards on lonely observation peaks, trappers, and mountain miners generally.

Meanwhile, Miller, with John Cram as chief assistant, was supervising the sinking of the Yellow Jacket prospect shaft. The men had returned to the Huntley. Fred Crawford was pushing the work there with Sandy Anderson as his foreman. The camp was flourishing. Then down went the diamond drills and on a day late in October, Miller sent forth a messenger to find Hartland who was in the Big River country in the high Rockies.

The messenger reached Hartland a week later. Hartland tore open the envelope and unfolded the single sheet of paper. Then he read:

Come back. We've got the copper.
                                                    Miller

When, some ten days later, they rode into Silver City, they were given an ovation by a crowd that accompanied them to the bungalow. Hartland, somewhat dazed, permitted his hand to be grasped by scores. Gradually he learned they'd got it in the Yellow Jacket. Wright & Harris, who had taken charge of the reorganization of the Consolidated, had changed the company name to the Hartland Mines & Milling Company and the stock was soaring in price with none to be had. Already it had been decided to change the name of the town to Copper

City. The railroad people were waking up. The boom had become a fixture.

Miller came at last and Hartland met him on the porch.

"Is it true?" Hartland asked excitedly. "Have we got it?"

Miller swelled out his chest. "I always said," he began, "I always said. . . ."

"Shut up," said Hartland, grinning. "Joe, get my horse."

A volunteer rider had dashed with the news to the Cram place and Margaret was waiting for him in the little yard when he arrived and flung himself from the saddle. He stood above her with his hands on her shoulders. She looked up at him—bronzed, clear-eyed—and saw something in his gaze that brought her heart into her throat.

"You . . . you stayed away so long, Roger," she said.

"So you would be sure when I came back," he answered. "Are you sure, Margaret?"

"Yes." He hardly heard her whisper.

Then he had her in his arms and she was clinging to him. He kissed her almost savagely. "I guess I'm not a misfit," he said whimsically. "I got a big thrill out of the camp when I got back, and another from you. Margaret, by the gods of these everlasting mountains, I love you!"

John Cram came riding in from town. Roger Hartland and Margaret did not see him until he was standing before them.

"What's this . . . what's this?" the old man blustered.

"We're getting married next week, if Margaret says so," said Hartland.

"Indian summer is as good as June," Margaret said.

"I expect that makes it unanimous," said John Cram dryly. "Well, I've only known it was going to happen for something like five months."

Roger Hartland and his wife were sitting in a comfortable chair before the fire in the bungalow. The scented dusk of Indian summer had long since given way to night. The wind was singing down the valley. *Creeps Hallow's spirit*, thought Hartland, and his arms held Margaret closer.

All Copper City had attended the wedding that noon. Sheriff Currie had been there; Ross Milton had been best man. Squint Evans, now a permanent fixture like Monocle Joe in the gaming rooms, had presented the bride with the first dozen genuine orchids ever seen in those mountains. John Cram had given his daughter away. 5,000 men, women, and children of the town and from the lowlands had given their blessing. Now they sat for the first time in front of their own fireside. Later, they were to go East and abroad. But always they were to come back.

Fredricks entered, inspected the lamp on the table, coughed slightly. Hartland looked up at him; his bride peered slyly over his shoulder.

It was a different Fredricks she saw. The face was tanned and had lost its flabbiness. Fredricks now could pack a horse as well as ride one. He could bake biscuits by the coals of a campfire. He could even swear. But he hadn't forgotten that he was a gentleman's gentleman.

"Begging your pardon, sir," he said with great dignity, "but could I ask for the night off, sir?"

Hartland smiled and looked at Margaret, who hid her face in his shoulder. She was laughing silently.

"What's the big idea?" Hartland asked, frowning fiercely.

"Joe wishes to take me downtown so I can learn . . . stud poker, sir," said Fredricks, elevating his chin.

Hartland laughed outright. "Go to it," he said. "I hope you've got enough money, Fredricks, because that crowd'll pick you clean as a whistle."

"Very good, sir," said Fredricks, bowing.

Hartland gathered Margaret in his arms, as Fredricks left, and kissed her. "Joe believes in the code of the East"—he chuckled—"get the money."

But the sally recalled an unpleasant memory. "What's the code of the West, Roger?"

"You'll have to tell me," he said.

"Be square," she answered. "We'll always be that with each other, won't we, Roger?"

"Yes," he answered simply.

Fredricks and Monocle Joe looked back when they reached the bridge. They saw the yellow gleam of the lamp go out. Only the dull, flickering light of the fire showed in the windows of the bungalow. They went on into town.

About the Author

Robert J. Horton was born in Coudersport, Pennsylvania. As a very young man he traveled extensively in the American West, working for newspapers. For several years he was sports editor for the *Great Falls Tribune* in Great Falls, Montana. He began writing Western fiction for *Adventure* magazine before becoming a regular contributor to Street & Smith's *Western Story Magazine*. By the mid-1920s Horton was one of three authors to whom Street & Smith paid 5¢ a word—the other two being Frederick Faust, perhaps better known as Max Brand, and Robert Ormond Case. Many of Horton's serials for Street & Smith's *Western Story Magazine* were subsequently brought out as books by Chelsea House, Street & Smith's book publishing company. Although virtually all of Horton's stories appeared under his byline in the magazine, for their book editions Chelsea House published them either as by Robert J. Horton or by James Roberts. Sometimes, as was the case with *Rovin' Redden* (Chelsea House, 1925) by James Roberts, a book would consist of three short novels that were editorially joined to form a "novel". Other times the stories were serials published in book form, such as *Whispering Cañon* (Chelsea House, 1925) by James Roberts or *The Prairie Shrine* (Chelsea House, 1924) by Robert J. Horton. It may be obvious that Chelsea House, doing a number of books a year by the same author, thought it a prudent marketing strategy to give the author more than one name.

Horton's Western stories are concerned most of all with character, and it is the characters that drive the plots rather than the other way around. It is unfortunate he died at such a relatively early age. Many of his novels, after Street & Smith abandoned Chelsea House, were published only in British editions, and Robert J. Horton was not to appear at all in paperback books until quite recently.

"When you think of the West, you think of Zane Grey." —*American Cowboy*

ZANE GREY

THE RESTORED, FULL-LENGTH NOVEL,
IN PAPERBACK FOR THE FIRST TIME!

The Great Trek

Sterl Hazelton is no stranger to trouble. But the shooting that made him an outlaw was one he didn't do. Though it was his cousin who pulled the trigger, Sterl took the blame, and now he has to leave the country if he wants to stay healthy. Sterl and his loyal friend, Red Krehl, set out for the greatest adventure of their lives, signing on for a cattle drive across the vast northern desert of Australia to the gold fields of the Kimberley Mountains. But it seems no matter where Sterl goes, trouble is bound to follow!

"Grey stands alone in a class untouched by others." —*Tombstone Epitaph*

ISBN 13: 978-0-8439-6062-4

OUTLAWS
PAUL BAGDON

Spur Award Finalist and Author of
Deserter and *Bronc Man*

Pound Taylor has just escaped from jail—and the
hangman's noose—and he's eager to get back on the
outlaw trail. For his gang he chooses his former cell-
mate and the father and brothers of his old partner,
Zeb Stone. Pound wants to do things right, with lots
of planning and minimum gunplay, but the Stone
boys figure they can shoot first and worry about the
repercussions later. Sure enough, that's just what
they do—and they kill a man in the process. With
the law breathing down their necks and the whole
gang at one another's throats, Pound can see that
hangman's noose getting closer all the time. Unless
his friends kill him first!

ISBN 13: 978-0-8439-6073-0

LOUIS L'AMOUR

For millions of readers, the name Louis L'Amour is synonymous with the excitement of the Old West. But for too long, many of these tales have only been available in revised, altered versions, often very different from their original form. Here, collected together in paperback for the first time, are four of L'Amour's finest stories, all carefully restored to their initial magazine publication versions.

BIG MEDICINE

This collection includes L'Amour's wonderful short novel *Showdown on the Hogback*, an unforgettable story of ranchers uniting to fight back against the company that's trying to drive them off their land. "Big Medicine" pits a lone prospector against a band of nine Apaches. In "Trail to Pie Town," a man has to get out of town fast after a gunfight leaves his opponent dead on a saloon floor. And the title character in "McQueen of the Tumbling K" is out for revenge after gunmen ambush him and leave him to die.

ISBN 13: 978-0-8439-6068-6

The Classic Film Collection

The Searchers by Alan LeMay

Hailed as one of the greatest American films, *The Searchers*, directed by John Ford and starring John Wayne, has had a direct influence on the works of Martin Scorsese, Steven Spielberg, and many others. Its gorgeous cinematic scope and deeply nuanced characters have proven timeless. And now available for the first time in decades is the powerful novel that inspired this iconic movie. (Coming February 2009!)

Destry Rides Again by Max Brand

Made in 1939, the Golden Year of Hollywood, *Destry Rides Again* helped launch Jimmy Stewart's career and made Marlene Dietrich an American icon. Now available for the first time in decades is the novel that inspired this much-loved movie. (Coming March 2009!)

The Man from Laramie by T. T. Flynn

In its original publication, *The Man from Laramie* had more than half a million copies in print. Shortly thereafter, it became one of the most recognized of the Anthony Mann/Jimmy Stewart collaborations, known for darker films with morally complex characters. Now the novel upon which this classic movie was based is once again available—for the first time in more than fifty years. (Coming April 2009!)

The Unforgiven by Alan LeMay

In this epic American novel, which served as the basis for the classic film directed by John Huston and starring Burt Lancaster and Audrey Hepburn, a family is torn apart when an old enemy starts a vicious rumor that sets the range aflame. Don't miss the powerful novel that inspired the film the *Motion Picture Herald* calls "an absorbing and compelling drama of epic proportions." (Coming May 2009!)

☐ YES!

Sign me up for the Leisure Western Book Club and send my FREE BOOKS! If I choose to stay in the club, I will pay only $14.00* each month, a savings of $9.96!

NAME: _____

ADDRESS: _____

TELEPHONE: _____

EMAIL: _____

☐ I want to pay by credit card.

☐ **VISA**   ☐ **MasterCard**   ☐ **DISCOVER**

ACCOUNT #: _____

EXPIRATION DATE: _____

SIGNATURE: _____

Mail this page along with $2.00 shipping and handling to:
Leisure Western Book Club
PO Box 6640
Wayne, PA 19087
Or fax (must include credit card information) to:
610-995-9274
You can also sign up online at **www.dorchesterpub.com**.
*Plus $2.00 for shipping. Offer open to residents of the U.S. and Canada only.
Canadian residents please call 1-800-481-9191 for pricing information.
If under 18, a parent or guardian must sign. Terms, prices and conditions subject to change. Subscription subject to acceptance. Dorchester Publishing reserves the right to reject any order or cancel any subscription.

GET 4 FREE BOOKS!

You can have the best Westerns delivered to your door for less than what you'd pay in a bookstore or online. Sign up for one of our book clubs today, and we'll send you 4 FREE* BOOKS, worth $23.96, just for trying it out...with no obligation to buy, ever!

Authors include classic writers such as LOUIS L'AMOUR, MAX BRAND, ZANE GREY and more; plus new authors such as COTTON SMITH, JOHNNY D. BOGGS, DAVID THOMPSON and others.

As a book club member you also receive the following special benefits:
- 30% off all orders!
- Exclusive access to special discounts!
- Convenient home delivery and 10 days to return any books you don't want to keep.

Visit **www.dorchesterpub.com**
or call
1-800-481-9191

There is no minimum number of books to buy, and you may cancel membership at any time.
*Please include $2.00 for shipping and handling.